SPELLCASTER

About the Editors

Elen Hawke lives in Oxford, England. She has pursued many spiritual philosophies, among them Wicca and Druidry, into which she was initiated, and her beliefs continue to be fluid and eclectic. Aside from writing, her passions are for photography and reading. She is a professional photographer and illustrator, having produced work for both exhibition and publication.

Martin White was born in Northampton, but now lives in a tranquil setting on the edge of the peak district in Derbyshire, England. As well as reading and teaching tarot and runes professionally, he also runs courses across the county in subjects such as meditation and relaxation, Qi Gong and Reiki. When not writing or teaching, Martin is also a qualified hypnotherapist and NLP practitioner, and uses these skills to help people overcome their difficulties and regain control of their lives.

To Write to the Authors

If you wish to contact the Spellweaver Collective or would like more information about this book, please write to the author in care of Llewellyn Worldwide and we will forward your request. Both the authors and publisher appreciate hearing from you and learning of your enjoyment of this book and how it has helped you. Llewellyn Worldwide cannot guarantee that every letter written to the authors can be answered, but all will be forwarded. Please write to:

Elen Hawke and Martin White

℅ Llewellyn Worldwide

P.O. Box 64383, Dept. 0-7387-0634-5

St. Paul, MN 55164-0383, U.S.A.

Please enclose a self-addressed stamped envelope for reply,
or $1.00 to cover costs. If outside U.S.A., enclose an
international postal reply coupon.

Many of Llewellyn's authors have websites with additional information and resources. For more information, please visit our website at www.llewellyn.com.

Edited by Elen Hawke & Martin White

SPELLCASTER

Seven Ways to Effective Magic

Martin Duffy • Anna Franklin
Poppy Palin • Morgana SidheRaven
Leah Whitehorse

Llewellyn Publications
St. Paul, Minnesota

First Edition
First Printing, 2005

Book design and editing by Karin Simoneau
Cover design by Kevin R. Brown
Llewellyn is a registered trademark of Llewellyn Worldwide, Ltd.

Library of Congress Cataloging-in-Publication Data
Pending

Llewellyn Publications
A Division of Llewellyn Worldwide, Ltd.
P.O. Box 64383, Dept. 0-7387-0634-5
St. Paul, MN 55164-0383, U.S.A.
www.llewellyn.com

Printed in the United States of America

This book is dedicated to the pursuit of tolerance, a climate in which we may celebrate and respect our differences rather than disapprove of and condemn those who think, believe, and act differently. Let not our differences be a cause for the assault of others and the destruction of that which they hold dear. In the past, this way of thinking has deprived us of much of our collective heritage, and even in modern times the devastation continues.

What, then, is tolerance? Let us leave that answer to a French philosopher whose writings epitomise the Age of Enlightenment, and someone who saw intolerance as one of the greatest scourges of society: Voltaire.

> What is tolerance?—it is the consequence of humanity. We are all formed of frailty and error; let us pardon reciprocally each other's folly—that is the first law of nature.
>
> —Voltaire

Contents

Introduction

We are a group of authors who have come together under the name of the Spellweaver Collective because we are concerned about the current tendency of the media to trivialise magic. We feel that there are too many overcommercialised works out there at present. We are also concerned about the way spells are packaged by publishers in an off-the-shelf, luridly presented "cookbook" style, intended to attract the very young, the desperate, or the sensation seekers. This is not to say that people shouldn't practice magic, or that it shouldn't be fun, but it is important that magical practitioners proceed with some prior knowledge of how occult energies operate.

Our book intends to set magic firmly back into the overall holistic context of the Craft, giving people the guidelines and tools they need to create spells that are tailored to their own unique requirements. We hope that readers will realise there is more to magic than a quick fix, that magic is part of an overall spiritual path, that it should be practised ethically and with regard to safety, and that it is not a pill to be thoughtlessly taken as a panacea for life's problems. Magic is indeed an art and a craft that draws on an understanding of universal energies, the elements, and much more.

We come from a variety of pagan traditions and from different countries, and our ages cover a wide range. There is no intention among us to censor or restrict each other's work. We all have different approaches regarding how we practice and where we draw our ethical boundaries, and we feel this adds to the value of the book as it shows people that there are many ways of working and many different viewpoints. Sometimes the work of one of us will contradict that of others in the group; this is because everyone has different life experiences and views. We invite the reader to keep an open mind and absorb the material before deciding which approach is personally applicable. At other times the different pieces will be in agreement.

Our aim is to give the reader sound rules that will help to empower and reassure him or her. People have a right to safe, ethical, imaginative guidelines for their magical work, regardless of their age, background, and Craft experience. The aim of this book is to provide those guidelines as clearly as possible, in a way that will foster confidence and inspiration whilst exploring seven different but complementary ways in which magical goals can be achieved.

Song of the Star

LEAH WHITEHORSE

When I first began walking the witch's path I was oblivious to the whys and wherefores of spells. They were something belonging to the dark horror movies of my teenage years, the pages of storybooks and fairy tales. Spells were about power, seduction, control, and perfection. Of course I was utterly fascinated, a little scared, and completely clueless. My first "proper" spell involved the obligatory unrequited love situation. I found a spell printed in some antiquarian booklet, diligently followed everything by the letter, chanted my chant, and got my man . . . for one night only, after which I was ceremoniously dropped from a great height whilst the Goddess giggled in the background. I came to know this as my first spiritual handslapping.

The partial success of my crafting inspired me, whereas its demise frustrated and disappointed me. Not only did I feel let down by the poor guy in question, but I felt utterly betrayed by spirit. The success led me to feel that there was something to all this magic stuff; the failure led me to question why.

Looking back at this situation, I realise that this was the beginning of my journey toward understanding the nature of magic. I pondered what I had done to change the fabric of the universe and bend it to my will. I feared retribution, questioned my motivation and intent, raged at the skies, and cried into my pillow. Somewhere there was an "answer," and I was determined to find it.

My dream life has always been vivid, and it was the nature and laws of the dreamscape that would eventually tutor me in the ways of magical practice. Spirits, Guides, and ancient gods populated my dreams from early on, and often my magical inspirations and understandings have been triggered by my nightly wanderings. I experienced lucid dreams as a child, and for a long time I didn't differentiate between that reality and the one of the waking world, despite being told the difference by others. My dreams were simply "my other life," just as real and meaningful as the everyday world. I quickly learned that I could fly at will and manipulate the scenery to my own design. It was this latter curious ability that really caught my attention, as I had an inkling of recognition that this in some way related to the structure of the waking world. I noticed that sometimes I could dissolve or transform the monsters and demons that haunted me, and other times I could not. I questioned why.

In my early twenties I began to work with astral projection/out-of-body experiences triggered by sleep paralysis and lucid dreaming. These journeys provided further food for thought from Guides and other entities that dwell in the astral worlds who put up with my childlike endless questioning and occasionally granted me glimpses of the greater pattern.

What I offer here is my understanding of the process of magic and how it shapes and changes us when we choose to cast spells. I have a firm belief that whatever spiritual path we follow, each step along the way needs to be matched with personal development. By "personal development" I mean the process of delving into the far reaches of the mind to understand why we act, think, feel, and respond as we do. The magical path is one that increases and demands self-awareness.

I have a particular view of reality and ways of working that I wish to share with you. I do not profess to know the truth, for we each hold our own individual truths. Instead I offer what I have learned so far on the journey in the hope that it will facilitate you on your own magical path and inspire you to seek greater meaning as to what magic means to you.

I rarely perform actual spells nowadays—that is, if you define a spell as using the various tools and paraphernalia available. Yet I live a magical life in which I notice the great web unfolding and changing endlessly with my thoughts. I am in awe of how the universe is constantly in communication with us and how the Goddess hears my whispers on the wind.

The Rise of Spellweaving

The Lady watched as I lit a candle and quietly seated myself
at the centre of the circle.
She smiled gently and through my chant
I heard her say,
"Child, don't you know you have it all already?"

Over the past few years there has been a growing interest in witchcraft and the magical arts. The media has caught on to the public's fascination with the Craft, and despite the fact that witches and their beliefs are often still heavily misrepresented and misunderstood, more and more people are curious to explore this seemingly new avenue. One of the unfortunate side effects of this has been the tendency toward "quick fix" magic. Your lover has left you, your finances are a mess—here's a spell to make it all right again. Certainly when I first came to the Craft it was useful for me to be able to look at spells written by others. As a solitary practitioner it would have been difficult for me to learn without the wide array of books on the market. However, without the deeper understanding behind spells, the chants and instructions had little meaning to me. I learned correspondences and planetary times, charms and talismans, trees and herbs, but knowing how to put all these together didn't make me a skilled magical worker.

Yet another aspect of the rise of spellweaving is *power.* Take a look at any popular self-help book and it won't be long before you find the word "empowerment." To be empowered, however, means to be strong within your self rather than to have power *over* anything else outside of you. On the whole, many people I speak to have a sense of being powerless in society. Certainly in the West we live in democracies and our vote is counted, but overall it is hard to be heard amongst the clamour of politics and profit. Literature and the media feed us tales of heroes and heroines who battle the forces of darkness, conquer the bad guys, and save the day. Our daily battles are fought in the mind and in the movies as work, children, mortgages, relationships, and money eat away at time and energy. A spell that offers the power to change your life, to make you heard, seen, loved, or rich is undoubtedly attractive at surface level.

The quick fix approach is perhaps indicative of the mood of society as a whole. We are presented with "buy now, pay later" offers, fast food and cars, lotteries, sales, and the desire to have it all *now*. Yet at the same time underneath it all is a growing tide of spirituality, the desire to return to our roots, create communities, care for the earth, consume organic food, and conserve energy. The path of the witch is more than spells, but magic holds an important place in our practice. For me, spells are empowering. I do not seek to control the environment around me to suit my will. I seek to know myself, shed the beliefs that disempower me, and thereby change the way I respond to the world. I strive to commune rather than control.

What Are Spells?

The Goddess rolled over as I floated beside her,
sobbing my sob of frustration.
"Take heart, child," she whispered.
"If you can hear that what you have done
is out of time with Time,
then you are blessed
because you have heard the song of the Universe
behind the din."

A spell is something beyond planetary times, chanting, and incense. It is beyond tools and deities invoked. A spell reaches out across the fabric of time and changes it in an instant. In the process I am changed, as is everything I perceive. A spell is a thought made manifest.

The word "spell" comes from Old High German *spel,* meaning "talk" or "tale." It is the words of a spell that contain the power, whether spoken or unspoken. In the Bible it says, "In the beginning was the Word, and the Word was with God. . . . And *the Word became flesh* and dwelt among us . . . " (John 1:1 and 1:14; italics mine).

Words are the way we communicate with others and with ourselves. Words give meaning to our thoughts and feelings. Words are powerful. The world has been changed by words spoken in a moment of passion, inspiration, and anger. Words can cut deep. Notice that "words" is an anagram of "sword." We can use words to attack, defend, or protect. The occult philosopher Piobb earlier this century said, "Magic is the science of the word."

Nowadays we use "spelling" to mean putting various letters from the alphabet into an order that creates a word that has meaning. The very act of giving something a name or description contains remnants of magic. By giving definitions to objects or people we make them real.

In the *Merriam-Webster Online Dictionary,* "spell" is defined as "a spoken word or form of words held to have magic power." In a sense all words have power, whether spoken or unspoken. All words stem from thoughts, and thoughts form beliefs and responses to experiences. When you give voice to those thoughts you create the world around you.

Simply put, a spell is a thought defined in words that have meaning to you. The spell is then sent out into the universe with energy and intent. The universe receives it, and your desire is created. Unlike the movies, things are not created out of thin air (much as I think that would be a nifty ability to have!). My understanding of the process is that everything is energy. What we see around us is energy: the table, the chair, the cat, the computer, the wind in the trees. Everything is energy that has been given a form and then a name so that we can recognise it. Often I notice that in order to receive, something must leave. To bring in the new, the old has to pass out of my life. This shows me that whatever manifests in my life is simply energy transformed from one state to another. The prefix *trans* means to go beyond, across, or through. When we work a spell, our consciousness must *transcend* the physical reality and reach out to other dimensions.

Life vibrates around us and within us. We are each an expression of matter and all of us vibrate at different levels. For any community large or small, human or otherwise, the members need to function in harmony with each other so that the group can survive and prosper. The universe is like one giant orchestra playing the greatest and longest musical. When you weave a spell you are weaving a new song into the whole. Your melody is the intention, the tools you use the harmony, the time you choose the rhythm. For a spell to work well it needs to fit in with the cosmic musical. Spells can be discordant. The discord is easily seen and felt, like an untuned violin. It jars at the senses of those directly in line with it. My first spell that went so wrong put my teeth on edge and made me sit up, take notice, and start listening.

The Nature of Magic and Reality

Science separates and studies. It says, "I am not that . . ."
Magic joins and communicates. It says,
"I am all that and more . . ."

Magic

Many within schools of magic and occult traditions have defined magic as the ability to manipulate the forces/energy of the universe. The idea of what magic can do, however, has changed over the centuries. In antiquity the supernatural ruled the world. Hidden forces moved across the landscape—some governed by gods, some by the power of the shaman or magician. These forces were feared and respected because they could bring life or death. Mother Nature was something tangible and intelligent, and could be communicated with in all manner of ways. There was no question, then, in these times that magic brought about physical changes in the world—whether sickness or wealth or love. Magic was courted, danced with, dabbled in, and snippets of knowledge fell into superstition.

With the Age of Reason, science took over the domain of the mysterious. Suddenly there were explanations, physics, biology, chemistry. The supernatural no longer existed, everything could be explained, and that which couldn't would be in time. Time became the great equaliser, and when science still didn't come up with the answers, humans once again began to turn to other means.

In today's modern world we live in an uneasy coexistence with science and the magical. Science has of course explained many things that were once seen as the domain of the gods. We know how rain falls and crops grow, how volcanoes erupt and disease spreads. Yet there is so much that science cannot explain, so much it refuses to contemplate.

Essentially, magic is an act of creation. Perhaps it is this that makes magic such a contentious issue. Our stage magicians reflect the attitude to magic as a whole. The audience ponders how the trick is done and the Magic Circle closely guards the secret. We grow up with the attitude that somehow magic is only for the select few. It is complex and skilful, mysterious and scary. However, we also know that the stage magician has somehow fooled us into thinking that he or she has made something appear out of thin air. We breathe a sigh of wonder and relief—relief that even though we can't figure it out, we know it is simply an illusion. The magicians haven't stepped into the realms of the truly mysterious, for there lies the path to madness, infinity, the absolute unknown—deity.

Many occultists use a different spelling to denote the difference between stage magic and trickery from real magic—namely, magick. The addition of the letter *K* is fascinating in itself. *K* is the eleventh letter of the alphabet. In the tarot this corresponds to the Justice card, symbolising cosmic balance and truth. In astrology, the eleventh house is ruled by Uranus, "the awakener." The eleventh house rules communities and the cosmic. Numerologically speaking, $1 + 1 = 2$—the number of the High Priestess in the tarot and associated with the God in witchcraft. Eleven and two are about balance and union.

When any two are brought together in union they naturally create a third state—a state of togetherness, a child, a relationship, or an identity that differs from each individual state. They become more than what they were separately. Magic, then, is about creating something beyond what we currently see, using the energy of what is available and transforming it. The art of spellweaving is connected to bringing balance and awakening to a new state of being.

As a witch I believe that the divine is within as well as without. I am not separate from my Goddess and God. The divine spark resides within me. It is this divinity within that creates when I cast a spell. My spirit and soul are inextricably linked to the Otherworlds. To work a spell I must be in touch with my spirit. I must understand how it speaks to me and in turn how it relays my thoughts back to the universe.

There has been some debate about whether the result of magic is simply a change of consciousness or a solid physical change. Some say that a spell only alters perception, and is rather like being given a spiritual placebo. Certainly spells can be used in this manner—to reinforce internal changes. However, I believe that, ultimately, magic changes both consciousness and reality.

Reality

I said to the Goddess,
"What is the most important thing I should remember?"
And she said,
"The difference between infirm and inform is the I."

As different species view the world differently, so do we. Take any single event witnessed by ten people and you will have ten versions of the "truth." Some actions may be described in a similar way, others may conflict—either way, the "truth" of reality begins to break down. The reality outside of oneself is uniquely bound within one's own perceptions and beliefs. Your beliefs about the world and about yourself will govern your reactions and responses to the world around you. Your reactions and responses will create your experience of the world. Change your response and you change your experience. Many years ago I was given a dream in which I was told, "You cannot change your past but you can change your perception of it." Suddenly the past was no longer a place of fear; it was a place where I could choose to be afraid or not afraid.

My reality, then, is constantly in formation. I form my reality from my understanding of the *information* I receive. My understanding will feed information back into the universe, and so the world around me is created anew. Life is constantly in-formation. How it forms will be up to you and the information you feed from and feed back. The Buddha said, "We are what we think, with our thoughts we make our world." This is echoed in the Bible: "For as he thinketh in his heart, so is he" (Prov. 23:7).

Whether I see my world as sick or healthy depends on me. As the Goddess told me, "You are the key." I can look around me and say the world is full of hardship and loss, grief and sorrow, or I can look around me and say the world is full of potential, beauty, strength, and vibrancy. My emotions tinge my sight according to what I believe at the time. When I first realised that I create my own world I struggled with this concept and in fact used it as a stick with which to beat myself. My understanding at that time made me feel that if my life was difficult I had only myself to blame. Certainly that can be empowering on one level in that it is up to me to change my world and I have the power to do so, but on another level it forgets that we are not islands. My reality is intricately woven with other people's. Another person's worldview can conflict or converge with, or complement, mine.

I had a dream one night that I was walking through a strange house with several friends. We started to separate and look in different rooms. Suddenly I became aware of an old vampire in one of the rooms. I remember shouting, "Come back—before he shifts your reality. If you're there too long he will change your reality because you will believe his illusion."

This dream illustrates how easy it is to take on the perceptions of others, how easily our worldview can be altered, sometimes moment by moment. In therapy terms it is an example of how we absorb the values and beliefs of our parents, family, and friends—introjected values. Often these hide the real you. So *your* worldview can in part be shaped by the beliefs of *others*. In light of this it becomes clearer that this is an important issue when embarking on a magical path.

It is the human struggle to live as a community in a multitude of realities all being lived at the same time—and that's without myriad other dimensions! Also, the fact that I create my own world does not divorce me from my emotions. I have learned that part of the process of creation is to take note of my feelings and, more importantly, just allow myself to *feel* them. Therefore, I am not devoid of hate, guilt, anger, shame, jealously, despair, pain, anxiety, or frustration. All these emotional states teach me about how I view the world. They remind me that I am alive. Dark emotions challenge me to reform my worldview and my self-concept. They ask me to look again.

In lucid dreams we consciously interact with the environment we find ourselves in. We are consciously aware that we are dreaming. It is possible to interact with the landscape you find yourself in and change it at will. I have noticed on my travels that sometimes it is harder than other times to change the scenery. There seem to be various levels of lucidity. Sometimes I am completely aware that I am in a dream and I assume control, and other times I seem to have some awareness yet I cannot control the dream.

There is another curious state of lucidity that I have noticed. In this state I have a sense of being completely "awake." I am clearly conscious that I am in the dreamscape, yet the place where I wander is unfamiliar to me. I know that somehow this is not my world. Here I cannot change what is around me—the landscape seems fixed. Perhaps I have wandered into realms created by other dreamers or communal places or dimensions I have yet to understand.

In magical terms this illustrates that spells cannot change that which isn't meant to change. There are certain laws in the universe, karmic laws, laws of destiny and alignment, that cannot be broken. There are patterns in the great cosmic web that must remain as they are. If I try to change them I am repelled by an invisible yet sentient wall.

Song of the Star

Is all that we see or seem
but a dream within a dream?

—EDGAR ALLAN POE

Life to me is a dream within a dream. What we believe to be solid and unchanging isn't so. We have simply agreed to the consensus that there is an ultimate reality around us.

Life is like dreaming. If I focus clearly on what I want and it is in agreement with the rest of the universe, it manifests. If I am lucid in a dream I can create whatever I want, as long as I know what that want is and can hold the image of it in my mind. If it's confused, then what manifests is blurred or different from what I intended. I intend for a wild stallion to appear so I can remember my days of riding through the fields when I was a child, but what I get is a crippled old nag that can't carry me because somewhere along the line I remembered that I haven't ridden for years and fear I might fall off. Underneath that runs my constant weight monitor who hasn't yet accepted that I will never be a size eight and leaps at any opportunity to make itself heard! Your conscious desires may conflict with your subconscious and unconscious desires. You might be casting a spell to find a partner because consciously that's what you want. However, your subconscious may be telling quite a different story—it may whisper that you have been hurt and relationships can be unhappy. Maybe you find it hard to trust, or fear that a new relationship will change your life for the worse. These feelings, these emotional stories, are all heard by the Goddess, and inevitably the message becomes conflicting. This is why self-awareness is so important in magical work.

In *Conversations with God*, Neale Walsch gives a rather humorous example of why we need to be clear in our desires and what we say to the Gods when he talks about the nature of "wanting." If I feed the universe with a desire such as "I want money," then what is created is my want for money. I don't get the money, I get the *wanting*! Many spells suggest that once the spell is done you shouldn't think about it or talk about it. This is to let the energy of the spell flow out into the universe and create. If you keep thinking about what you have done and what it is you desire, the energy is never released. You may know the phrase "to know, to dare, to will, *to keep silent!*"

The waking world is the same as the dreamworld, only it takes a little longer for the manifestation to happen because the physical world has a heavier vibration. When I am completely in tune with the universe, however, I notice that physical manifestation speeds up, as if life has answered my call and has already set things in motion. It can be the simplest of things. For example:

> One day a vicious wind and lashing rain proved too much for my umbrella. I dumped the twisted remains in a bin and sheltered for a few moments. I needed to be somewhere and look presentable when I got there. Soon a friend drove up to me in his car and offered me a lift.

That is fast and simple manifestation motivated by a strong desire. It is a spell of the quickest kind.

The waking world and the states of awareness within it are a mirror to the dreamworld. I can be utterly unaware that I am dreaming as I can be utterly unaware in waking life. When I "wake up" in a dream everything comes into focus. Colours exist that I previously could not perceive. I am conscious of the ease with which I float through space and time and the exhilarating clarity of mind. I sense a great peace within me and feel like I have finally "come home." I can wave my hand across the landscape and where my hand passes snow falls or flowers blossom or the fields become stained glass windows shattering and reforming like a kaleidoscope.

Likewise, in waking reality when I become truly aware of myself, my environment, and my connection to it, I perceive different options. I feel more deeply and sense more intuitively. I belong. I'm in the right place at the right time and everything is as it should be. I am a perfect being in a perfect body.

If I live my life as if I were in an ordinary dream state then I simply accept reality as I find it. I interact with it, live in it, and let it lead me wherever. In other words, I just accept what I see. In that accepting, I may be drawn into casting spells to change the "reality" because I see no other way of it changing. I have the choice, however, to "wake up" to the world and live as if the world is as fluid as the landscape of a lucid dream. In that state anything and everything is possible, and limited only by your own imagination and the greater pattern. Spells in this state flow. Indeed, I have come to wonder whether life can be one long spell—the world recreating with each new story you tell it, with each level of self-awareness explored.

As I move through the world I am constantly receiving information through my body and through my spirit. My body feels the gentle breeze on this summer's afternoon, hears the hum of traffic in the background, sees the clouds rolling past my window, and tastes the cup of coffee I drink. In my interactions with others I send out all manner of signals—from the expression on my face to subtle body language. These signals, this language, this information triggers responses and reactions from others that, in turn, I react to.

Spells and Personal Development

There is only now . . .

If spells are just desires, then why is it that I haven't won the lottery or found the perfect partner or succeeded at everything I set out to do? This is the question I most often hear from those who come to my workshops or ask me about doing spells. It was a question that I asked myself over and over.

As I follow the spiral path of the witch in the outward world, I also follow the spiral inward. As I pass through each point of the Wheel of the Year I come to know myself a little better. Each Sabbat represents a stage of development, and we can use these markers as a trigger to work on personal issues. The journey is naturally cyclic. I come back to certain aspects of myself and issues over and over again. Each time I move deeper into the nature of myself, my beliefs, and my self-concept, and challenge those aspects that work against my innate desire to flourish. It is like removing layer upon layer of dust that clouds my spirit—the real me. With each layer cleared away I feel a shift in my consciousness.

It is not an easy journey. Throughout time witches have been known to be healers and keepers of wisdom. Perhaps it could be said that the journey of a witch is toward self-healing, self-understanding, and self-acceptance—being wise within and without. Many, if not all, of the disciplines associated with witchcraft heavily accent self-exploration. Tarot, astrology, healing, meditation, visualisation—all are methods of unlocking the doors of the mind so that your spirit shines. All ask you to question yourself.

As I explained earlier, for a spell to work or for your desire to manifest, you need to be clear and focused on the purpose of your spell. Every aspect of you needs to be in agreement of the desired result and comfortable with the consequences of the working.

In many ways, the beginnings of a spell can be likened to goal-setting. When you set a goal you need to think about your desired outcome and the steps you will take to get you there. It is also important to think about the obstacles, both internal and external, that may block your progress. Note that thinking *too* much about obstacles can in fact impede your progress because they can seem so daunting that your mind tells you it's just impossible. Many times I have found that if I cast a spell (or send up a desire to the universe), the obstacles shift or change or dissolve in ways I couldn't have possibly imagined. Be aware, but remain open to solutions.

Much of popular psychology emphasises the need to explore your subconscious desires and motivations, as these often carry far more weight in the outcome than your conscious wish. In terms of spellweaving, I can personally admit that it is no use screaming to the Goddess that I am utterly bored in my job and want another if all she hears is that other voice from my subconscious that says, "Yes, but changing jobs is so stressful and I might hate it and I have to leave all my friends and blah, blah, conflicting blah." Consciously you may be thinking and planning one thing, but if you have not allowed yourself to examine your true motivations you may find that your spell works in a way you didn't anticipate at all. The universe is very insightful. It can easily pick out your true feelings and beliefs, and it is those it uses to create with.

The process of casting a spell is an opportunity for increasing self-awareness. For example:

> I long to live in the countryside where it is quiet and pretty and the air is clear. Currently I live in the middle of a city where streetwise wisdom is learned quickly and the sound of cars and music are ever present.
>
> Some years back I decided enough was enough. Financially, I wasn't in a position to move; obstacles seemed everywhere. I pondered the idea of a spell. Rarely one to rush into ideas, I decided to meditate, then sleep on it.
>
> That night I dreamed I found a beautiful house. The house was old and white, with bright windows and high ceilings. Wind chimes tinkled in the garden and the sound and smell of the sea enchanted me. As I walked up the steps, keys in hand, a neighbour stopped me.
>
> "So you bought the old house, then?" Her question was loaded with trepidation. "You do know it's haunted, don't you?"
>
> I blustered something about not being bothered. I could handle a haunting. It seemed a fair trade for such a wonderful place. However, as I walked up the steps and into the house I felt a growing sense of "evil." Lights flickered on and off, my pets wouldn't come into the house, and suddenly I felt desperately alone. The evil presence enveloped me until I struggled to breathe. Finally I woke up.
>
> I instantly knew from my dream that this was not the time for a house-move spell. The "evil" in the house was my unacknowledged (or, more accurately, skated over) fears that spoke of isolation if I moved away from my friends and connections. The

neighbour brought the fear to my conscious mind. The lights going on and off were a warning sign—like a lighthouse. The fact that the house was "old" suggested that my motivations were based on something in my past rather than in my present. I did not take the dream to mean that I mustn't move ever—just that now wasn't the time. There were issues I needed to look at and I needed to be honest with myself concerning the reasons I was living in a place I insisted I hated. My dream highlighted my true feelings and hidden motivations for staying where I was. It was not magic I needed, it was self-exploration.

The next day I went outside and looked at the street on which I live. I noticed the people I say hello to every day, heard the bark of dogs I know by name. I thought about every person I had met whilst living here, and how those people had influenced my life. I wandered through the community gardens, the park, and looked out from the bridge onto the city skyline. Everything was familiar, and I suddenly realised that despite myself I did think of this place as home.

Beneath my desire for the countryside was a deep sadness at the thought of leaving. It was this that I needed to work with in order to free myself to move on. My spell became a spell for courage rather than lifting obstacles outside of myself to help me move.

In accordance with universal law that what is created internally is created externally, a mindful technique at the beginning of a spell is to invert the desire or intent. So, for example, say you wish to do a spell for love. Turning this inward would mean asking the question, "Where is love within me?" A spell for money could be turned inward by asking, "What do I value within me?" In my previous example I was led to find "home" and what that meant to me on the inside.

When you make a request to the universe, remember the infinite internal universe. What is it that you wish to manifest in the physical external world; how does this affect the psychic internal world? What you seek on the outside you seek within, also. What you ask to manifest on the physical plane is also liable to manifest on the inner plane. What is changed here is changed in the other worlds, and vice versa. Personal development through magical work is like following the double spiral associated with the horned god and the equinoxes.

As you follow the spiral path outward you also follow the spiral maze within—ever turning, ever searching, ever questing deeper and deeper into your soul. You are the microcosm.

If You Desire a Lover

- What does love mean to you?
- Whom do you love?
- How do you express love?
- What form does love take?
- What is love?
- Where in your body do you feel love?
- When love is showered upon you, how do you feel? Can you explain the feeling exactly?
- How does being loved by another change, shape, or define your life?
- What would it mean not to have this love?
- Can this love be felt without a partner?

If Your Desire Is Money or Financial Security

- How much are you worth on the inside?
- What do you value about yourself, others, and the world?
- What does "secure" mean to you?
- How much energy (psychic money) do you expend each day?
- How much is in your energetic account?
- Are you overdrawn (tired, sick, stressed, anxious)?
- What certainties are you looking for?

- Are there any certainties?

- Where lies your internal power?

- What are your strengths and weaknesses?

Asking these questions and others will lead you to the internal landscape. This landscape is linked to the astral worlds—those worlds that you connect with when you work a spell. The world is not separate from you. You are an intricate stitch in the fabric of time. If you change the stitch you change the pattern. You change all that has been and all that lies before you.

The first step to the working of a spell is *deciding* whether or not to work magic. Actual spells are a last resort. Work needs to be done on the physical plane to achieve the things you desire. You need to be going to places where you might meet that special someone, or applying for a new job, or putting your house up for sale, or taking an assertiveness course— and it is even more important to do these things once the spell has been cast. All these actions fuel the spell.

Our common perception of spells is that we cast a spell upon another or over a situation to force our will upon it. Any reality that conflicts with mine is moulded into something more acceptable to give me room to move in the way I desire. Examples include spells to attract a specific person, job, or experience. There are ethical dilemmas to be considered here. Casting a spell on another is certainly possible, but in what circumstances can this be done without harming another—or oneself, for that matter? Harm can be read as physical, emotional, or spiritual harm—harming the life-path of another in order to create a situation that you want. These are questions that are unanswerable because what constitutes harm to one person does not to another. We all have differing ethical standpoints, although some we have a consensus on; for instance, we don't do spells to physically or emotionally hurt someone just because we have been hurt by him or her—even that, though, is debated by many. Personally, I am not against petitioning the Goddess for quick justice if I have been the victim of a crime. How that justice manifests I leave to her. However, within this I also look at what I have learned from my experience. I seek to hand back my anger and pain to those that heaped it upon me—no more, no less. I am responsible for how I respond to being a victim. The perpetrator is responsible for his or her actions and the consequences of them.

Spells to attract a specific person or situation are minefields that I refuse now to walk into. After my first ever spell I realised that I could not presume to force my will upon another. Forcing my will also assumes that I have no trust in the greater pattern, or that I can learn from the experiences that come to me naturally. Now I would rather have someone love me for who I am than be in love with a glamour. I would rather listen to what life is trying to teach me.

What I consider to be of most importance is the process by which you decide to actually perform a spell and the questions you ask yourself along the way. A spell that hums to the tune of the universe is one that really comes from your heart.

Weaving with the Pentagram

I echo the maiden above,
the curve of my belly against the ground,
her light and a thousand sisters penetrate my mind . . .

As a child the stars captured me. I gazed up into space and counted as far as I could. Sleep came when a thousand lights had been pointed at and included. My dreams would be filled with stars wheeling above me forming endless dot-to-dot pictures that I would join together. A new sky would be born with each dream—a new world of opportunities with each creation.

When I look up into a brilliant clear night sky my body thrills to the tune of mystery and magic. I feel an overwhelming sense of connection, an infinite longing to understand, a wild dream that I can journey to this place and beyond. I look out at stars that have long since died, and a velvet canopy that hides those being born. The pattern of the constellations seems eternal, yet each is shifting away from the alignments I know and love and commune with. The sky lures me into thinking that this is the one thing eternal in our restless world, yet I know that isn't the truth. Each star seems to send out little lines of attachment, to me, to the ground beneath me, to every living thing. I am part of something so vast I cannot comprehend it, yet I sense it somewhere deep in my soul. I long for it, work with it, name it, and change it. I ask it questions and it throws back more in return. The stars remind me that I am a tiny being yet a giant soul.

Stars have enchanted the human mind since time began, and it is no surprise therefore that one of the most potent and well-known witches' symbols captures the mystery of infinity. Here on earth the magic of the stars is expressed in the perfect symbol: the pentagram.

The pentagram is a symbol that is popular amongst modern-day witches, but its history is far older. It is found in ancient Palestine and was used by the Sumerians. The word itself comes from the Greek *pente,* meaning "five," and *gramma,* meaning "a letter." Followers of Pythagoras called this shape a pent-alpha because it looks like five As weaved together. The letter *A* in many languages is a letter of power. It encompasses all beginnings and, by nature, all endings. The Babylonian goddess of beginnings was simply called *A.* Birth, death, and rebirth are the constants of a magical path. The river Styx, a place symbolising death and rebirth, had an alternative name: Alpha.

The upright pentagram has often been likened to the figure of a human with arms and legs stretched out—man as microcosm. The five points represent the five elements: earth, air, fire, water, and spirit. Contained within a circle the pentagram becomes a pentacle representing the five elements and the infinite; humankind in communion with the divine. Often in magical thought the pentacle is used as a symbol for earth—whether on the altar or in a tarot deck. All elements combined become physically manifest. The fifth element, spirit, is the breath that gives life to all.

In numerology the number five signifies change. In astrology the fifth house is ruled by Leo. Leo is ruled by the Sun, which signifies the *I*. The Sun gives life to planet Earth. The fifth house of the natal chart shows us our ability to create. In the tarot, the fifth card of the Major Arcana is the Hierophant, and in many decks it is symbolised as the Pope. He is shown holding a key—the key to the doorway between heaven and earth. This stems from, "I will give you the keys to the kingdom of heaven. Whatever you bind on earth shall be bound in heaven; and whatever you loose on earth shall be loosed in heaven" (Matt. 16:17–19).

The word "key" has a numerological value of five. The key is an emblem of St. Peter. The Papal flag includes two keys. Sometimes these are silver and gold (feminine and masculine, perhaps?). Even on a simple level the word "key" immediately links to "unlocking."

The pentagram, therefore, is the key to creation. Within this simple pattern is a profound understanding of the universe. Five is a number rarely found in inorganic structures, but it is prevalent in organic life. You only need to look at your hands and feet, flowers and starfish. We are blessed with five physical senses: taste, touch, smell, sight, and hearing. The basic outline of the pentagram is used to denote luck or fame, and we still use the phrases "thank your lucky stars" and "wish upon a star."

Muslims pray five times a day and see the pentagram as a symbol of creation. In medieval times, the "endless knot" was the symbol of truth, as it was also to the Hebrews. To the Egyptians the pentagram was the underground womb.

The old folk song "Green Grow the Rushes, O" sums this up rather well: "five is the symbol at your door." It refers to the fact that people would use the pentagram as a sign of protection in their homes, but I read it on a deeper level. The pentagram becomes both the key and the door.

To understand the nature of spirit we need to open the four gateways to the elements. If you reduce fire, water, earth, and air to a single number in numerology, you are left with the number five. The four elements of the physical world are a doorway to the spiritual world. By understanding the spiritual teachings that each of the mundane elemental guardians have to give, we come to know the fifth element. When we communicate with our spirit we become the Creator.

For me the pentacle is a unique symbol that touches upon every aspect of my magical work. It is earth, change, infinity, wisdom, connection, the visible and the invisible, the mundane and the spiritual. It is all things.

Connecting with the Elements

The North Speaks
Earth

I am mystery. I am the snow-driven fields that show nothing of the promise beneath. I come to you when you are lost and ask, "What is your question?" I am ice—the keeper of memories. I am absolute silence.

I am the long nights that ask you to be still with your own darkness. I am the age-old bear wheeling in the sky, the compass and the map. I am the sorrow that steals upon you at midnight when all around you sleep. I am the shadow that escapes your gaze. I am the hidden face of the moon and I reside within each eclipse of the sun. I am the velvet darkness of eternal rest. I am the Cailleach that strips bare the trees in winter, the mountain summit that haunts you, the quiet earth beneath your feet. I am wood and stone, coal, peat, and precious metal. I am the footprint that remains for a million years in stone. I am far memory and your ancestry—your genetic makeup, both physical and psychic. I am old.

I am there in your employment, your career, your job. I notice how you value yourself and others as you value money and material possessions. I offer patience and strength when you think you cannot go on. I am the solace of an embrace and the violence of a volcano. I am within the walls of your home, in the flowers you tend. I am the fertile womb, muscle and bone, and the food you eat.

I am the stability you seek, the success you gain, and the creativity you express. I am the crystal keepers of wisdom and the power-animals' care. I am woodland, hedge and fence, field and plough. I am the orbit and the steady turn of the earth. I am the Keeper of Time, yet know time is an illusion.

I am the manifestation of thought.

Connecting with Earth

Walk barefoot on the grass, through woodlands and forests. Lie on a hillside face down, like the snake, and listen to the heartbeat of the Mother. Sit beneath a tree and lean your back against the bark and see what thoughts come to mind. Meditate in a cave. Watch for stones that speak to you through their shape or colour. Plant seeds and tend to your garden, balcony, or houseplants. Eat organic food and eat mindfully. Play with clay or carve sustainable wood.

Consider the animals that you are drawn to and those that repel you. Watch nature programs and notice the wildlife in your immediate environment—whether urban or rural. Nature is everywhere!

Be aware of your home and what it expresses about you—each room relates to aspects of yourself. Try to see it through the eyes of a stranger—what does it say about you? Think about what money and security mean to you. What are your strengths and weaknesses? Are you comfortable with silence and darkness? Sit in a dark room—what do you see, sense, or hear?

Visit stone circles and sacred spaces. See if you can tune in to the energy of these places or just note your immediate impressions. In your own neighbourhood, see if you can sense the subtle energy shifts, the lines of power, the places where energy is drained. What does winter mean to you? Read up on the astrological signs Taurus, Virgo, and Capricorn.

The East Speaks
Air

I am the dawn of all things, beginnings, buds, whispers on the wind. I am the sunrise that follows the night you thought would never end. I am the kindling of orange on the horizon that heals old wounds. I am anima—the breath of life. I am your voice and your ability to think. I am in your desire to communicate and express. Come to me when you are lost for words. I sat by your side when you learned to tell the time. I am memory and concentration. I was there in your first friendship and first flirtation and I am in those special moments when you know you are understood.

I am the hawk that rides the breeze and calls to you to look up—to see the great dome of blue and welcome the sunshine. I am the lark that gave you your love of music and melody. I am the clouds that paint great pictures in the sky, the soft balloon that you let loose as a child. I am the eddy that spirals across the field and the hurricane that makes all things bow. I am the voice of the trees, leaf upon leaf, that comforts you.

I am found within truth and justice. I stand for universal balance. I am the call to invent and discuss, theorise and decide. I am in every decision you make. There is no right or wrong way—the decision itself is the teaching I offer.

I remind you that the earth is a community, a neighbourhood of souls; that there are realms beyond this one and that language comes in many forms. I am the ability to rise above what is known and see beyond the next horizon. I am illumination.

Connecting with Air

Feel the breeze on your face. Take a balloon ride. Notice how the wind passes through and around you. Be aware of the changes in pressure that bring rain or shine. Notice the clouds and how their forms glide and change. Write down the pictures you see within them. Gaze into the vastness of a blue sky and compare it with that of the night sky. Learn to recognise constellations and direction: north, south, east, and west.

Watch how a bird rides the wind, how a flock of birds gracefully folds over and over. Throw a feather into the sky. Get up just before dawn and meditate or dance to the sunrise. Allow your senses to open up as the sun's rays grow longer.

Listen to yourself when you speak. Be aware of your thoughts. Consider how you deal with conflict and decision making. Learn a new language or take up a course that challenges you to think beyond where you are. Be aware of your breath—breathe slowly and deeply three times, inhaling and exhaling to a count of eight with a slight pause before letting out the breath, and see how the tension leaves your body.

Turn to face east and imagine flying high up into the sky. What do you see? Think of spring and what this season means to you. Read up on the astrological signs Gemini, Libra, and Aquarius.

The South Speaks

Fire

I am passion. I am the heat of the noonday sun and the force of a super-nova. I am summer in all its glory. I am the blood that courses through your veins, the brilliant red of love, rage, war, and life. I am the pulse and the rhythm you dance to, the beat of the shaman's drum, and hooves upon the sand. I am the King Stag silently watching from the woodland clearing, the clash of antlers, the duality. I purify and I destroy. I urge you in your desires. I am the wild embrace of lovers and the soft candle flame of a kiss.

I am there when you race to the finish line, see the mountain to climb, and I honour your individuality. I am there when you fight for what you see as the truth. I am within that flash of inspiration that warms your belly and sparks your mind. I am in your vivid dreams that show you the way. You seek me when you have a thirst for knowledge and when the horizon glistens with the promise of pastures new. I give you courage to forge your own path.

I am the hearth fire that soothes, the bonfire, the bel-fire, the torch and lightning. Watch my flames and I will show you a story of how humans befriended me but never tamed me. I have no definite shape, yet I am defined by my nature. I am fierce, a warrior, a traveller, a storyteller, an entertainer, an explorer. I am and I create. I am the curiosity of children, the thirst to survive, the hunger for more, and the primal scream. I am complex, combustible, terrifying, and lifesaving. I am inner light—the divine spark within.

Connecting with Fire

Gaze into the flame of a candle, bonfire, hearth fire, or campfire. What pictures do you see? Listen to the song of the fire. Retell your own stories—those you have lived through, those you have heard. Imagine your inner light growing brighter—commune with it, connect with it.

Feel the heat of a warm summer's day, the warmth of hot food in your belly. Get up and dance and sing; move with whatever rhythm inspires you. Be aware of your sensual and sexual nature—relax with it, own it, delight in it.

Play with your children, play children's games, or recall your own favourite childhood pastimes. Paint pictures or compose songs.

Go to new places—it doesn't matter how near or far away they are. Experience new concepts and ways of being. Take up a cause that is close to your heart; support a charity that works for positive change. Honour the truth. Remember when you have been courageous. Read up on the astrological signs Aries, Leo, and Sagittarius.

The West Speaks

Water

I am the tide. I am soft showers and wild flood. I am the ocean—the history of the human race. Within me are buried treasures; across me are smooth waves to carry you and quieten you and lull you. I remind you of your life in the womb. I am the Great Mother.

I am sister to the moon and between us we set the pace of life—the gentle cycles of body and soul. We are set and yet we stand for fluidity. I am the place where the sun sets; I am the dissolving of light—the in-between of life and death. I am there in your grief, your tears in each rise and fall of emotion. I am despair and sorrow, compassion and love. I am unconditional love.

I am memory and remembrance, the Land of the Young and eternity. I am there in those moments when you know you have been here before. I am the recognition between you and a stranger. I echo the depths of your mind and the wonder and fear you find there. I can wash away all that has been and reshape the landscape. I purify. I overwhelm. I am the mysterious call of whale and dolphin.

I am security and the oasis. I am mystery, taboo, and procreation. I am the unknown, the hidden, and the lost. All things return to me. I am reflection, healing, and intuition. I am poetry, art, and the desire to leave something behind. I am that which cannot be expressed in words. I am unconscious desires, dreams that show you the way, prayer and absolute peace.

I am connection.

Connecting with Water

Take a bath. Pour water over your hands. Go out in the torrential rain at the height of summer and feel how it washes you clean. Find a safe beach and float on the ocean or just walk by the water's edge and listen to the hush and shy of waves breaking. Drink at least eight glasses of water a day.

Tune in to the moon phases. Record them with your thoughts and dreams. Compare each new, full, and dark moon with your emotional state and general life. Do you see any patterns emerging?

Think about those you love. What is it that you love about them? What do you love about yourself? Unconditional love is a powerful healing energy.

Practice scrying or other forms of divination. Be aware of communication in the form of synchronicities and symbols appearing. Watch the sunset. Go out for a walk in autumn. Read up on the astrological signs Cancer, Scorpio, and Pisces.

Ways of Weaving

Castles in the air vanish in the midday sun.
Be still and gather strength, for there is much to be done.
You are the Art, the Message, and the Song.

A spell can be as simple as a thought directed, lighting a candle in a quiet circle, or as elaborate as a full-blown ritual, creating talismans on a specific tide and decorating altars. When you wish upon a star you are performing a spell. As the star falls from the heavens it carries the wish to earth, where it can manifest. When you send up a prayer for healing, when you gaze at your lover's photo, saying "Call me!"—these are spells. Essentially there are no right or wrong ways of performing spells (although awareness of psychic protection is advisable), just different methods of working. I have worked in many different ways and all have manifested the desired outcome. Typically, however, I work alone with the things I have at hand and music in my heart. Despite living in the city, my country-dwelling roots often show themselves in the way I work. I may collect flowers or pieces of wood that suggest themselves to me. Sometimes I gather stones or use my tarot cards as a focus for my ritual. Sometimes I create the ritual way in advance of an actual working; at other times it is spontaneous. Whatever method you choose, the goal is to achieve focus, raise energy, and direct that energy to the desired outcome.

The majority of spells performed work with what is termed *sympathetic magic*. This means that the tools or objects you use correspond to the intention of the spell. For example, red is the colour of passion, determination, and motivation, so you might use a red candle when you want to work a spell to increase energy and drive. White is the colour we associate with purity and cleanliness, so you might use a white candle to work a cleansing spell for the body or for your home. The colours are in sympathy with the energy you call upon.

There are many books on the market and sites on the Internet with tables of correspondences for you to look up and work with. These are useful, but I prefer to work with tools, symbols, and colours that have personal meaning to me. I want to understand why they are present rather than just have them there because they are said to be of a similar vibration. This way I feel that every part of my working is unique to me. Every part contains my essence and my voice.

The most universal language we all have access to is symbolism. Our dreams contain layer upon layer of symbols that convey complex messages, intuitions, and information. Learning to work with symbolism is one of the most basic and necessary skills when walking a magical path. The other skills I would suggest as being vitally important are the ability to visualise and the ability to be still and focused at any given moment.

When you perform a spell you are creating a microcosm of the world—as the pentagram symbolises. Each tool, each motion you use enhances and amplifies your intent. Magic is created in the mind, but we use tools and ritual to focus mind, body, and spirit on the matter at hand. A spell puts you in touch with the forces of the universe, the myriad worlds that crisscross their way through our hearts and minds.

Devising Your Own Spells

Personally, I prefer simple spells and small rituals. Sometimes I use tools, and other times I cast using only my mind. You must choose a method that suits you best.

One quick technique I use to cast a spell is to visualise a protective circle around me, then visualise a pentagram. Into the pentagram I put my desire, then I visualise the gateways of the four elements opening and flowing out toward me. I form the centre point of the cross. I am careful not to use my own energy in the process, otherwise I will be drained after doing the spell. It is the same as when one is channelling healing to another—you are a channel for the healing, not the source. I call upon the Goddess and the God and ask them to bless my desire. Once I feel the energy building I focus it into my pentagram. Sometimes I also send Reiki into it. When I feel that I have channelled enough energy, I release the pentagram like a balloon. I thank the deities and elements, lay my hands upon the floor to ground any excess energy, and the spell is done. If I still feel a little disorientated afterward, I eat lightly to bring me back to earth. Mostly I cast at night so I can sleep after a ritual. I prefer to work with the moon so that she can pass on my message to the sun. This symbolises the internal becoming external, the unclear becoming clear, the fluid becoming solid.

If I need to cast a spell very quickly I simply use the pentagram balloon alone. I visualize a pentagram made of light that floats in the air above me as if a fine cord is attached to it. I hold this cord in my hand. I then visualize my desire in the centre of this balloon. I do this by reducing my desire to a symbol—something simple and to the point, such as a coin for money, for example, or a rune that embodies the kind of energy I am looking to draw to me. By doing this, my desire is enfolded by earth, air, fire, water, and spirit. I then thank the Goddess and release the balloon. It is done. This could also be done with a real balloon. Write down your desire—in code, sigils, or as a drawing, and tie it to a balloon. You could use a corresponding colour for your balloon, if you wish. Then simply take it outside and release it into the air. Watch as it carries your message up to the gods, then, once it is out of sight, forget about it.

A spell can be broken down into several parts. These are just some suggestions for how to proceed with each. They are not carved in stone and I heartily encourage you to go with whatever feels right for you.

Desire and Intent

You need to be able to name and clearly visualise your desire in as much detail as possible. Without a clear focus your spell is a nonstarter. Think about what it would be like to have achieved your desire—how it would feel. Whilst thinking about your desire, notice your reactions in your mind and body. Do you feel tension anywhere, or bubbling excitement? What do these feelings mean to you? What is your overall intention?

Try to describe your desire succinctly out loud, as long lists become complicated. The classic list is something like, "A partner who has brown hair, a good job, a car, is a vegetarian, a nonsmoker, has no children . . ." How about simply, "The right person for me"?

Generally I meditate or sleep on a spell before casting. Another option is to divine using tarot, astrology, runes, or whatever method appeals to you. This can bring to light things you hadn't previously considered and raise issues that you need to be aware of. In some circumstances—such as in my idea to cast a spell to move home—it can change the focus of your spell altogether.

Timing: When to Work a Spell

Spells can be worked immediately or can be planned around a specific time that links to the purpose of the spell. Days of the week and hours of the day are assigned different planetary rulers, and the planets rule over different aspects of life and contain certain virtues and attributes. The moon tides are also very important in spellweaving. The phase of the moon is clearly visible (when it isn't cloudy!) and each phase marks a different energy. New moon, for example, is a time to start new projects, full moon brings things into fruition, and at dark moon we banish what isn't needed. In time as you work more closely with the Moon Goddess you will find that you don't even need to see her to know which cloak she wears. All of my spells and rituals are noted in my Book of Shadows, along with moon phases and signs, so that I can see any patterns that emerge. I do find certain moons more difficult to work with; some electrify me with energy, some make me cry. Working with these cycles puts me in touch with my own rhythm.

Cleansing/Purging

Cleanse the space that you wish to work in, and cleanse yourself. You may find that going on a day-long fast, taking a long walk in the countryside, or taking a long bath helps to set the mood. Quite often I begin a spell with a big house tidy. I throw out anything that I don't need, sort through papers, and generally make sure everything is in order. This is my method of purging—making way for the new. You can smudge the room with lavender or sage or ring a bell to dispel stagnant energy. Take the phone off the hook, put a note on the door, and clear children and animals from the room if they will distract you.

Casting a Circle

Use salt, a cord, tea-lights (be careful!), stones, crystals, or simply visualise a circle of light. This is to create a safe, undisturbed area for you to work in. When you perform a spell you are opening yourself up to the Otherworlds and all manner of energies and vibrations. The circle protects you from attracting unwanted energy that can leave you feeling drained and confused. It is also a sacred space between the worlds and time. As you cast the circle you may wish to say out loud what you are doing. For example, I say:

> I cast this circle in the name of Father Sky and Mother Earth.
> Within it no harm will come to me.

I usually walk the circle three times and recite as I do so.

Invoking the Elements

Find something to represent each element—typically incense for air, water for water, soil or stone for earth, and a candle for fire. Use a compass so that you know which direction to face, but if you don't have one don't be too concerned if you end up facing east when you meant to face west. I've done it and I'm sure others have, too, even if it's never mentioned. It is your intention that counts! In time as you perform rituals more often you will find that your sense of direction improves and that you quietly take note of where the sun rises and sets.

When I call upon the elements I imagine a doorway opening and the Guardian of each doorway walking toward me. Often I see them as animals, but some use the names of the archangels or sense or see them in other forms.

Invoking Deity

You may call upon the divine generally (such as I often just call upon the Goddess) or use a particular goddess and/or god that feels appropriate for the spell you want to do. So, for example, if I am working a spell to make the way clear I might call upon Ariadne to throw me a line through the maze or call upon Brigit to help me with creative projects.

Some people are drawn to particular pantheons and traditions such as Celtic, Egyptian, Greek, or Norse. Others may draw on a broad range of deities according to their own intuition and feeling. For me the Goddess and her many names and aspects are a personification of whatever the intelligence of the universe is. She may actually be a deity, a sentient energy that pervades all, an alien, or something else altogether! I feel no great need to define to myself which it is—it is enough to know she is there.

Read up on the myths and legends of those pantheons that attract and inspire you. Call upon deities who have a connection with your purpose for a spell. Invocation, like all else in witchcraft, can be as simple or as complicated as you wish. Let the words you use bubble up from your spirit. As I call upon my Goddess and God I light candles to represent them—their *light* is present and with me.

The following was written on April 28, 2002, after I had been bereaved. I felt disconnected and disoriented. I decided to work a spell to reconnect to my spirit, and these words came spontaneously as I quietly asked the Goddess to help me heal from my grief.

Lady be with me
Beneath my feet
Above my head
To my left, to my right

Lady be with me
In my past
In my future
Before and behind

Lady be with me
As I wake

As I sleep
Day and night

Lady be with me
In my thoughts
In my words
In my deeds

Lady be with me
In my heart
In my soul
In my dreams

Lady be with me
As I tend
The quiet earth
The blazing hearth

Lady be with me
As I walk
As I work
The witch's path

Generally during an invocation you call upon the deity of choice and ask him or her to bear witness to the purpose of your ritual. Your invocations do not have to rhyme. I find it easier to say something that rhymes because it is easy to remember and contains a rhythm that helps me focus. If you prepare beforehand and you are stuck for words, try writing down single words that you know you want to say; for example, for a spell to clear the air after an argument you might want to use the words like peace, clarity, friendship, and so on. Now think of each word you have written down in turn—what images come to mind? When I think of peace I think of a gentle, calm sea; clarity makes me think of the sun; and friendship calls to mind love, understanding, support, and joy.

So, my invocation might be:

Song of the Star

Mother Goddess, hear my prayer
Now that words have been spoken and harmony broken.
The ocean is stormy. The skies are dark.
May my rite bring peace, calm water, and light.
May my anger and hurt be dispelled on this night.

Okay, not the perfect poem, but it was right off the top of my head! I used this after an argument had occurred in my home. The spell was not intended to "put things right between me and my friend," as that needed to be done on a real and physical level with eye contact; rather, it was to clear my house of angry vibes so that I could think clearly about what had happened between us and try to understand the source of my anger. The words and images you find are your own and unique to you and the spell you work. It is between you and your gods, so you are free to express yourself in whatever way you choose.

Raising and Directing Energy

Dancing, drumming, and chanting are some of the ways people raise energy for a spell. You can also simply strongly visualise energy being channelled into your desire. Only you can judge when enough energy is raised. It comes with intuitive practice. You may channel the energy into a thought form or something that symbolises your intent. Some people may place a cauldron at the centre of their circle and use this to receive energy. Commonly I use a candle whose colour corresponds to my purpose, perhaps carving a few words or a picture into the wax. As the candle burns down the energy is released to do its work. Some people use a cord or a talisman, a piece of paper that is then burned, a crystal, or any other suitable object. Another method that I find works well is to set out tarot cards that tell the story of what I want to achieve or that symbolise achieving a goal—the Star and the World and the Ace of Wands have been used many times for different purposes! Once I feel that enough energy has been put into the spell I release the energy by imagining that the cards are doorways opening and all the energy I put into them flows out into the Otherworlds to do what it's meant to do. Sometimes I imagine handing the energy directly to the characters displayed on the cards, as though they are little helpers that will take the energy where it needs to go.

Closing the Circle

Once the energy is released the spell is finished. Thank the deities and elements for attending, and imagine firmly closing all doors you have opened to the Otherworlds.

Snuff out any candles that you have used (unless you are leaving a candle that has been used as the focus of your spell to burn down in a safe place). Ground excess energy and partake in a little food or water/wine to come fully back to earth. The circle itself will disperse naturally.

I am an act of creation.
I am the result of my parent's desire to have a child, nature's desire to survive.
I am the creation of a millennia of desires, actions, and inactions—
chance meetings, missed moments, decisions taken, steps into the unknown.
I am a creation of body, mind, and spirit, physical, mental, and spiritual.
I am something that sits, thinks, sneezes, and sleeps.
From the moment I was placed on my mother's stomach I created havoc with
my screaming, peace with my suckling, contentment with my smiles.
As I lay in my cot, a billion eyes looked down upon me.
Me, the result of their creation.
I am creation.
I create.

My life is one long spellweaving, something unbreakable yet delicate—changed in a thought. Ariadne has allotted me a line of destiny to weave as I will in accordance with universal law. Above me Arianrhod takes up my thread and throws it out to the sea of stars. When I am still and centred I notice where there are patterns emerging in the whole—places where I can make my stitches. When my heart sings I hear her voice echo and a glorious harmony rings out. I weave when I must and trust my heart to choose the right colours. Magic is in every moment and every breath.

I honour your path and your creation.

Acknowledgments

Nadia Muscaty, for her comments regarding the connection between the nature of reality and the Dreamworlds. Thank you!

Bibliography

Walsch, Neale Donald. *Conversations with God: An Uncommon Dialogue, Book 1*. London: Hodder and Stoughton, 1997.

Frazer, Sir James George. *The Golden Bough*. Hertfordshire, UK: Wordsworth Editions, 1993.

Adler, Margot. *Drawing Down the Moon*. Boston: Beacon Press, 1986.

Merriam-Webster Online Dictionary.
Quote on page 5 used by permission. From the *Merriam-Webster Online Dictionary* © 2004 by Merriam-Webster, Incorporated (www.Merriam-Webster.com).

Nataf, Andre. *The Wordsworth Dictionary of the Occult*. Hertfordshire, UK: Wordsworth Editions, 1994.

Nature and Magic

ELEN HAWKE

If you go into almost any high street bookshop in practically any major city in the Western world, you will see an assortment of spell books with plush covers, wildly embellished typography, and lurid, colour-saturated illustrations. The magical focus of these books is often love, career, or money—the three most common concerns for many people. Not far away, probably even on the same shelves, you will also find some extremely serious-looking magical tomes, probably in black, dark blue, or brown, with plain white lettering, and bearing such titles as Grimoire, Ritual Magic, or Book of Shadows. The contents of these books may seem very studious and obscure, and may be written in archaic or pseudoarchaic language, with complicated-looking lists and tables and the odd sigil here and there. In between these two extremes are dozens (stocked from a choice of literally hundreds, if not thousands) of books on witchcraft and other forms of paganism, some well written and informative, some racy and sensationalist in Wicca-meets-Hollywood style. In a culture that highly values scholarly pursuits and academic qualifications, and also, conversely, glamour and glitz, it is perhaps unsurprising that we expect to acquire our knowledge of spellwork in the same ways.

Of course, there are some excellent books on magic. If you are studying ritual magic or one of the other old magical systems, then you will need to apply yourself diligently to some of the expert writings on the subject and gradually learn about planetary hours, the watchtowers, and other arcane matters, and will almost certainly be working within an occult lodge or with a teacher, or at the very least by careful study. (If you aren't prepared to put a huge amount of time and effort into learning this type of lore, then you are dabbling and are behaving foolishly and possibly dangerously.) Similarly, if you have already done a fair bit of training within one of the pagan systems such as witchcraft or druidry, either of your own volition or with a teacher or group, and have acquired certain basics such as the elements and correspondences, then you will find it easier to make proper use of books on subjects such as candle spells or herb lore. Indeed, many books on magic, as well as general Craft books that include spells, are excellent starting points for the fledgling spell crafter, as long as it is understood that they need to be incorporated into an overall practice where learning is gradual and careful. Unfortunately, careful, meticulous hard work is not the message indicated by a great many of the magical books on the market; instead, they seem to promise the attainment of your every desire, all achieved by dramatic flourishes and incantations, on a par with the performance of the witches in popular films and television programmes. The books that treat the subject seriously, on the other hand, are likely to appear complicated and obscure, leaving all but the most precocious and foolhardy of would-be practitioners intimidated and overwhelmed.

So how do you steer a middle course between these two extremes, while taking the best from the published material and putting it to work? The answer is simple. Magic is a part of nature, as much a function of life as rain and wind and sun, or the very acts of sleeping, eating, and breathing. Magic obeys the same natural laws as these things, and to utilise magical force we only need to tap into the universal energy flow, but we need to do so respectfully and in the right way. Although it requires hard work, concentration, and dedication, weaving magic is something that all of us can learn. In fact, many people probably practice magic without realising that's what they are doing. Have you ever wished for something with all your heart, thought about it all the time, visualised it, obsessed about it? If you have, then you were employing the very techniques used to bring a magical goal to fruition.

It is also important to realise that magical work is not something that can be reasonably split off from other elements of the Craft. Indeed, along with being very much rooted in nature, it is also about growth, the spirit, and self-realisation. Whether or not that was your original intention, practising magic will lead to deep and profound changes in your life. I will say that again: magic will change you, sometimes in ways you had not anticipated, so be prepared to work positively with those changes. Not only that, but how you work magically will affect other people, too, for we are not isolated beings but are part of the vast web of creation within which everything is linked; so your spellcrafting must be responsible, ethical, and careful.

So how do we utilise the natural forces that are necessary for spell-work? There is a current trend for books on magic to stress the use of ritual tools, candles, and other props. These things are fine, and in fact a bit of drama will enhance your spellwork and put you in the frame of mind to succeed. However, they are not strictly necessary, and becoming dependent on them will limit your magic and turn it into something lacking in depth, understanding, and purpose. Furthermore, some modern spell books tend to either overcomplicate or overexplain the process, leading to an eroding of personal creativity and a lack of confidence. An intricate spell requiring specific ingredients put together at a strictly appointed time may sound very impressive, but it is likely to make the inexperienced practitioner fearful or anxious. Conversely, a spell that is handed to you on a plate, so to speak, may be ineffectual or only partly successful because it has not asked for the application of sufficient energy and willpower, or has failed to fire the imagination. It is perfectly possible to work magic without recourse to either of these alternatives, and the secret lies in reconnecting to the natural world, the seasons, the phases of heavenly bodies, including the moon. It also requires the use of observation and common sense. Along with these ingredients, it may be useful to borrow techniques from other spiritual systems that have made long studies of how to employ cosmic energies, such as the chakra system.

Moon, Sun, Stars, and the Natural World

To the practitioners of folk magic in times gone by, their art was not separate from their daily lives. People lived very close to the soil, depending on an acute observation of the climate, animals, insects and birds, plant growth, and a host of other factors in the course of producing their own food and keeping sheltered and in good health. Their magic was interwoven with these things, so that herbs, charms, potions, and cures were part and parcel of the mundane round of living. They probably employed their observations of the seasons, the moon's phases, and weather lore to aid their farming and gardening, and out of this may have grown an appreciation of timing for spells and healing.

Present-day witches, druids, and other pagans work with these natural cycles, too, aligning their magic with the rhythm of the monthly and seasonal tides to take advantage of the ebb and flow of the cosmic process. The following categories show how this timing takes place and how spells benefit from it. Going with the flow is always easier and more successful than working against it, so a knowledge of natural cycles is important if your magical efforts are to bear healthy fruit.

The Moon

Modern pagan myth breaks the moon's cycles down into three major phases that are attributed to the three life stages of women, and the three faces of the Goddess. These are new, full, and waning, and relate to the Maiden, Mother, and Crone stages of women's lives. There are at least three other phases that can be worked with, including dark moon and the quarter moons, but for the sake of clarity I won't pursue them here, though it would be well worth your effort to look into and experiment with these extra phases.

When the moon is new, everything is filled with vitality. This is a time of beginnings, of enthusiasm, a time for planting and watching things grow. This is the best time to cast spells that are concerned with fresh enterprises, such as looking for a new job or a new direction. If you are a gardener, then seeds do best if planted now as well.

The full moon brings culmination and harvest. Spells to bring a definite, fully realised result, or to empower the culmination of an ongoing goal are best suited to this moon's phase. It is also a time to celebrate, with so much exhilarating energy available. Magic now is concerned with specifics rather than ideas; you will be working on a definite goal, not looking for the right one out of many possibilities. In field and garden, as with magic, this is the time to reap what you have grown.

The period when the moon is going from full to dark is better suited to winding down, letting go, or getting rid of the unwanted or outworn. You should see this time as a release, when all that has outlived its purpose can be gently relinquished. Try to visualise this as a dark, restful, inward period when you recuperate, ready for new growth. You may find such activities as scrying, meditation, and spiritual learning productive now. Examples of spells that would be appropriate are those for banishing unwanted conditions, including illness, or for releasing a relationship that has ended, thus setting both partners free of the negative bonds that may still be holding them back from forming new links. If you are a gardener, you will find that this is the best time for pruning dead wood from plants and trees; the life force is ebbing and the plant can rest to recover from your surgery. Weeding is appropriate now, as the diminishing energies make it harder for pernicious weeds to revive.

A positive way to work with the lunar cycle is to clear the ground while the moon is waning, using some sort of banishing spell to release that which is no longer needed (you might banish illness or excess weight, for example, prior to working on building up your health), then beginning a positive regime, or planting novel ideas when the new moon comes, finally reinforcing the spell or stating a precise intention when the moon reaches full.

The following simple example will help to demonstrate how a spell can be timed to the moon. It doesn't matter if you don't adhere to the instructions precisely, and it can be adapted to suit other goals as well.

Spell to Find a Suitable Job

Let us assume that you are unhappy or dissatisfied in your present employment, or perhaps that you want to relocate to another area and need to find work there, but that all attempts to find something by mundane methods have failed. If you haven't looked in the paper or at job centres or any other outlets for finding work, then you are possibly wasting your time with magical means, which should be used as a last resort. Believe me, magic takes much more effort.

Find out from an ephemeris, calendar, or almanac when the moon is waning, or go and look at the night sky—the waning moon shows increasing dark on the right-hand side, with a diminishing lit crescent on the left. Spend some time while the moon is waning meditating on whether there are any blocks in yourself, such as fear of the unknown, anxiety that you may be about to do the wrong thing, fear of change, and so on, that may be holding you back. Sitting in a quiet space with a candle lit, then closing your eyes and gently thinking about changing jobs, being alert for any worries and signs of inner resistance, will probably make you aware of factors you hadn't perceived before. You may even realise that you don't want to change jobs at all, and that what is needed is a reassessment of your current employment, along with consideration of what might be done to improve your work situation, your own performance, relationships with bosses or fellow workers, or whatever else is not totally satisfactory, including possibly a raise in pay. You could even discover that the job isn't the issue at all, but is an area of your life upon which you have projected anxieties about some other matter of which you have not been consciously aware.

You must consider ethics throughout this magical exercise: it is wrong, unkind, and dangerous to try to deprive someone else of his or her job or status in pursuit of your own needs. Any magic worked to harm, deprive, or otherwise negatively affect another person will always rebound on the one performing the spell.

Two or three days before the new moon, when the old moon has waned to a very thin crescent or is completely dark, collect some earth from the garden, or obtain some compost. You need enough to fill a small bowl. If you are using compost, please try to find some that isn't peat based, as peat is a rapidly dwindling resource, and peat bogs, a part of our environmental heritage, are being dug out of existence to produce commercial gardening products.

When it is dark, take your bowl of soil to a quiet place where you can sit undisturbed for a while. Hold the bowl in your hands, bring to mind all the blocks, fears, and worries that are surrounding your quest for an improved job situation, then visualise these blocks as clearly as you can for several minutes. Now imagine that all those negative factors are flowing in a murky, sticky stream out of you, down through your arms and hands, and into the bowl of earth. Let this process go on till you feel it is time to stop. Try to visualise the sticky dark stream as vividly as possible, but allow yourself to let it flow unimpeded.

When the flow has finished, keep holding the bowl and tell yourself that the negative factors you have projected into it are like decaying material that will be broken down into a useful growth medium. Many things return to the soil: the corpses of once-living creatures, ourselves included; rotting vegetable and plant matter; the shells of snails and hard outer skeletal cases of various insects; leaves; weeds; spent seed pods. Sometimes this organic waste is unpleasant and distasteful, but it all mulches down to make sweet, health-giving loam in which new plants will grow. Your doubts, fears, blocks, and worries will mulch down, too, metaphorically and in terms of energy, and can be used to promote growth as well, as we shall see shortly.

Put the bowl of soil on a shelf or shrine. Leave it there till the new moon crescent can be seen in the sky (or two to three days after astronomical new moon—if the sky is too cloudy to see the moon, look it up in the appropriate tables). You will need a small handful of easily sprouted seeds, such as sunflowers or nasturtiums; don't worry, these will germinate indoors at any time of the year. Take up the bowl and sit with it in your lap, in the same quiet space you used before. Light a candle and incense for relaxation and concentration, if you feel they would help. Cup the seeds in your hand and tell yourself that they are the seeds of fresh opportunity in your search for an improved employment situation; make sure to specify that you want the right solution for your personal needs, and that no one be harmed or deprived in its fulfillment. Concentrate as hard as you can for as long as necessary on visualising these seeds growing and taking root, establishing your goal. Then sprinkle them over the surface of the earth, trickling a little of the compost over them to lightly cover them, or gently pressing them down with your finger. This is a fairly standard form of seed magic. The point of it is in the symbolic intent, so don't worry if your plants don't come up or don't do well.

At the next full moon, transplant your sprouting seeds to a larger container or individual pots, visualising the fulfillment of your goal as you do so. If the seeds didn't take, simply scatter the earth in the garden or some local green space, again thinking about the object of the spell. Now put the spell out of your mind and wait. I promise that you will get results, though they may not be what you had in mind when you started the process. They will, however, be what you need.

You can see that this way of working takes advantage of the ebb and flow of the lunar cycle, as well as using natural ingredients, a little bit of psychology, some symbolism and some visualisation, plus the direction of energy—all fundamental parts of most spell work. It's more common sense than hocus pocus. As Granny Weatherwax, the famous witch from Terry Pratchett's Discworld novels, says, magic is largely headology.

The Sun

Just as magical work can be timed to take advantage of the rise and fall of lunar energies, so can it be made to follow the solar cycle, though this is much longer than that of the moon. Put very simply, the energies of nature rise from midwinter (Winter Solstice) to midsummer (Summer Solstice), then gradually decline once more from midsummer to midwinter, so it is possible to do long-term magical work wherein you initiate projects after midwinter, then eliminate or banish after midsummer. This can be better broken down into a pattern of growth and harvest that follows the eight pagan festivals. From Samhain, at the beginning of November, to the Winter Solstice, just before Christmas, clear the ground for new projects, just as in the waning moon period of the aforementioned job spell. From the Solstice/Yule, begin to sort out new ideas for the year ahead. At Imbolc, the beginning of February, symbolically purify your life so that you can eliminate any personal deadwood and allow your seed ideas to germinate. At the Spring Equinox/Oestara on March 21, do some magic using real seeds to symbolically plant your germinating ideas. At Beltane, at the beginning of May, celebrate the growth so far and give your goals an added influx of magical energy. At the Summer Solstice, or midsummer, review your progress and send more power into your projects. When Lammas comes at the beginning of August, reap the rewards of any goals that have become reality, just as the farmers will be gathering in the grain harvest round about now, and mentally let go of anything that is clearly not going to work out. Mabon/Lughnasadh or Autumn Equinox, which begins in the last third of September, is the time to gather your remaining harvest and allow any spent ideas to go back into your unconscious, just as the debris of autumn begins to sink back into the earth at this time of year. You are ready to begin the clearing and eliminating, which reaches a peak at Samhain once more.

The Stars

If you know anything about astrology, then you will know that some planetary configurations lend themselves to growth while some seem to block our efforts, so that, for example, Saturn transiting the eleventh house of friendship and groups in your natal horoscope may make this area of your life more serious or restricted for a while, whilst a similar transit involving Venus will render you the life and soul of your friendship group and have you brimming over with fun. Similarly, when the sun or moon is occupying certain zodiacal signs, there is a greater chance of success or failure within magical work, according to the signs involved.

The following list will give a brief idea of the forms of magic that are appropriate to each sign of the zodiac, so if you have an ephemeris or other source that lists the sign positions of the sun and moon, you can consult it for timing your spells. Don't worry too much about this, as many people work successful magic without recourse to astrological timing. I simply give this information so that you can look into it and use it if you so choose; the most powerful tools in your magical repertoire will always be will, imagination, and firmness of intent. Strictly speaking, all the earth signs can be used for prosperity and growth, all the air signs for ideas and communication, all the fire signs for activity and creativity, and all the water signs for emotion, empathy, compassion, and psychic matters. Those who find they want to work closely with astrological factors might find it worth their while to look at the planetary hours as well, so that they can time spells to the hour of the day when a compatible planet rules.

Aries: Spells to begin things or to bolster courage, sport.

Taurus: Growth and prosperity.

Gemini: Learning, communication, and short-distance travel.

Cancer: Home, family, getting pregnant.

Leo: Courage, creativity, command, enjoyment.

Virgo: Harvesting, diet, health, attention to detail.

Libra: Social life, fun, justice, equilibrium, partnerships.

Scorpio: Uncovering secrets or keeping them, healing, getting to the bottom of things.

Sagittarius: Long-distance travel, higher education, religion, sport, the outdoors.

Capricorn: Ambition, organisation, initiation.

Aquarius: Friendship, groups, intuition, original ideas.

Pisces: Clairvoyance and other psychic activities, devotion, meditation, creativity.

The Natural World

Within the Craft, much magic can be carried out with particular success by aligning it with natural forces. If you wish to disperse something, for example, try shouting it into the wind so that it is blown away. Or you could ask the rain to wash your cares away, or the sun to bless you with life force and power. Seeds to represent magical aims can, as has been suggested, be grown in the earth. A wish, or something to be destroyed, can be committed to the fire, the first so that the energies are released and symbolically carried on the smoke and flame, and the second by letting fire consume and purify. Water can wash away negativity, especially when combined with salt, or it can be poured into a bowl to make a natural scrying surface (scrying is a form of divination carried out by gazing into a surface, usually reflective). Magical tools, jewellery, and other objects can be cleansed by being passed through smoke and flame and then sprinkled with water and earth or salt.

Observation of the seasons will inspire and inform you. If the leaves are budding and plants are thrusting through the surface of the soil, doesn't that suggest growth and new beginnings to you? How about the quiet endings of autumn, or the cosy contemplation of winter? Or the mellow richness and well-being of late summer?

You can build up a vocabulary of signs that have divinatory meaning for you as well, all drawn from what you see around you. A flight of birds may have a certain significance for you, as may the sudden appearance of a wild animal or insect. To me owls stand for dark feminine mysteries and wisdom; the hawk or kestrel tells me of clear seeing or of swiftly attaining what I'm seeking; while a butterfly represents the mystical life force that returns again and again through all of the myriad forms of creation. These symbols may have the same meaning for you, or something different altogether. It's important to make your own decisions about this, using imagination and instinct, as well as seeing what other people have to say about the subject.

Be aware that many spell ingredients can be grown naturally or picked in the wild, saving you money and tuning you into nature at the same time. A little research with some magical books or sources explaining how to recognise herbs will provide a wealth of ingredients not only to pep up your magical work but to heal you or supplement your diet as well. A few words of warning, though: be very careful not to consume anything, or inhale it or put it on your skin, unless you are absolutely sure that you know what it is, and that it's safe (some toxic plants look very similar to edible ones). Take care not to pick wildflowers—not only is this illegal in many parts of the world, but it contributes to making some species rare or extinct. Also, do not trespass onto private property or gather growing materials from public parks and gardens without permission. Be a conscientious magician with an awareness of the earth we live on, and respect the rights of other people. Consider not only what you can take from the world, but what you can give to it.

Although it is fun and useful to work spells with ingredients such as coloured and shaped candles and other fairly ritualistic materials, many spell supplies can be found in the natural world.

Learn some simple correspondences or see what certain objects suggest to you. A symbol can have more than one meaning, or may come to mean something different over time. Research, reading, and intuition, plus a measure of common sense, will help you form your own list.

Try out some of the following:

- Shells to tune yourself into water and the realm of emotional and psychic things
- Oak leaves for male fertility, as oak is associated with the God (oak can also give associations of strength and wisdom, and to the druids it was said to be the gateway into Otherworlds, or the door between summer and winter)
- Eggs to suggest pregnancy or a fresh start
- Wheat or other grain for prosperity or health
- Feathers for clarity, freedom, or travel
- Earth for grounding and stability

Your magical practice can and ideally should form a part of the fabric of your daily life. You should be able to flow with seasonal changes, aligning spells and spiritual work with the weather, daylight or darkness, growth or decay, just as our ancestors did.

Sympathetic Magic

Deep in the hearts of caves, where the light never reaches, beautiful, flowing art has been discovered on the rock walls. These pictures were put there by our remote ancestors before recorded history, and they seem to tell the tale of the hunts that supplied the tribes with food. Herds of antelope, bison, and deer fleet by, captured in ochre and black; shamanic human figures, clothed in the skin and horns of beasts, crouch with weapons raised, or appear to sleep or trance, or even copulate with the animals. It is thought that the acts depicted in the painted scenes are examples of sympathetic magic. Dancing humans, dressed in the hides of the animals they wished to kill, would mimic those creatures in an attempt to psychically draw them near; walking into the dream world would have allowed the shaman to contact the spirit of the quarry and do it honour, asking permission to take its life, ensuring it willingly sacrificed itself to the hunt, therefore granting the hunters an easy kill; symbolically mating with the animals would be a way of magically energising the natural increase of the herds. We can't be sure whether the scenes depicted show a record of actions taken by the people who painted them, or whether they are a kind of pictorial spell, with the art itself being the magical focus.

As with the previous examples, sympathetic magic is based on the assumption that like attracts or affects like. An example of this would be weather magic, where one might sprinkle water on the ground to imitate rain in the hope that the rain will happen in actuality. In another example, one might write the name of a desired object or goal on a piece of paper and carry it around, possibly in a pouch containing other artefacts that are linked with the goal, so that a coin tied up in gold cloth would be thought to attract wealth because both the coin and the colour gold are associated with money. Some people say there is no inherent magical power, other than natural life force, in the objects used for this type of spell work, while others claim that there is a potent energy in the symbolism, which resonates on the astral plane, thus bringing your spell to life. The truth is probably a blend of both, but the potency is in your belief that the objects will attract the thing they represent, or in your willingness to assign a particular meaning to them for the purpose of your work. There is no doubt that symbols that have been in use for hundreds of years will have built up a powerful etheric charge, which we can tap into and use, but personal symbols also acquire effectiveness with use, and a correspondence that is deeply meaningful on a personal level will always be the most valuable, whether or not it has universal validity as well.

You might also use such objects to assist spiritual investigation, meditating on them in a way that unlocks layer upon layer of subconscious symbolism. Sophisticated forms of this type of magical imagery are runes and other sign systems. They have taken often-used qualities and broken them down into abstract glyphs that encapsulate the original interpretations; one example of this is *b,* or Berkana, which is a birch tree, whose associations are birth and other beginnings. The following is a brief list of possible associations that may help you to appreciate this way of working, and may provide a basis for compiling your own:

- Grain can represent sustenance
- A stone might be carried to remind its owner of stability or the need to remain earthed
- A piece of quartz, apart from any healing properties it possesses, could stand for clarity
- Seeds are growth or beginnings
- A broom represents cleansing, as do water and salt
- An image of a cat could be feminine intuition or wildness
- Lion images are metaphors for strength
- A bull could be strength, determination, or endurance
- Rabbits suggest fertility because they are prolific breeders
- Water might stand for emotion or intuition

Take a look at children's story books, fairy tales, and television adverts, all of which give examples of imagery used symbolically, sometimes in quite subtle ways that might bypass our rational minds and go straight to the subconscious. Magic draws on the same well of instinctual imagery.

Using occult correspondences is a highly sophisticated form of sympathetic magic in which one consults lists of colours, incenses, and so on and assigns some to a piece of magical work; the purpose of this is to match a colour, odour, or other quality to the work being done, in the belief that it will help magnetise those very qualities into your spell. For example, you might want to attract prosperity and you find that patchouli oil is associated with monetary gain, and that furthermore burning a green candle will enhance the magical work. This is because patchouli and the colour green have become associated with prosperity and are therefore used in the belief that they will attract it into one's life. What is happening in actuality, at least on one level, is that having a symbolic vehicle to ride upon, the mind and imagination believe that the goal will be more easily attained. Belief is a huge part of successful magical work because it begins the process of altering reality, shaping it into that which is needed or desired. On a deeper level, the symbols themselves work on the psyche, opening new vistas of understanding, further shaping what could be.

The following exercise will demonstrate one way of working magically and spiritually with an object of symbolic significance. I want you to imagine that you are seeking to discover more about your own spiritual nature, how you fit into the overall scheme of things, and the direction in which your path is taking you. For this you would need to find a beautiful spiral-shaped shell or an ammonite. This pattern is common in nature, from shells, to growth patterns in plants, to DNA (the basic blueprint for all life), and has been portrayed through many cultures and historical periods as an emblem of spiritual growth. Indeed, our development often seems to resemble a spiral, moving round in wider circles of understanding, returning us to a point that shows us all we have absorbed, time and again leading us to wider vistas that give a view of our development so far. Furthermore, we may seem to travel into the centre of the spiral from time to time, seeking our own spiritual source, then travel out again to bring what we have discovered back into our daily lives.

The first thing you might want to do is form a bond with the spiral object so that you can more easily tune into its shape and energies. For this you could carry it in a pocket or medicine bag, or sleep with it under your pillow for a while. Take it out and look at it from time to time, turn it over and over in your hands, feel its contours and smoothness with your fingers. Try portraying its image pictorially through drawing and painting, or let it suggest words or poetry that you can write down and later read. Let that spiral shape sink into your mind so that it becomes familiar. You might want to do this for several days, or even longer.

Eventually you should create a little shrine for the object, or make room on an existing shrine, making sure it is visible when you are seated in meditation. Place flowers near it and light a candle. Now sit down before it, gaze at the spiral shape for a few minutes, then close your eyes. Hold the image of the spiral before your inner eye for a while, then begin to trace its shape with your mind. Imagine that you are setting out along its curving path. Do you naturally start from the outer arc or from the innermost point, and what significance do you place on your choice? Let your consciousness free-wheel and observe any images, thoughts, or impressions that come to you. When you have finished—and you will know when it's time to stop—you should write down your experiences, then eat and drink to thoroughly ground yourself.

This part of the exercise could be repeated on subsequent days for a while. Gradually but surely, the spiral symbolism would begin to trigger a response from your inner self, probably resulting in a series of informative dreams, meditative visions, or intuitive insights leading to the discovery of relevant reading material or other sources of information, all helping you to understand your own spiritual nature.

To conclude this work, you might want to hold the spiral and ask it to help you to understand the spiritual direction that is appropriate for you at this time in your life. This is a very simple little bit of magic, but an evocative one. At this point you would probably feel motivated to carry the spiral object around with you while the magic takes effect. You would be using the spiral imagery to unlock information about your spiralling spiritual journey, assuming that, using the "like attracts like" theory, the object would energise your own spirituality or attract a spiritual ambience to you.

You may prefer to work with a different symbol, and that's perfectly fine. The reason I have chosen the spiral is because it is recognised as being a strong spiritual key, and has probably been so since mankind's earliest times.

Other examples of this type of sympathetic magic are:

- Carrying the feather of a bird whose qualities you admire or wish to assimilate

- Carrying the leaf of a tree whose magical qualities you wish to absorb (you might want to study systems such as the Celtic Tree Alphabet for more information on this subject)

- Inscribing, on a stone or piece of wood or paper, the image of an animal whose characteristics you wish to absorb or emulate

- Meditating on a tarot card that symbolises such qualities as strength, justice, or hope

- Burning a yellow candle to attract sunny weather

- Composing a script made up of runes or other symbolic sigils that together form the name of something you need

- Pouring water slowly from one container to another to free up the flow of your life, or to dissolve blocks

- Blowing on a candle, then lighting it to attract a refreshing breeze

- Using herbs associated with certain qualities to bring the corresponding things into your life

So-called sympathetic magic is one of the most widely used forms of spell work. It is effective, even when our rational minds know it is based on the symbolic rather than the actual. The reason it is so effective is that it gives the intuitive part of us something to fix on and work with, thus bypassing any scepticism we might hold.

More About Correspondences

It is wise to think carefully about any correspondences you use in magic because a colour or incense, for instance, is not going to work for you if you don't identify with its assigned qualities, no matter how many ancient occult tomes attest to its validity.

Some correspondences are new, and some have been built up over the centuries. The ones that you should work with are the ones that feel right to you, though many correspondences will be universally applicable and may have been in existence for thousands of years, and there is something to be said for drawing on the accumulated power of anything occult that has gained force through constant repetition. Some correspondences will alter according to the period of history and the geographical location within which they have been used. To give examples: the behaviour of the twelve zodiac signs seems to be fairly consistent through various cultures; however, planetary attributes can be very different between Eastern and Western systems of astrology; the colours for Jupiter, for instance, are purple and royal blue in Western astrology, but gold, yellow, and orange in Vedic or Hindu astrology, and this may very well reflect the predominant colours worn by religious figures in these places, as Jupiter has rulership over exoteric spirituality; holy men in the Far East tend to wear orange or saffron, while religious dignitaries in Western countries often wear sumptuous blues or purples, as in the case of Catholic bishops. Similarly, the European sun is perceived as being life-giving and nurturing, but in India, where the heat dries up water and vegetation, the sun is thought to be malevolent, merciless, and cruel. Further examples demonstrate how correspondences can be personal and built up to suit one's environment, emotions, and so on. Within occult systems, water is often seen as blue or green, but to you it could be amber or brown if you live near peaty moor land, steel grey if you are located near the ocean in a region subject to storms and rain, or shades of purple and mauve and white if reflecting mountains. Do you see fire as intoxicating, exciting, and welcoming, or harsh, relentless, and unpredictable? How much are your ideas about it influenced by your life experiences and where you live?

The originators of the tables and lists of correspondences used in the various occult systems will have worked from a wide spectrum of sources, among them the chakras, the effects colours have on mood and emotion, perception of energies in use, and many others. Above all, they will have operated on the maxim that if it works, use it. The best way to build up a personal set of correspondences is to read widely, using your intuition as well as trying things out, then begin to observe how they work for you. For example, look at different colours, meditate on them, observe your responses to, say, red as opposed to blue or green; get outside on a windy day and experience air; do some gardening so that you are in tune with the energies of earth; test out the other elements, too; sample different incenses and essential oils and carefully monitor your emotional reactions so that you can differentiate between myrrh and patchouli, or jasmine and sandalwood (other than by smell!). Try to experience the whole spectrum of emotions or feelings that a specific colour or scent or object suggests to you. Correspondences can be used effectively to bring in something you are lacking, or to balance out an excess of something else. For example, red may make you feel cosy and warm, but it may also make you feel more aggressive, and so could be employed in a spell to help you fight for your rights; blue, which has a soothing influence over most people, may be used successfully to calm you if you are going through a phase when you can't seem to control your temper—try wearing blue clothing or lighting blue candles around your home.

You might find it useful to keep a notebook to copy any correspondences you come across, especially if they seem valid to you, and then expand this with your own experimentation and observation. The following are some suggestions for further increasing your personal working correspondences:

- Choose an array of incenses. It's best to use the granular type sold in jars or packets rather than joss sticks or cones, as these are purer and give a cleaner and more pleasing aroma. A starting list could include benzoin, frankincense, myrrh, cedar, and damiana. Try burning one each day for several days, meditating on the images, thoughts, and feelings they evoke, and writing it all down carefully afterward. Then you could try mixing them in combination. Try burning herbs as well, but only a little at a time, and never anything toxic. It's also worth tuning into the atmosphere in the room afterward, to see what the energies feel like. Some incenses are known purifiers, like frankincense, and some are used to induce moods or meditative states. See how they work for you, then try to imagine what use they could be put to magically. If a certain smell makes you feel sleepy or relaxed, then perhaps it could be incorporated into a spell to combat insomnia, or to help you unwind and leave your workday stress behind.

- Make a study of the colours known by psychologists to trigger certain states of mind or responses. This technique is used widely in fields such as interior design, and is especially used by businesses, shops, restaurants, and so on. Fast food chains will often choose colours that aren't too relaxing so people don't linger too long filling seats that could be taken up with new customers; work places may be decorated to keep employees alert and productive; a dentist's waiting room needs to be relaxing and soothing. See how these colours can be incorporated into spells to gain various effects.

- Another use of colour would be gained through a study of the seven main chakras. If you want to increase your visionary capabilities or clairvoyant powers, then violet (purple) would be a useful colour to work with as it relates to the third eye, the seat of psychic imagery. Spiritual growth might be helped along by burning white candles dedicated to the purpose, because white is the crown chakra colour in some systems. Orange could bring you prosperity, well-being, or confidence, according to the emphasis you place on it, for these are all qualities associated with the orange-hued navel chakra.

- Take a look at fruits, flowers, herbs, minerals, and any number of other categories. What does the smell of cinnamon suggest to you? How would you use it in a spell and to what end? Do you, in common with most other people, find lavender calming, and if so, how could you utilise it? Which animals make you think of courage, or speed, or industriousness; would an image of one of these, or a strand of its fur or a feather, make a difference to a spell you are working on to increase these qualities? Please don't go around murdering cheetahs or wolves or other wildlife to rob them of their qualities, or buy illegal imported skins, fur, horn, or ivory! Such actions would just bring you a dose of unwelcome negative karma. Be aware also that some birds, such as eagles and ospreys, are protected, and even picking up their feathers from the ground is illegal—you can be fined or go to prison for being in possession of eagle feathers in some countries!

With all the above suggestions, take your time and think of different ways to explore the potential correspondences. You might want to draw and paint herbs, leaves, or flowers that suggest certain associations to you, or write about them, or try them out alone or in combinations with other things. Have a look at tarot cards, planetary tables, and astrology, too, to see what other people have discovered and made work for them.

The Tools of the Trade

A word might be appropriate here concerning magical tools, ritual paraphernalia, and so on. There are some evocative and compelling myths attached to modern paganism, some of which have their roots in ancient forms of practice and some of which are recent inventions or exaggerations or half truths. That people should want some sort of validation for pagan practice is understandable; after all, we are coming out of a period of mistrust and misunderstanding when the "establishment" frowned on anything occult, and the pagan revival has been happening after centuries of suppression when the original foundations were all but eradicated. Not only that, but having a body of supposedly ancient rules and legends makes paganism seem more real, more acceptable to many people. We live in a world where many of the mainstream religions have the distinction of being extremely old and of having supposedly been received from a higher source, and are therefore respected as authentic. Therefore, it is tempting, understandably so, to search for or even invent some sort of history or pedigree for neopaganism, while, of course, editing out such nasties as human sacrifice, augury using animal entrails, collecting the heads of your enemies (yes, the Celts did this), and any other less than savoury but unquestionably genuine ancient pagan customs.

One particularly prevalent and popular myth runs along the following lines:

> In olden times, in Europe, during the Burning Times, witches met in secret. They met at the full moon because that way they didn't need torches to light their way. Peasant and noble alike belonged to the coven, and so rites were conducted skyclad since then there would be nothing to distinguish the privileged from the poor, and nobody would be recognised out of the context of their everyday lives (so all were safe from betrayal). Their tools were mundane implements so that they would not give the coven away in the event of discovery: the cauldron was the family cooking pot; an ordinary kitchen knife was used as an athame (the magical knife witches use to direct energy); the pentacle was made of wax so that it could quickly be thrown in the fire, there to melt, thus destroying all signs of witchy use; only a nobleman would own a sword, and for this reason one of such station would cast the circle and lead the coven, for he and he alone could legitimately wield such a weapon without arousing suspicion in the eyes of the authorities (so he got to pull rank after all!); records of spells and rituals were kept in secret code, such as Theban script, in the Book of Shadows, lest they be read by the Inquisition and identify the owners as members of the Old Religion. Nor, on pain of death, must the brothers and sisters of the coven reveal each other's identities, even under torture, lest they join the millions being burned at the stake all over England. For this reason, each was known by magical name only, so that if the pain of torture became too great and the prisoner broke down, he or she would not be able to betray other witches.

The above is an example of a wonderful modern folk myth. There is no evidence that medieval witches met in covens, though several writers have tried to prove that they did. Furthermore, why would meeting naked prevent the peasant members of the coven from recognising the local gentry, and vice versa? As for using ordinary implements as magical tools to avoid the authorities realising they had stumbled on a witches' coven at work, don't you think a group of people leaping around naked, causing a huge conflagration by throwing a large wax pentacle on the fire, might arouse a fair measure of suspicion? I'm sure black Books of Shadows kept in Theban might look fairly suspect as well. As the peasant members of the mythical coven would have been illiterate anyway, one wonders how they managed to write Books of Shadows in the first place. Also, the majority of people murdered during the witch hunts were not witches at all but ordinary people who, incidentally, probably died by the thousands rather than millions. In England they were mostly hung, though burning at the stake was employed in Scotland and Continental Europe.

The truth is that many of the myths of modern paganism were invented by Gerald Gardner, who was the founder of Gardnerian Wicca and responsible for much of the witchcraft revival in the early to mid-twentieth century. He claimed to have been initiated into a traditional coven in the New Forest, and there is some evidence to suggest that this was true. However, he was also known to have links with Freemasonry, Ritual Magic, and druidry, and Gardnerian Wicca draws from all these sources, especially in the use of magical tools such as the athame, and in the practice of casting a circle within which to work. His Books of Shadows are written in language that is made to look old-fashioned, but much of the content is drawn from recent sources, including the works of Aleister Crowley, and Rudyard Kipling's poetry. Even the Wiccan custom of working skyclad, or nude, almost certainly originates in Gardner's liking for Naturism.

The old country practitioners of spell and herbal lore used apparatuses that were part of their everyday lives, perhaps brewing up herbal potions in an ordinary cooking pot, making charms from ingredients we would find repellent, such as the feet of small rodents, the internal organs of large animals, and bottles of nails filled up with urine. Knives, wands, incense burners, swords, and other paraphernalia derive from ritual and ceremonial magic, and have come into the Craft via people like Gerald Gardner and Alex Sanders, both of whom had a background in more formal practice. This doesn't mean we shouldn't use their methods, but we need to keep an open mind, realise that such tools were not a part of spell work till recently, and above all try not to rely on them exclusively. Using magical tools is fun and can be very effective as long as you don't confuse the props with the real tools. Athames, wands, pentacles, and the like are wonderful for directing energy, adding drama to your work, and putting you in the right mood to do magic or ritual, but the real power comes from your own mind.

The first part of most magical workings is to call on the powers of the imagination to strongly visualise the object of the spell. Sometimes this alone will bring about the desired result; in fact, if you look back, you may recall times when you have wanted something so badly that you have been unable to stop thinking about it, fantasising, and daydreaming, only to find that that which you desired so strongly appears to have come about of its own accord, often against all odds.

The next step is to summon up an absolute determination to succeed. For most successful magic you need to put aside any doubts, because these will dilute your sense of purpose. You have to tell yourself that there is no way that you will not be able to attain the goal you have set for yourself. This is one reason why people who are confident often do very well in life, despite any obstacles in their paths. Again, you may be able to recall times in your own life when you have been so desperate for something to happen that it has! The more you want something, the more likely you are to get it, which is one reason why doing spells on someone else's behalf is often less successful than the magic you work for yourself.

The last step, which often forms part of the first two steps as well, is directing energy into your spell. This energy is present all around us, and is also contained in food, water, living creatures, plants, and so on. It has various names—*prana* and *chi* being but two. Whether you channel power through an athame or wand, or simply use your hands, your mind is the tool that does the work. However, you must take care that you draw this power in first, rather than relying on your own energy. Universal life force is inexhaustible, but ours is limited, so relying on our own power alone will lead to exhaustion and illness. When you are visualising a magical goal, and when you are putting yourself into a determined frame of mind, a certain measure of energy will inevitably accompany the work. During the final part of the spell, you need to apply imagination and will power once more, this time to mentally "see" yourself pulling etheric energy into your body and then directing it in a stream toward the spell. Different people perceive this energy in various ways, but one method is to imagine that you are surrounded by clouds of silvery or golden white light, and you suck these clouds into your body through your skin via your breath or through your hands. Then you push this power out again down your arms, or through a pointing finger, wand, athame, or whatever, and into the object that symbolises your desire (for example, a candle). You would visualise the power as a brilliant stream of light (you will find that you have your own colour for this; go with what seems most obvious to you). Alternatively, you could cup the spell material in your hands and infuse it with power.

Other spell materials, such as candles, are also props. Many magicians find that they rely less and less on the outward tools of the Craft over the years, till eventually they don't deliberately work magic at all—though they still manifest the results they desire.

I hope I have gone some way toward helping you to see that magic is not a dramatic art, but is a part of our lives, not *super*natural but an extension of nature, relying on the forces that surround us at all times. However, because it relies on a focusing of imagination, desire, and intent, it forces us to look at ourselves and what we want. Furthermore, by utilising an expanding vocabulary of symbols in our magic, we begin to initiate deep changes within ourselves that have far-reaching effects on our psyches, leading to growth and change, whether or not that was our original intent.

Bibliography

Pratchett, Terry. *Equal Rites*. London: Corgi Books, 1987.

What Is Magick?

MARTIN WHITE

Magick is a deeply personal thing; it is something that most people do unconsciously all of their lives, instinctively and without any need to be taught or told when to do it. Our whole world is filled with magick. There is no right or wrong way to "do" magick, no one single path to success. We all need to find the way that works best for us as individuals, not to blindly copy someone else. This is especially true if we have no real idea why others are saying or doing the things they say or do. The way to discover your own path—for a journey of discovery it most certainly is—is to read widely, meditate on what you read, learn to trust your own instincts above all else, and experiment and find out what works for you. Eventually, slowly, your own magickal truth will start to emerge. In the pages that follow, it is my intention to explain my path, my journey. The path I follow favours the old gods and goddesses of the north, the Aesir and Vanir. It is one that reveres ancestry, acknowledging that everything I am or have stems from them. It is a wild, free, and feral path, reflecting the nature of the forces that empower it. Having read it, you may decide that my path is not your path; but, as I said, magick is a deeply personal thing.

So what exactly is magick? It has often been described as "the ability to affect change in accordance with will." In fact, if you think about this, almost any act, including making a cup of tea, may be considered magickal to a degree. Even for the simplest tasks we undertake, we generally need to

think about them beforehand—thought always precedes action. Following this train of logic, a spell may be seen as a "deliberate act to focus the will." Now, back to our mundane example of a cup of tea. Our spell for quenching thirst has such ingredients as a tea bag, water, and possibly milk and sugar. From this we can already see that there is a fair bit of latitude. For example, what type of tea, how much milk (if any), and can I still cast the spell without sugar? The actions in the spell will be filling the kettle, boiling the water, and combining the ingredients, until at the end we have achieved our goal—a thirst-quenching liquid. How ludicrous you would think someone if he or she told you this "spell" could only work with Earl Grey tea, or that it could not possibly work without *two* sugars. Yet I have heard people say that because a "real" spell they have read in a book calls for pink ribbon and they don't have any, it can't possibly work—nonsense! It can work if what you *do* have is enough to focus your will and intent, and that may very well be different for you than either me or the person who wrote the spell in the first place; as I keep saying, magick is a deeply personal thing. I guess by now you're thinking this is all very well, but making a cup of tea isn't particularly stretching for the will, and doesn't seem particularly "magickal" (although you would do well to consider how magickal your kettle boiling might have appeared to someone a couple hundred years ago). Before we leave the example, however, there are a couple of other things it clearly illustrates that are worth pointing out.

First, *the laws of the physical universe cannot be broken.* By this I mean that for a spell to work it needs to have a means of manifesting into the physical world that does not contravene the laws of physics. Magick that stays in the realms of thought, such as spells designed to work on your own personality, have a great deal of flexibility, but spells required to have a tangible result in the "real world" must obey physical laws. Casting a spell for more money will not make it drop out of the sky; merely chanting at your tea bag will not transform it into a steaming beverage—magick isn't magic!

Second, *magick is not an exact science.* From the earlier example we can see that there was a good deal of flexibility in the ingredients. We can also obtain very satisfactory results from varying the quantities of those ingredients. We could also use electricity or gas as a power source for the spell (more on this subject later), and we could even use a device that makes the drink automatically at an appointed time in the future (for example, to be ready when we wake up in the morning).

When considering the nature of magick, there are a few other things we should bear in mind. *Magick follows the path of least resistance.* Like flowing water, magick will tend to find the easiest way of working. Because of this, it is important to consider very carefully what you are working for. For example, casting a spell for more money could lead to you winning the lottery, finding a penny in the street, getting a pay raise at work, having an elderly relative die and leave you something in the will, or a multitude of other possibilities. The actual outcome would partly depend on how much money you were subconsciously thinking about when you worked the spell, and what in your specific case was the easiest way for it to come about.

Magick comes at a price. The universe is a complex place, and one of its rules of operation seems to be to try to keep in balance. Therefore, if you upset this balance with a spell—which, to work, inevitably must happen to a degree—you should then expect to pay an appropriate price (this, unfortunately, you rarely get to choose). For example, you might get the great new job your spell was worked for, but the added responsibility keeps you away from home, placing a strain on your relationship. Or the partner of your dreams appears, but turns out to live halfway across the country, so your sacrifice would be one of frequent travel. The possibilities for "repayment" are endless.

I hope you can see by now that magick isn't an easy option. Casting any spell requires forethought, ingenuity, a strong will, and even a little luck. It most certainly is not simply a case of getting the "right ingredients," repeating a few words from a prewritten page, and sitting back to let the good times roll. Personally speaking, I tend to use magick as a last resort after I have tried all the mundane options first, because by and large they are more predictable, with no hidden costs associated. There are times, however, when only magick will fulfil the need, and when it does, the spellcaster needs to be capable of limiting the possible negative side effects while giving the spell as many chances of coming into manifestation as possible. It isn't always an easy balance to achieve, but it is a skill that can be mastered with time and practice.

Constructing the Spell

In my mind, the only sensible way to judge a spell is by asking, "Did it work?" All the exquisite prose and poetry, all the aesthetic quality of the candles, ribbons, robes, and "cutlery waving" count for nothing if at the end the spell didn't work. I'd like to illustrate this with a personal example of what I would now consider an act of spellcasting, but which came from a time in my life before I was consciously aware of magick at all. I was in a job that was making me desperately unhappy and depressed. Each evening I would come home and sit brooding about my situation. After a while, though, I started fantasising about what my ideal job would be like. Each evening, I would retreat into this fantasy world and add more and more detail to the picture in my mind's eye until it became almost as real to me as the rest of the world around me. About three months later, I received a letter through the post offering me a job based on an interview I had had six months earlier. I had completely forgotten about it, and my vague memory of the interview was that it didn't go particularly well. It ended with a heated disagreement with the person chairing the interview. The position turned out to be remarkably close in every detail to my fantasy ideal job, and I had many happy years there. I know now that my fantasising was an act of visualisation; my power for the spell came because I desperately wanted the outcome. The spell found the easiest path open to it, and as I wasn't applying for any jobs at the time, it needed to rekindle an old spark of one I had attended and botched, which shows to me just how much energy I must have put into the spell. By my benchmark this was a very successful spell, conducted without a single magickal prop or invocation, but by force of will alone. I now of course know that I could have made it much more efficient and painless, but I doubt the end result could have been any better.

Casting a spell, then, is a little like lighting a fire. You set the spark and it takes, but where are you? In a tinder-dry forest, perhaps? What is the wind speed and direction? How much fuel do you need? Is there enough to keep it burning until the purpose is achieved, or so much fuel that it will consume everything in its path, including you? Realistically, you can't expect to control the flames of a fire exactly, nor can you control the effects of a magickal act exactly, but you can still have a safe fire with the right precautions, and the same is true of spellcasting. If we take the analogy a little further we can see that there are a number of factors we need to consider for our safe fire. Is the fuel dry? Is it too windy? Is it raining? What can we use to contain the fire? What will we use to ignite the fire? The analogies in magick are as follows. The will of the spell-caster equates to the fuel. Is your desire strong enough and your concentration good enough to sustain you throughout the spell? Obviously, a short, simple spell with lots of opportunity to manifest will be easier than one with greater complexity and fewer opportunities. The energy level raised might be equated to the wind speed, and we shall return to this point in more depth later. For now, consider that we need only enough energy to manifest the result and not so much that all sorts of side effects become possible. Astrological conditions may be equated to weather such as rain, sunshine, and so on. Ideally, you should light your fire when it is dry, and ideally you should cast your spell when the planetary conditions, moon phase, and sun tides are conducive. As you might build a stone hearth for a fire's containment, so in magick it is common practice to cast a circle to hold the energy raised before its release. Finally, the method of ignition will be the intent of the spell and the carrying out of the spell itself.

"Stage Props"

In my opinion, most of the paraphernalia associated with casting a spell are mere stage props. They act as an aid to focus the will, but no more. You can cast effective spells with just your mind, as my previous example shows, but you can never be effective by simply carrying out the acts and saying the words if the *will* and *intent* aren't there. Pretty much anything can be used as a focus for the will in spellcasting, and some of the more common items are candles, cords, crystals, poppets, and tarot cards. Some of these can be enhanced to act on many layers of consciousness at the same time. For example, lighting a candle can be an act of focus, but the colour may have added significance: green for wealth, pink for love, and so on. They may have even been picked for planetary correspondence: green for Venus (and wealth or love), orange for Mercury (and communication). You may have used specially prepared oils to consecrate the candle beforehand, with the ingredients of the oil also selected to correspond to the task at hand. You might even mark the candle with special symbols before burning it to add yet more meaning to the act. Some items such as tarot cards act on very deep subconscious levels with their imagery, and there is evidence to suggest that this is at a level where all of us share the same in-built imagery. As I said at the beginning of this chapter, I am drawn to the gods of the north, and therefore my preferred method of focus is through a set of symbols known as the runes.

The Runes

There are actually several sets of symbols known as runes, each having some common elements and some only used in their particular system. The number of symbols varies from sixteen to over thirty, depending on the system used. For my part, I use a system known as the elder futhark, which has twenty-four symbols. The runes are sometimes referred to as an alphabet, and indeed they were used for this purpose, but we need to remember that language itself was considered magickal at one time, and the runes were probably used for magick long before they were relegated to a mere alphabet. Like the tarot cards, the symbols of the runes are deeply rooted in our subconscious, and with some effort and patience the spellcaster can access the meaning of each for himself or herself. One of the reasons I use runes is because they are associated in my mind solely with performing a magickal act, so the mere fact that I am using them puts me in the right frame of mind for spellcasting. It is not my intention to go into the meaning of each rune in any great detail here; there are many excellent books that have already done that (see Bibliography on page 93). For those readers who are coming to runes for the first time, however, here is a very brief list of the elder futhark runes and some associations. Please note that each rune has far wider meaning and application than I show here, but to do justice to each would take a book in its own right. A couple of points are of particular interest. First, the divinatory meaning isn't always about the same thing as the magickal application, and second, the magickal applications fall into two distinct categories: those that are for a particular type of spell and those that perform magickal operations.

Runic Symbol	Name	Divinatory Keyword	Magickal Application
ᚠ	Fehu	Wealth	Power up a spell and "send" the energy
ᚢ	Uruz	Strength	Increase strength or courage
ᚦ	Thurisaz	Destruction	Achieve breakthrough or set up defence
ᚨ	Ansuz	Expression	Increase eloquence or persuade
ᚱ	Raido	Travel	Safe travel, both physical and astral
ᚲ	Kenaz	Knowledge	Create an opening or gain illumination
ᚷ	Gebo	Exchange	Bonding, partnerships
ᚹ	Wunjo	Joy	Empower wishes
ᚺ	Hagalaz	Disruption	Hexing
ᚾ	Nauthiz	Need	Developing the will, overcoming addictions
ᛁ	Isa	Static	Blocking and binding
ᛃ	Jera	Steady growth	Fertility or steady increase
ᛇ	Eihwaz	Endings	Past-life work
ᛈ	Pertho	Secrets	Divination
ᛉ	Algiz	Protection	Protection
ᛊ	Sowulo	Success	Success or healing
ᛏ	Teiwaz	Justice	Obtain justice
ᛒ	Berkana	Rebirth	New ventures
ᛖ	Ehwaz	Cooperation	Heal rifts in partnerships
ᛗ	Mannuz	Self-knowledge	Improve mental powers
ᛚ	Laguz	Go with the flow	Dream work
ᛜ	Inguz	Gestation	Storage of power for magickal use
ᛟ	Othila	Home	Pull together for common goals
ᛞ	Dagaz	Sudden change	Enlightenment

So how can the spellcaster get to know the runes well enough to use them for effective magick?

The first step is to obtain a set of runes for your *sole* personal use. The most common forms that may be obtained commercially are inscribed on stones, burned into wood, or are sold as a set of cards with appropriate images on them. The first set I used included cards with images, and I found that in a similar way to tarot, the images themselves helped in understanding the symbols. However, the symbols have many, many layers of meaning, and there comes a point when the images start to limit the subtleties and nuances of understanding contained within the rune. This stage may be recognised by a feeling that you know all there is to know about the symbol, and it has become "static" in your mind. It is time then to move on to a set of symbols without images, again obtained commercially, or, better still, ones you have made yourself. At first this will probably feel like going back to square one—it certainly did for me! However, you will find that with patience, the associations you had already learned with the cards return, and then start to expand. After many years of working with runes I still find fresh new insights into their meaning.

Let's suppose you have obtained a set of runes in a form that appeals to you; what then can you do to gain an understanding? First, I would recommend that you link yourself magickally with them, achieved by an act of cleansing and consecration. You might also want to dedicate them in service of deity as well. Following this, in my opinion there is no substitute for reading widely about the meanings contained within each symbol, and you should strive to read as many books on this as you can find. You will notice that while they broadly agree on the general meaning behind each rune, there will be subtle differences as well. Start by memorising the broad meanings, come up with a set of keywords for yourself, or use the ones given in this book. Pick only one word or short phrase for each rune to start with, and spend time looking at the runes and thinking about the keyword until you get to a point where the keyword springs to mind instantly as you view the symbol. While you are undergoing this process, get into the habit of picking a rune at random each morning, and then in the evening, think back to what has happened during your day that may associate with the rune you picked. Use whatever books you have to help you make these associations. You will be surprised at how often there is a clear correlation between the rune you picked and what happened during the day. In fact, you will probably find that after a few months, the rune you pick can predict the events of the day; this is a definite sign of progress and an indicator that the symbols are starting to take root in your subconscious. You might also find that your dreams begin to throw up runic symbols as well, and for those interested in dream work, the runes offer an excellent tool for communicating ideas between the conscious and subconscious mind. The other task you should assign yourself during these early months of assimilating the runes is to keep records. I would recommend that you split your records into a few pages for each rune. Keep a diary of your associations regarding "rune of the day," and note any dreams that you can associate with the runes. The pages for each rune should contain its symbol, the keyword you have associated with it, and then, over time, add things you learn about the rune. For example, you might find out which herbs are associated with each rune, or what deity it is associated with, or what day of the week it corresponds to, or what magickal properties it has. The list here is virtually endless, and for that reason a looseleaf folder is a good choice for your record keeping.

Once you get to the point where your mind automatically associates each rune with its keyword, it is time to use meditation to expand the meaning; this is where you will gain your own personal insights. Remember from your reading that each author had slight differences in interpretation. It is these differences that show the author's personal insights, and you should also spend time now considering *why* the author has made any particular associations. I would recommend picking a rune per day, possibly the same one you pick at random for the day's events, and spending at least ten minutes meditating on the symbol and noting in your records any insights you get concerning that rune. There is also a system that was developed by German occultists in the last century that is a form

76

of runic yoga. In this system, the practitioner uses body posture to mirror the shape of the rune while concentrating on, and drawing into him or her, the essence of the rune. There are also associated sounds that may be intoned at the same time. If you have an interest in Eastern philosophy and wish to see for yourself how this has been translated into a northern context, then I again refer you to the works mentioned at the end of this chapter. *Any* work spent in gaining further insights into the runes is worthwhile and will be rewarded in the long run. The exercises described here are enough to give you a good understanding of the runes, but if you want to expand your knowledge further and faster, I would recommend using them for divination as well. Again, there are many good books that deal with this aspect of rune work.

After a few months to a year, depending on how much effort you put in, you will be ready to use the runes effectively in magickal operations, and I will now outline a few ways that this may be done. My own techniques are not the only ones, and I have read and tried many others. The ones listed here I know from practical experience work, and given the level of experience you should now have, they will provide positive results for you. For each technique shown I will assume that you have already made a sacred space and prepared yourself physically and mentally for magickal work, having selected the rune or runes you require for the spell.

The first technique is executed entirely with the mind. Sit in a comfortable position and go into a meditative state. In your mind's eye, see the situation you wish to bring about. Play it through like a movie until you get to the point of completion, then superimpose each rune in turn on this picture, considering the property you want it to bring to the outcome, and let it sink into the picture, possibly making it glow for a while until it is absorbed. When the last rune is absorbed, let the picture fade and know that the outcome has already happened. This technique does require a bit of practice, but it has the advantage that it can be performed just about anywhere with no equipment needed; remember, sacred space can be cast in the mind alone.

The next technique involves empowering an object with runic energy. As with all runic magick, you will need to spend a fair bit of time thinking about what runes to use and why, meditating on them, and looking into yourself to see if your motives are pure. Once you have made your choice of runes, you need to select the object. This can be pretty much anything you like. In the past I have empowered letters, gifts, walking sticks, and clothing, to name but a few. One thing I have found that works extremely well is empowering crystals or stones, also picked for sympathetic associations with the purpose of the spell. For example, I might use rose quartz in association with Gebo, Wunjo, and Jera to promote harmony between two parties, or substituting Othila for Gebo to create a joyous atmosphere in a room or house. Once you have selected whatever object you choose to empower, stand before a representation of the power source you wish to utilize to bring the force of the runes to bear. This source may be a particular deity, an ancestor, or it may be elemental in nature, and we shall discuss the pros and cons of each later. Taking the object in your left hand (which, magickally speaking, is the one used for receiving), hold it out to the source in an open palm and request that it empower the object with the first rune. In the request, state clearly why you have chosen this rune. See or feel the tingling as a stream of this runic energy flows into the object. When the sensation subsides, repeat the procedure for each rune until all have been absorbed. The object should now be placed in an appropriate place where the imbued energy can work. For example, the piece of rose quartz referred to earlier might be placed in the room or building, or given to one of the parties involved. This method has the advantage of hidden energy; the object may be kept in plain sight without attracting too much attention. A variation on this technique would be to inscribe the object with the symbols. This can be quite effective with jewellery such as rings, for example, or magickal items such as wands. The empowering process would be the same as before. A further variation on this theme can be used when there is no particular place to put an object; for example, when working a spell to attract wealth, or a partner. In these circumstances one method is to draw the runes on a piece of paper. Traditionally, you should use red ink and use your will to impart the energy of the rune while you are drawing it. Once completed, you may either visualise the outcome while holding the paper, or empower it with the chosen power source, whichever you feel is more appropriate. Next, burn the paper and see the spell dispersing through the cosmos to bring about the result.

In the previous techniques I have talked about combining runes, and, again, there are many ways to do this. The simplest is to draw or imagine them one at a time, and this is effective. When, however, the overall meaning depends more on the blend of the chosen runes than the sum of their individual energies, there is a technique known as *binding*. Essentially, this technique involves joining the chosen runes together into a single symbol. There are only two rules when doing this. First, you should strive to keep the number of lines to a minimum, which means using the same line for more than one rune. Don't worry here too much about relative size—each rune can be a different size if you can reduce the number of lines drawn. The second rule is that the overall symbol should be aesthetically pleasing, which may mean joining runes at an angle to each other, or increasing by a line or two your minimal efforts from rule one. In the end, trust your intuition—when you have a symbol that is combined effectively you will just feel it and know. The end result is known as a *bind rune,* and can be used in any of the techniques previously described.

Sources of Power

We talked in the last section about power sources, and now it is time to consider these in a little bit more detail. Where exactly does the power for your spell come from? Well, there are several possibilities, and rather than leaving it to chance, the spellcaster would do well to consider this question before operating and make a conscious decision. The first and easiest power source to access is you. You take subtle energy in all the time from the surrounding universe—it is called *ki* in Japan, *qi* or *chi* in China, and *prana* in India, but the concept is the same. It is poor occult practice to use your own power reserves as a source, though. If you use your own reserves of energy you will feel drained and unwell at the end of the operation; effectively you have become a drained battery and will need to be recharged. In the long run, continued use of your own body's energy for magick can lead to more serious conditions. Furthermore, it is a very limited source, and as a result not particularly effective.

The next source of energy to consider is elemental force, the neoplatonic system of earth, water, air, fire, and spirit. Depending on the spell, you may channel one or more of these forces, and they can be very effective. They are particularly useful for cleansing or blessing operations, which are often simple, localised events, and this gives a clue to their weakness, which is that these are pretty much "blind" forces. I feel that they are less effective where the spell is more complex, requiring an intelligent power source. Still, they are forces that every serious spellcaster should become familiar with and be competent in using.

Moving up the intelligence chain of possible sources of energy, we come to ancestors. But what do we mean by ancestors? Do we mean the other people on our family tree, now in spirit? Do we mean the people who lived where we do now? Or all the people bonded in some way by a common cause or set of beliefs? Actually, it is all these things. For me, the ancestors are those who went before without whose blood, sweat, and tears I wouldn't be sitting here now, in a comfortable home, typing these words. Quite literally, I believe we owe them everything, and as such, they are worthy of our love and respect. We are each linked with our ancestors through the common cause of humanity, and they are ever at our side in times of need, to protect, guide, or assist us in our endeavours—and that includes spellcasting. They are intelligent, so the energy they lend to a spell carries intent as well as power, and is more suited to complex spells, or ones whose goals are abstract in nature, such as working on your own personality.

Finally, we come to the highest form of energy, that of deity. There are numerous gods and goddesses in the lands in the north, many of whom are associated with different aspects of human nature. For example, Odin is associated with persuasive speech in one aspect, Freyja is associated with love, sex, and magick, Tyr with truth and justice, and so on. Before considering working with the energies of the deities, however, you really need to know them well, their unique natures and attributes. Just knowing their names isn't nearly enough.

This brings us to an important question; namely, how do we get to "plug into" these various power sources? Starting again with the self, where all aspiring spellcasters should start, there are a wide variety of exercises for increasing personal energy awareness and capacity. Systems such as Qi Gong (pronounced "Chi Kung"), Tai Chi, and hatha yoga are all designed to work with the body's subtle energies. Healing systems such as Reiki and Sekhem are also excellent ways of increasing personal energy capacity and the ability to channel energy, which is a vital skill to have, especially when dealing with the higher energy sources.

Once the individual has a sound awareness of his or her own body's energy, he or she is in a better position to experience external forces, the first of which should be the elements. The ability to sense elemental forces can be built up over time by first understanding what attributes each of the elements represents and what their correspondences are, then spending time meditating on them. It is common practice to experience each element in turn, often starting with earth, then water, fire, air, and spirit, taking several weeks on one before moving on to the next. You should try to utilize as many of your senses as possible when getting to know an element. For example, when experiencing earth, go outside, preferably barefoot, so that you can really feel what the earth is like, take a handful of dirt and smell it, or go outside after rainfall, close your eyes, and drink in the heady scent. Feel the stability beneath your feet, for stability, strength, and support are what this element is all about. Get out in the countryside and walk at different times of day and during different seasons. Really get in touch with the element until you can determine, with your eyes closed, what time of day it is, what season it is, or if it has rained. For water, spend time near a lake or stream, put your hands in and feel how it moulds round your fingers; look out to sea at sunset and let your mind join with the element to understand the true nature of emotion. For fire you might try scrying into an open fire if you are lucky enough to have one, or really take note of your body when you are exercising and feel energised and alive; force and courage are the nature of fire. When experiencing air, meditate upon a clear blue sky or stand on a hilltop on a windy day, close your eyes, and really feel the air against your skin. I'm sure you, the reader, can think of dozens of other exercises that will allow you to personally experience the elements.

When we come to the ancestors, in my opinion, contact can only really be achieved out of doors. I have found sunset to be an ideal time, probably because of its association with death. Stand and call to them aloud or in your mind, with your eyes closed, and see what happens. If you do this with respect and an open heart, they *will* respond. Leave offerings of water and bread or cake out for them; get into the habit of honouring them with libations after your ritual practice. Ask their opinions on decisions with which you are faced; make them a part of your life and you may be surprised at the many ways they choose to show you their presence.

It should go without saying that any deity needs to be approached with love, respect, and humility. As I have said previously, you really need to understand the nature of the particular god or goddess you wish to work with. You can achieve this by reading about them (the more books, the better), meditating upon them, and linking each of them to the corresponding emotion you feel, then look deeply into the myths that surround each one to extract its true meaning. I must make it clear here that I do not perceive gods as "big people"; they are far, far more than that, although it can be useful to see them in a human form during meditation. Always remember that though they can occupy the form you have given them, they are *not* the form itself. The closest I can come to describing the gods and goddesses is as varying frequencies of energy, but an energy that has intelligence and purpose. This is something that you must experience for yourself to fully appreciate.

As we are talking here about the northern pantheons, you might try the following pathworking to meet the goddess Idunna in her orchard. The goddess Idunna is the only one to survive the Ragnarok (end of the world); she sinks down into the roots of the world tree Ygdrassil to emerge when the destruction is over and the world is born anew. She is the bearer of the golden apples that keep the gods youthful.

Create your sacred space and make the following plea to Idunna:

Idunna, goddess of the golden apple;
She who survives the very end of the world, to be born anew,
I ask for your help in understanding the mighty ones of Aesir and Vanir.
I ask for your guidance through the mysteries of the north.

Then go into a meditative state and imagine yourself walking across a meadow. Feel the sun shining down upon you, hear the gentle sounds of summer, and feel at peace. As you are walking, notice a mist coming up all around you, light at first, but getting heavier until you can't see more than a foot or two in front of you. You know this is a magickal mist and something wonderful is about to happen. You sense the mist clearing in front of you and with courage you continue walking. All at once you are standing in a beautiful orchard. You notice that the apples are golden in colour and there is a fair-haired maiden with a wicker basket over her arm picking them from a nearby tree. You walk toward her and she turns. She is the most beautiful maiden you have ever seen, and she is smiling at you. You kneel at her feet and know that this is the goddess herself; you feel blessed in her presence. She touches you on the forehead with her cool hand and instantly communication takes place—you are aware of a message from her. Wait now until she has given you her message. Eventually, you stand in her presence and she embraces you, smiling, and you know that you will always be welcome here. Then she fades from view and the mist descends again. You walk forward into the sunny meadow, but remember everything that has happened. Slowly return to your own space and time. Clear your sacred space.

During another session you might try asking her to introduce you to one of the other gods. Take several sessions with each until you have a good understanding before moving on to the next. During this process I would suggest that you do not mix and match pantheons; take your time with this one before considering others. A teacher of mine suggested waiting two years before tackling a second, and from my own personal experience I would endorse that statement. Of course, it might be the case that the gods come looking for you, as I discovered.

When I was about four years old I used to have a recurring nightmare in which my father was trying to give me away to an old (and quite scary) woman in a long black dress with a matching cloak that obscured her face. I used to wake up terrified. Many years later, not long after I took up the study of magick, I came across a short piece about a goddess named Holda. It said that she was the face of the goddess who gathered all the souls of the children who had not been christened in the name of the old gods. My childhood nightmare immediately came to memory, although I hadn't given it a thought in over thirty years, and I *knew* it was Holda who had been holding her arms out to me all those years ago. I no longer think of those dreams as nightmares, but rather as blessings; Holda is a goddess with whom I now have a very close relationship.

One final thing to consider before we leave the subject of energy sources, and that is attitude. You can only *request* the help of the higher powers, not *command* it. You should treat all power sources with the respect they deserve. When working with ancestors and gods in particular, remember that it is a partnership. They will expect your loyalty and allegiance in return for their help. You can't simply pick them up and discard them on a whim. Having said that, I wish you well in your own personal journeys to contact the higher powers; the rewards are more than worth the effort.

Magickal Ethics

Whatever motives you may have for wanting to learn the arts of magick, you will inevitably find that through the process of acquiring the skills necessary to become effective, your personality will change. You will probably find that the things that drew you to it in the first place, especially if they were material goals, no longer seem important, and spiritual growth becomes the goal you will treasure beyond all else.

The laws that govern magick seem to have an in-built code of ethics, which you will only notice when looking back with hindsight. So what exactly are these ethics? Well, they seem to me to be based around three basic tenets. The first tenet is one of service, both to others and to deity and the cosmos in general (which may well be the same thing). You will find yourself drawn to the healing arts, and it is quite likely that your paid employment, unless it has a strong element of service or a motive to help others, loses its attraction. It is also likely that you will start to reach out (or, more accurately, inward) toward deity, feeling a need for some kind of contact and guidance. The second tenet, which stems from the first, is one of not wishing to harm others. This may extend to all forms of life, especially as you become more aware of the life current in everything around you, and your "connectedness" with it. An important lesson here is that *to sustain life you must take life,* and it can be a very uncomfortable lesson to learn; remember, plant life is sacred life, and no less important than animal life. The third tenet, and some would say the most important one, is that of free will. Like it or not, you have free will, and with it comes complete and total responsibility for your thoughts, words, and deeds— twenty-four seven! All of us at one time or another have laid blame on others or on events beyond our control. How many times have you said, or heard someone say, "I had no choice," or "They made me do it." The practice of magick will make you realise this to be an illusion, and that you *always and without exception* have a choice—not always a palatable one, but a choice nonetheless. Once this realisation sinks in you will feel both uncomfortable and liberated at the same time: uncomfortable because laying blame makes us feel absolved, and we are no longer able to do that—no longer willing to hand over control of even the tiniest part of our lives to another; and liberated because we start to see things clearly as we take up the mantle of our own power and become completely self-determining.

There are two closely related phrases that neatly sum up magickal ethics for me: "Do what thou will, shalt be the whole of the law," which was coined by a great occultist of the late nineteenth and first half of the twentieth century named Aleister Crowley, and "An it harm none, do as ye will," which is also known as the Wiccan Rede. The "will" referred to in both of these is often misconstrued to mean "do what you like," which couldn't be further from its actual meaning. What both of these phrases mean by "will" is the will of your spiritual self or higher self, as it is sometimes known, which, being divine, is true to the laws that bind the universe. The life purpose of every person should be to determine what his or her "will" is, which is often far from obvious and takes real effort to determine; one must then devote all efforts to its execution. Another term you may come across regarding magickal ethics is the Law of Threefold Return. Basically, this implies that whatever energy you put out will return to you threefold, good or bad. It is quoted as a reason for not doing harm to others, but as I have already stated, "going with the flow" as far as magick is concerned will prevent this anyway; more of that later, however. To my mind, this law doesn't stand up to close scrutiny because it breaks the laws of the physical universe—where is all that extra energy supposed to be coming from? What will happen to fill the void it leaves? If it were true, I think the universe would be a very unstable place indeed. I have heard it said in its defence that "threefold" refers to once in the physical world, once in the spiritual world, and once in karmic terms. I have no doubt that the act, good or bad, will reflect back in proportion to the magnitude of the act, but I do not believe it to be threefold. However, you have free will, and you must make up your own mind on this. One last point to consider regarding the "boomerang effect" of magickal acts is its relation to karma. Karma is the action and reaction that takes place at a spiritual level. Karma has nothing to do with crime and punishment, but rather a cosmic harmony or neutral balance. Karma can be worked out by the individual soul over many lifetimes; any "karmic debts" built up now can be repaid in a later life. One thing that the individual following a magickal path will notice is that the effects of karma seem to speed up. That is, any act performed gets its reaction right here and now in this lifetime, not in a future one. This is a sure sign that spiritual progress is being made, and at a much accelerated rate.

I briefly touched upon "good magick" and "bad magick" in the previous paragraph; now it is time to look at this more closely. Consider the following example: Imagine that you are a powerful magician and the year is 1665, the place London, England. One in three people across all of England is dead from the great plague, with the death rate even higher in the cities. You decide to cast a spell aimed at eradicating the plague and call on all the powers you know to do so. A short time later, we have the great fire of London, which kills hundreds of people, but eradicates the plague once and for all in the city. The spell worked, but think . . . would you consider this an act of good or bad magick? Moreover, if you had known the way the spell would work in advance, would you still have cast it? If the answer is still yes, presumably you would also be prepared to face the consequences and take responsibility for the deaths caused by the fire as well as those lives saved by the eradication of the plague. Think about it. The point I am trying to make here is that magick is not good or bad, but rather neutral. Good and bad are perceptions we put on the intent, and often change according to your perspective. If you can cure, you can curse—they are opposite sides of the same coin. I have stated that I believe the underlying laws of magick flow in the direction of service and not harming other life. So while it is quite possible to do harm, it is a little like swimming against the tide; if you try to do this for too long, however, you will get swept out to sea and drown. I firmly believe that magick has its laws that reflect these principles.

Casting the Spell

Now that we have looked at what magick is, what is needed to perform it, and the associated ethics, we are in a position to consider how to actually cast a spell. There are a number of clear logical steps involved in this, so let's look at them in turn.

The first step is to consider carefully what you want to achieve. Think about the end result and articulate it clearly to yourself, mentally or in writing. If you can't do this, there is no point in continuing, because you won't be able to bring the necessary degree of focus to bear. Also, consider what you *need* rather than what you *want*, because the two things do not always coincide. Step two is the spell design. Take your time over this, and make sure that everything you use in your spell means something to you. If you do decide to use someone else's pre-written spell or part of one from a book, you must fully understand why you are using the ingredients listed and/or performing the acts stated. When you have designed the spell completely, take time to consider all the possible outcomes of the spell, good and bad. This step is essential, so do not pay lip service to it. You might also think about those things that are most likely to happen; remember, magick takes the path of least resistance. You will probably want to limit or completely eradicate the chances of all undesirable outcomes here, so a redesign may be necessary. Once you have your amended spell, go through the loop of considering outcomes again, preferably at another time to give you a fresh insight. Meditation is always a good technique to use at this point, as it can bring the subconscious to bear on the problem and may suggest some outcomes that you hadn't previously considered. When you are confident that there are no outcomes you need to prevent, and what you *do* want is encapsulated in the spell, it is time to look at it from a more practical angle. What I mean by this is that for the spell to work you must visualise the outcome clearly, with all the negative outcomes excluded. If at this point you discover the spell reads more like the small print of a legal document than a request to the cosmos, it is time to think again. It is not enough just to add empty phrases at the end of the spell, such as "and with harm to none," especially if you don't mean or really feel them. You must be able to *visualise the outcome clearly,* harming none. If there are so many exclusions mentioned that you can't possibly hold them all in your head, then it is time to consider again the question of whether you should be doing this at all. If the answer is still "yes," then it is time for another rewrite to simplify it. This may mean taking more risks and being prepared to accept the consequences of the outcome—but at least by going through this exercise you will have a pretty good idea of what the risks are and how likely they are to happen. Another point to consider during this final rewrite is that "God is a statistician," so the more channels you leave open for manifestation to take place, the more chance there is of the spell working. Now the spell is ready for use. Because of the time you have spent on it, you should know it completely, and you can expect to reap the rewards of that time well spent, as it is now firmly embedded in your subconscious mind. Next you need to consider *when* to cast the spell, the most favourable time. Some knowledge of astrology is helpful here, and the more factors you consider the better your chances of success. Having selected the appropriate time and place, you are finally ready to cast the spell. There should be no holding back, and it should be cast with all the emotion you can muster.

There is a saying associated with the casting of spells, and it goes: "To know, to dare, to will, and to keep silent." "To know" means that you have the knowledge of how to cast the spell and you know exactly what it is you want to achieve. "To dare" means that having considered all the possible outcomes you are still prepared to take the risk; remember, magick is not an exact science and you cannot fully control its flames. "To will" means that you just "go for it" wholeheartedly and without reservation. "To keep silent" is something we haven't considered yet, but it is a vital last stage, so let's look at it now.

When we cast a spell, energy is released out into the cosmos to do our will, at which point we have little control over it. A good analogy here is bowling: you move into position, swing your arm while taking aim, and let go of the ball. You have done all you can, and now you can only watch. If your aim is true, you will hit the target. A spell is like the ball, and the letting go is our "keeping silent." The worst thing we could do is hold on to the ball too long; if we do, it may never even leave our hand, or at best it will go straight into the gutter. When we cast a spell we must let it go *completely*. Any act on our part that prevents this will hamper the spell's chances of success. To hold on to a spell, we are likely to talk about it or think about it, but both of these acts *tie the spell to us*. You should *never* discuss a spell with anyone while it is still "operational." If you feel you must, then only do it after it has worked, or when you are convinced that it hasn't. Equally, you must get into the habit of not thinking about the spell afterward, which I know from experience is far easier said than done. However, with practice this can be achieved. Some tips I have for this are performing the spell and going to bed straight afterward, or writing the spell down in your magickal journal immediately afterward as an act of letting go. To keep your mind occupied, it is essential to plan on doing something completely different directly after casting the spell.

One other thing we haven't yet considered is the question of timescales. How long does a spell take to work? This can vary enormously. A spell can work instantly for the small, mundane ones you may like to try, like making sure there is a parking space at the mall, or can take a year or longer for something very complex. Some spells of course have an in-built "sell-by" date based on the nature of what you are asking for; for example, a piece of weather magick probably needs to work on a specific day. Sometimes you will have a timescale in your head either consciously or subconsciously, and this will affect how soon the spell manifests. On average, though, I would say that most spells take from one entire moon cycle to a season to work (one to three months), so, you see, magick is rarely a quick fix.

Clearing Up

So the spell is cast and you have written it up in your journal. What else is there to consider? The one thing left to do is tidy up. This not only covers the most obvious act of dispelling the sacred space, but also giving consideration to the things that are left over that are still magickally charged. Most likely you have used real water as a representation of that element; this needs to be poured onto the earth or into a natural body of water as an offering back to the unused power—don't just pour it down the sink. There might be candle stubs, and the tradition with these is to bury them on your property for magickal acts of attraction and growth, or off property for the reverse. Better yet, let them burn down to nothing. Longer term, you may have created an amulet or talisman, and there could come a time when this is no longer required. If you have such an item that is no longer needed, then it needs to be disempowered. There are many reasons for this. One is that you may want the intent encapsulated in the object to only work the once—for example, in attracting a partner; another is to avoid the magickally charged object falling into the possession of someone who does not understand what it is and thus being subjected to its intent. If the object is paper or parchment, this may be ritually burned and the power offered back to the cosmos in that way. If it is a solid object like a crystal or piece of jewellery, I recommend leaving it exposed to the elements for an entire moon cycle in a place where it will not be disturbed, but in contact with the earth, where rain, sun, moon, and wind can all reclaim the power. This can be done with a simple ceremony of asking that the elements take back their power from the object. Do not give magickally charged items away to people who have no concept of the occult arts, unless the item was intended as a gift in the first place. There is no telling what effect the item will have on them, but it is unlikely to be beneficial.

Magick and Spiritual Development

The final thing I would like to discuss is the role of magick in relation to spiritual development and belief systems. To someone not familiar with magick and the occult, this may seem like a strange link to make. However, as I have said previously, once an individual embarks on a magickal path it will have wide-ranging effects on his or her personality. It will also start to raise such questions in the mind as, "How does this work?" and, when power is being raised and actually felt within the body, "Where is this coming from?" It is a natural process to want to see how you fit into the great scheme of things, and at this point it becomes unavoidable to question the very nature of deity itself. Given this, the link between magick and spiritual development becomes an obvious one. Magickal energy is not bound to any specific religion. It is a natural force and process that all people tap into from time to time, even if they are not aware of what they are doing. All we have been discussing here is how to bring the process entirely into consciousness. We have seen that magick is neither good nor bad, but rather neutral. I state these things in order to make the point that magick in itself is *not* a product of some evil entity enticing us into its grasp; if it were, then I suspect it would be made a whole lot easier to perform. In fact, magickal practice is an extremely viable way for individuals to make direct contact with deity and discover for themselves what that word *really* means to them. Many spiritual paths incorporate acts of magick into their philosophy, prayer being another form of spell-casting, and you may find that you are drawn to one of those. Ultimately, the path you take is your choice; you have free will. No one can tell you what deity is; you must find that out for yourself.

I leave you with a thought that a very wise teacher of mine once said, and that is, "Once you take a step upon a path, it cannot be taken back." At face value this seems a curious proposition, but what it really means is that once you learn something, you can't easily unlearn it. As you tread a magickal path you will see many new and wonderful things; you will discover things about yourself that you didn't suspect, and not all of the discoveries will be pleasant. But whatever you do discover, you will know it to be the truth, and therefore it cannot be "taken back." You may decide to go no further along the path, but you cannot forget the steps you have already taken. If you do decide to follow the way of magick, I would like to wish you every success. May your gods go with you, and may you be rewarded in your search by attaining the truth.

Bibliography

Aswynn, Freya. *Northern Mysteries & Magick.* St. Paul, MN: Llewellyn Publications, 1998.

Starts with an in-depth discussion of each rune and how the runes relate to each other. Following this there is information on use of the runes for divination and magickal applications. The final chapters look at the most popular northern deities and feminine mysteries.

Ravenwolf, Silver, and Nigel Jackson. *Rune Mysteries.* St. Paul, MN: Llewellyn Publications, 1999.

The book is accompanied by a deck of cards called The Witches Runes; *in my opinion, this is the best set of rune cards around. Although the book deals largely with the use of runes in divination, and it does this in some depth, it is also a good source book of runic correspondences for magickal application.*

Thorsson, Edred. *Futhark: A Handbook of Rune Magick.* York Beach, ME: Samuel Weiser, 1984.

This book concentrates on the use of runes in magick. For those interested in learning more about the system that is analogous to yoga and was devised by German magicians, this book is highly recommended.

Occult Philosophy and Magic

MARTIN DUFFY

The aim of this work is to show how magical practice can be enhanced by the understanding and application of occult philosophy, but before launching into a discussion of magic, it is necessary to first set the scene so you may know where I'm coming from. The whole of this work is based upon the hermetic premise of "as above, so below," which, put simply, means that the spiritual world (as above) is directly linked with the physical world (so below), and that the two have an effect on one another. We also refer to the spiritual plane as the macrocosm (the "great world") and the physical plane as the microcosm (the "small world"). This of course is the basis of much pagan thought, but here I shall be exploring how this seemingly simple axiom underlies the process of magic.

The Microcosm

The physical plane is obviously the world within which we operate on a daily basis, including our workplace, our homes, and the environment around us. This physical world is made of four forces, and these are the elements of earth, water, fire, and air. I have not the space to devote to an in-depth appreciation of these four sentient forces, although I do hope to invest in you a basic grasp of their more obvious natures. The elements are named after states with which we are all familiar, and the physical manifestation is what gives us the keys to understanding their virtues. It must be understood that when we talk of the elements we are talking of forces, not the gross forms themselves; earth is more than earth, water more than water, fire more than fire, and air more than air.

To understand earth, simply note the impressions that arise within you as you think of it. More than likely you will resonate with its solid, substantial, firm, and "real" qualities. The saying "down to earth" may also come to mind, as might the fact that earth grounds electricity. All of these things tell us that the earth force is grounding and gives firm foundations upon which to build. It additionally brings security and realism, provides fertile ground in which to plant our aims, and encourages introspection (looking within our own earth/body).

If you apply the same method to water, typical observations of its nature might include its fluid, nonsolid state, its reflectiveness, the waters of birth (both the amniotic fluids of childbirth and the waters of the sea from whence humankind came), and maybe its associations with washing away the impure. Water is also passive, and this is because its shape is dependent upon the container into which it is poured. From this information we may deduce that the water force brings pliancy and the ability to transform from one form to another. It engenders cleansing, calming, and nurturing energies, encourages reflection, influences the emotions, and brings forth the psychic abilities.

Turning our attention to fire, we might say that it is powerful, destructive, single natured, uncontrollable, hot, and dry. Additional insight may also be gleaned by contemplation upon the "fiery" temperament. By similitude, we can say that fire gives us drive and ambition, and is purifying (it breaks down the physical form to release energy), releasing, cathartic, strengthening, and passionate. Whereas water was seen to be passive, fire is active; it has a "life of its own" and cannot be as easily contained as water. If we consider the fiery sun, we can also see the life-giving and growth-promoting energies of fire in action.

The last of the four elements is air, and the easiest way in which to understand this element is to consider the breath. When we are newly born the first thing we do is inhale, which informs us that air embodies inspiration, the initial idea and principle that we receive. When we apply sound to our out breath we gain the ability of speech, and so air is concerned with communication as well as the intellect that our words communicate. Furthermore, travel is implied by virtue of the fact that it is on the air that our sound is carried. Air can therefore be seen to bring new ideas, fresh approaches, strengthen the mind and intellect, and influence communication and travel.

In order to help you further, I shall also devote some space to the consideration of other qualities besides those perceived directly through attunement. Each of the four elements is related to a direction, and this is based upon a similarity between the virtue of an element and a direction. In short, these are air to east (the sun rises in the east, beginning the day, and air rules beginnings), fire to south (fire is the epitome of heat, and south is the position of the sun during noon, the hottest part of the day), water to west (water is calming, and when the sun is in the west it is getting to the time of day when one winds down), and earth to north (inside the earth is dark, and when the sun is in the north of the sky it is below the horizon, and so it is night).

Further to this, each element has a colour association, and so green represents earth, blue denotes water, red corresponds to fire, and yellow indicates air. Obviously, each element has secondary colours, and so all those colours that conjure up earth are of that element, which includes brown, for example. Other colours for fire might be orange and yellow, whereas water might include turquoise and sea green, with air also being represented by sky blue and white (for clouds).

The four elements may also be understood by another system that utilises the theory of the four humours (humour meaning "fluid"). In this approach each element is conceived to be a pairing of either hot or cold with dry or moist. Earth is cold and dry like the winter ground, water is cold and moist like a freshwater stream, and fire is hot and dry like a raging inferno, whereas air is hot and moist like steam.

This leads neatly to the concept of friendships and enmities. Both earth and water are of a denser nature than fire and air, as can be seen in the gross physical forms of the same name. Earth is the densest, being the ground on which we tread, whereas semisolid water is fluid and changeable, hence the next in line. In light of this, earth and water are said to have a friendship between them; that is, they work together. Fire is not as dense as water and is consequently more mobile in nature, which leaves air as the least dense and most mobile of all the elements. The mobility of fire and air makes them active, unlike the more passive earth and water; it is because of this that we say they have a friendship.

These friendships are additionally based upon the elemental qualities. Earth and water are both cold and so have a friendship; earth is also friendly with fire, with which it shares the quality of dryness; likewise, water is friendly with air on the basis of their mutual moistness. Fire and air have a friendship because both are hot, but fire has a second friendship with earth, and air has one with water (as mentioned above).

In occult philosophy, a friendship between two forces or items brings them together, so just as a magnet will draw iron and catnip will attract cats, an earth item will draw a water item and the two will happily work together, as will fire and air, and so on.

In metaphysics, as in life, disharmonious relationships also exist, and these are said to be *enmities*. There are only two enmities, and these are between fire and water and earth and air. Fire and water are the most obvious, because the calming water may douse the passionate fire, and the determined fire may boil away the passive water. This is seen in the qualities of both elements, wherein the hot and dry qualities of fire are the complete opposite of the cold moistness of water. Earth and air are also of opposed nature (cold and dry earth versus hot and moist air); one is passive and the other, active. Furthermore, earth, as the ground, is the densest of the elements, whereas air, as the sky, is the least dense, and so furthest away from the earth.

Enmities between two forces or items will result in a rebuff, and just as cats repel mice, so things of earth will repel those of air; likewise with water and fire.

There are other aspects to the elements that you may learn about through the personal effort of getting to know the elements yourselves. This of course is an effort that will yield far more rewarding results than merely reading about them ever will.

This, in short, covers the four building blocks of the physical world, and it will have been noted that the adage "as above, so below" has been employed in the above, whereby we sought the spiritual understanding through the physical embodiment of each element. This simple point also unveils the premise that spirit, the fifth element and material of the soul, is housed in all physical constructs.

The Macrocosm

Spirit is the building material of the spiritual world ("as above"), and to impart some sense of its nature would, again, take a book of its own. However, for the sake of this work it is enough to know that although it is a separate element in its own right, it also infuses the four physical elements and is within them. Spirit, in essence, is the energy of deity, the God and Goddess, and it is also the cloth from which all souls and spirits are formed. Moreover, it is the power with which we work when weaving magic.

Spirit can be separated into two polarities—the masculine and the feminine. It must be remembered that we are not talking physical gender traits here; these are merely terms used to denote certain qualities. The masculine force is positive, growing, and creative, and the feminine force is negative, decaying, and destructive. They additionally rule different aspects of physical matter, and so the masculine rules the right-hand side, fronts, and tops, whereas the feminine rules the left-hand side, backs, and bottoms. Furthermore, masculine works from the centre outward, and so is extrovert and repelling, whilst the feminine works from the outside in, and hence is introvert and attracting. When combined, the masculine and feminine form one neutral hermaphroditic force. It is also worth pointing out that neither force is superior; they are equal, although it should be borne in mind that "equal" does not imply "the same as."

We can now comprehend a world that consists of two interpenetrating layers, each affecting the other, and each with its own building materials. However, in reality the two aren't as easily separated; they are commingled, with the physical world acting as a containing vessel into which spirit can be poured. In the larger picture this is exemplified by the notion that the whole world is suffused with spirit, and on the smaller scale, the human is the house of a soul (which is a contained amount of spirit). The previous examples again show how the macrocosm ("as above") is a divine blueprint for the microcosm ("so below").

Everywhere around us we see spirit enclosed in physical vessels; it is in every animal, tree, plant, and rock, and it is this energy that we utilise when we employ an object in magic. In magic we can bring out the power inherent in natural objects and add our own to the object in order to make something that is more likely to occur.

The Law of Correspondences

The law of correspondences basically declares that certain items have certain uses, and that items are linked by shared qualities. Those who are not new to magic will have probably come across the idea of correspondences before and will more than likely have been presented with lists of ingredients with the uses to which the correspondences may be put. I am not going to give any lists for the simple reason that anyone is capable of discovering an item's correspondence with the application of a little effort, and this is not only preferable but an excellent means by which to interact with the world in a magical way.

For those unfamiliar with magic, the correspondence view of reality is that physical items are magically linked with specific virtues on the basis of some sort of similarity or connection. In short, everything in nature has its own spirit, and each spirit has specific areas of influence. The extension of this premise is that the use of certain physical objects in magic rites will add extra power and increase the likelihood of achieving the spell's aim. To discover the arena in which an item has its effect, one simply employs the same technique that was utilised when exploring the elements. It is through similitude that the occult spiritual nature of things is exposed; the physical body is the clue to the higher reality, "as above, so below." In other words, the occult virtue of an object is communicated to us through the language of symbolism.

The reasoning for the above understanding is quite simple. All occult power originates in spirit, and it is this power that one is using when performing magic. The spirit enters material objects on the basis of their shape, and so the container determines the nature of what is inside. There is consequently a direct relationship between the vessel and its load, and accordingly one may surmise the nature of the contents based upon the container's appearance, much as one may guess a present by studying the shape of the box.

To illustrate this point, let us consider a few examples. A plant with tongue-shaped leaves may help in magics concerned with communication issues, simply because the leaf is tongue shaped and therefore receives the force to affect communication. A stone with a hole, also known as a hag stone, may be protective because it symbolises the female genitalia, therefore the Goddess, and consequently feminine power. Water that flows from the north to the south becomes imbued with the powers of earth (as that is where it flows from), and so is useful in goals that relate to grounding, strength, and material abundance.

Second, every item in nature has an elemental ruler that to a large extent governs its area of influence, and this can be quite easily deduced. The physical vessel of an object determines the elemental ruler, and this will again help determine its occult virtue. A candle flame is obviously ruled by fire, and rain by water; however, some items may have secondary rulers that exert a different influence, thereby altering the basic virtues. An example of this is in plants and stones; these all fall under earth as a primary group but have individual rulers that differ based upon their specific nature. Cinnamon with its fiery taste is obviously fire, whereas the moist cucumber is water.

Now that we have the necessary tools, let's work through an example together so that we may see the theory in practice. To do this we shall use the instance of a crow feather. The first step is to find which of the four physical elements is its ruler, or which two of them, and this will tell us the general magical uses to which it may be put. In the case of the feather, it is obviously ruled by air, because not only do birds fly, but the feather itself is light like air. This tells us that the feather will help in air-based goals, such as those pertaining to inspiration, new beginnings, communication, and travel. The next step is its appearance, and the crow feather is black, which conjures up images of death, the night, and secrets. Black is also absorbing and powerful. One may subsequently surmise that crow feathers can be used in spells aimed at communicating (air) hidden knowledge (the colour black) to us.

The Planets

Planets have a very important part to play in occult philosophy, and this is because they exert a considerable influence on the world. It must be realised at the outset that by "planets" we are not referring to the mere physical bodies themselves any more than we considered the elements to be limited to their grosser forms. The planets have a dual nature, like humans; they are of both a material body and a spirit. It is from spirit/deity that the planets receive their occult power, and this is their supernal (heavenly) nature.

Additionally, the planets form an intermediary between the material or elementary world and the spiritual world (which contains intelligences, spirits, and so on), and make up the celestial world. The celestial world partakes of both material and spiritual qualities, as we have just discussed, and this is the reason for its intermediary position in the three-world structure—it connects above with below.

Traditionally there are conceived to be seven heavenly bodies, which are Saturn, Jupiter, Mars, the sun (or Sol), Venus, Mercury, and the moon (or Luna). Technically speaking, the sun and the moon are not planets, but that is not important in terms of occult workings; it is simply a term of convenience. We also now know of the existence of Uranus, Neptune, and Pluto, but these are not visible to the naked eye, and so were not known to occultists of the past. I shall not be dealing with these last three in this work, but if you are interested in adding them to your own practice, there are many astrological books that touch on this subject. We now turn to the planets themselves and each of their elemental rulers, and we shall do so by looking at them in the order in which they rule over the days of the week (Sunday by the sun, Monday by the moon, Tuesday by Mars, Wednesday by Mercury, Thursday by Jupiter, Friday by Venus, and Saturday by Saturn).

The Sun

The sun is technically a luminary, and not a planet, as such; however, it exerts a very powerful influence over both our physical and spiritual world. The sun is masculine in nature, and so exerts a virile force, as anyone who has lain in its rays for extended periods of time will know; it is also ruled by fire. Typically, exposure to the sun's rays will result in heightened passion, a fiery temper, and increased sex drive, but it also increases the sense of well-being and the inclination to extrovert sociable behaviour, and so all these things are influenced by the sun.

The sun rules life and growth; without it the earth would be a dead and barren planet, so solary virtues include those that inspire ambition, success, growth, prosperity, money, and health. The sun is the centre of the solar system, and as such it pertains to the microcosmic equivalent of our own bodies (that is, the self). Consequently, the sun's fiery rays may bolster self-confidence, self-esteem, an independent streak, and the sense of what one is about; the rays also work to influence our status and friendships.

Things that are considered solary (of the sun) are those items that imitate the sun through similitude. These include stones of its radiant colours, such as amber and gold, plants that open and close their petals to solar effulgence, as well as those of its colour, for example, marigolds, St. John's wort, and sunflowers. Other solar plants are those that are sharp to the taste, a little bitter, and cause a "contracting" feeling, such as cinnamon, clove, and basil, and those whose smell is a mixture of sweet and sour, such as orange, rose, and rosemary. The sun has dominion over the metal of gold, its colour being similar to that of the solar rays.

The Moon

The moon is feminine in nature and ruled by water (and earth, to some extent), which is seen in its gravitational pull on the tides of the sea (there is a limited pull on solid objects, also). The link to the feminine is strengthened by the fact that the moon takes twenty-eight days to orbit the earth, which is close to the length of the menstrual cycle, and so the moon influences women's cycles, fertility, and the feminine mysteries. The moon also impresses its occult power on birth, family, and children by virtue of its bond with femininity, and by reason of the sea, which it rules, being the place from which all life came.

We earlier saw that the moon has an effect upon water, which influences the emotions, and so by extension the moon does act upon the feelings. Because of its association with the night, this luminary also rules dreams, mysteries, the unknown, the intuition, and divination. Related to this, it holds sway over illusions (such as those of our minds) by virtue of the fact that although it appears to radiate light, it actually shines with the reflected luminosity of the sun, and not its own.

The moon shows three faces for each of its three stages; these are waxing (growing in size), full (fully illuminated), and waning (decreasing in size), although we could add a fourth to this, which is the dark moon (no illuminated face visible). This tells us that the moon rules change, natural tides of growth (waxing), attainment (full), and destruction (waning).

Lunary items include all those things of its silvery white hue, such as pearls, objects that are white or clear, including quartz and egg white, and anything reflecting the darkness of the hidden moon, such as black onyx. The moon has command over the metal of silver, whose colour is that of the shimmering moon. Among the lunar plants are those that are of similar colour to the heavenly body, including cleavers, saxifrage, jasmine, clary (which has whitish-blue flowers, the colour of the moon), and especially those that are succulent or have water associations, such as the willow, the lily, the lotus, and the mandrake. Furthermore, lunar plants have little or no aroma whatsoever, much like the element of water that rules this planet, and so the moon rules poppies, cucumber, lettuce, pumpkins, and melons.

Mars

The red planet of Mars is masculine and ruled by fire, and from this combination comes many of its associations. The colour red suggests blood, which is the source of our physical energy; consequently, Mars has dominion over courage, passion, drive, determination, strength, vitality, and lust. The symbolism of blood has a further connection with warfare, and the planet itself is named after Mars, the Roman god of war. This association informs us of the control that Mars has over instinct, defence, competitiveness, the will, assertiveness, power, problem solving, achievement of desire, and also violence, revenge, and anger. One further attribute that Mars has is the expression of the true self.

Martial objects include anything that is red, sharp, spicy, acrid, hot, dry, and strong—these qualities being reminiscent of martial virtue. Mars rules crystals such as ruby, bloodstone (heliotrope), and red topaz, and it commands the metal iron. In the plant kingdom, martial plants are those that are poisonous and produce a burning sensation, such as wolfsbane; those that cause pain, such as thistles, hawthorn, and nettles; and those that are otherwise bitter, hot, or tear inducing, such as wormwood, radishes, peppers, mustardseeds, hops, ginger, chives, and onions. The aroma of martial plants is bitter and sharp, and often astringent, such as that of pepper and tobacco.

Mercury

It is air and the fluid element of water that has dominion over the hermaphroditic (masculine and feminine combined) Mercury, and this planet is named after the messenger to the Roman gods. Indeed, from the earth Mercury appears to travel the skies at the fastest pace, an admirable quality for a messenger. It is from this association that the planet's many virtues arise, the most obvious being that of air-ruled communication, by which we are speaking of the larger sense of the word, that is, to make known, reveal, or pass on. In this respect Mercury comes to influence not only talking and letter writing, but also drawing, drama, education, orating, and prediction or divination. This heavenly body has an additional command over those virtues related to communication, such as information itself, logic, science, magic, and the fields in which they may be utilised, including business and exams.

Mercury as a messenger god has the ability to travel with news, and so becomes the ruler of journeying, travel itself being the means of *communicating* oneself from one place to another. One last important area of influence for Mercury is that of medicine and healing, and it is the caduceus of Hermes (the Greek equivalent of Mercury) that is often used as a symbol of medicine even in this age.

Mercurial objects are those that are fluid, like the element of water and the chemical mercury itself. They also tend to be many coloured, of mixed taste, or generally of mixed nature. Mercury has dominion over stones that are yellow, including golden-yellow topaz, and those that are variegated, such as opal and agate, which can come in a whole variety of hues. Of metals, it rules quicksilver. Some plants that have short leaves are mercurial, such as parsley and marjoram, as are those that have mixed natures and are of a mercurial colour (yellow or variegated), such as cinquefoil. Mercurial plants also have an aroma that can be described as clear, penetrative, and refreshing, and so include the calming herbs of lavender, marjoram, and valerian (which, although quite foul smelling, does have a penetrative camphorous note in it).

Jupiter

Jupiter is masculine in nature, and is under the dominion of air. Jupiter (or Zeus of the Greek pantheon) is the head of the gods in the Roman pantheon, and Jupiter itself is the largest of the planets, so his attributes are those one would typically associate with someone of his position. It accordingly comes to be that this planet has dominion over the virtues of authority, career, and education, all orthodox roles of a father, and by extension the related areas of knowledge, honour, law, money, philosophy, politics, and exoteric religious form. In the traditional view a father also provides all that is required for a family, and so in the macrocosm this planet provides what is needed when we call upon it, whether it be guidance, material means, or opportunity. Linked to this, Jupiter as the largest planet comes to represent expansion, growth, success, and prestige, although in excess this can become negative.

The jovial kingdom includes all those things that represent increase and nourishment of life, as well as those things that are blue or violet. Of stones, Jupiter rules those of a jovial hue, such as amethyst, lapis lazuli, and blue sapphire; of metals, it rules tin, by reason of the ease with which it may be worked (just as a child may be moulded by his or her father). In the plant world, we find those that are jovial by virtue of their subtle sweetness, slight sharpness, and astringency, and so included in his empire are the likes of meadowsweet, dandelion, nutmeg, mace, nuts (almonds and pistachios), pineapple, rhubarb, and lemon balm.

Venus

The planet of Venus is ruled by water and earth, and is obviously feminine in nature. Venus is the brightest heavenly body (besides the two luminaries of the sun and moon), and is often called the "evening star."

Its brightness in the sky links it to the goddess of love, after which it is named, and so Venus pours forth the many qualities it inspires. The areas in which Venus holds sway include beauty, love, lust, pleasure, relationships, children, and young women, as well as the related concerns of peace, harmony, sociability, friendship, and any other partnerships (business, family, and so on).

Those items that are said to be venereal are moist, attractive, sweet, pleasant, and seductive. In the mineral kingdom, Venus rules those that are green, such as emerald, jade, lapis lazuli (when it has more green than blue, otherwise it is under Jupiter's dominion), malachite, and turquoise, but also rose quartz on the basis of its association with the heart and love, and coral, due to its association with water. Of metals, she claims copper, which has the inclination to turn green (verdigris). Their attractive appearance, sweet perfumes, and sumptuous fruits identify venereal plants; examples of these are the rose, foxglove, hollyhock, orchid, columbine, daffodil, daisy, feverfew, primrose, the mints (including pennyroyal), thyme, mugwort, runner beans, blackberry, raspberry, strawberry, gooseberry, peach tree, plum tree, and pear tree.

Saturn

The last of the seven main planets is the masculine Saturn, whose regent is earth. Saturn moves around the heavens very slowly and takes just under thirty years to circle the zodiac, in which time the moon would have done so more than 1,100 times, and the sun ninety times. It is because of its ponderous measured pace that it symbolises maturity and a mastery over time. This basic nature informs us that Saturn rules ageing, death, grieving, hardship, stability, patience, perseverance, tenacity, self-control, restriction, reality, and wisdom, all of which are metaphorically represented by the image of Saturn as Old Father Time (the Roman equivalent of the Greek Cronos). These qualities are emphasised by the rings of Saturn, which act to restrict and control. This sense of permanence, stability, and endurance likewise gives Saturn a dominion over the land, the home, groups, property, money, and the outdoors—all things that last. Moreover, Saturn's wisdom makes him the regent of study and success.

Saturnine things are those that are moist, natural, dark, bitter, old, or dead. Of minerals, Saturn lays claim to those that are heavy, dark, and earthy; some examples are onyx, jet, the loadstone, and chalcedony. Of metals, Saturn is the regent of lead by reason of its weight. In the plant world, Saturn rules those that are dark and mournful, and especially those that are poisonous, such as deadly nightshade, the yew tree, the holly, the ivy (all of whose berries are toxic), hellebore, hemlock, henbane (all poisonous), hemp, and the fern (as it grows in damp places). Saturnine plants also tend to be mournful, sour, bitter, and sharp in taste or aroma; examples are the blackthorn (especially the sloe berries), patchouli, myrrh, cumin, and cypress.

This concludes our consideration of the influences of the seven planets; it now remains to gain an appreciation of how correspondences can be found in number and colour.

The Power of Number

Numbers, like planets, also receive an intelligence based upon their symbolic traits. We shall here consider the scale of the decad, that is, one to ten. Before this it would be useful to first consider the absence of number, in the form of zero. The character of zero is very much like a single point from which all comes forth. We could liken it to the seed, which, within itself, contains all potential for the future plant. The zero also resembles the glyph for eternity, as it is a complete circle, and in this it shares a similarity with the ouroboros (a serpent that is swallowing its own tail). The ouroboros symbolises the original state of things, in that it contains all things within itself. It also informs us of the fact that all life that proceeds from the source will return to itself, just as the head of the snake swallows its own tail, and so all life will be destroyed in order to provide the energy for future growth.

One

From this single point (the seed, if you like) grows a stem, the number one. Being the first number of the decad it comes to represent the macrocosm. The number one signifies unity, the self, concord, and friendship, for the simple reason that one is complete and cannot be split into a whole number. This figure also contains the power of impulse and beginnings, and is thus dynamic, for the simple reason that it is the first number and all others are made from it.

Two

The number two is unity (one) united (1 + 1), and this tells us that two signifies equality, love, marriage, partnership, and support. Besides being representative of partnership, it can conversely be a symbol of choice and confusion because it shows a choice of unity (one or the other). You could liken it to scales, whereby those that are balanced show equality whereas those that aren't are imbalanced. The key traits of the number two as choice and harmony are seen in the fact that all extremes are symbolised as two ends of one spectrum. The number two also influences the microcosm as a whole, as it is the first creation of one (the macrocosm).

Three

In three we see the first true number, as one and two are creative principles (odd and even, macrocosm and microcosm); therefore, three represents the physical world, which itself is a combination of spirit (one) and body (two). Its link with the physical world can be seen in the fact that it has a beginning, a middle, and an end; a past, present, and future; and length, breadth, and height. The number three combines the impulse of one with the support represented by two, and this formula results in creative growth, another key trait of three; it can further be seen in the fact that from the union of masculine and feminine, a child might result (1 + 2 = 3).

The last consideration of three we shall make here is its ability to create harmony through mediating, which can be seen in the addition of a one between the extremes symbolised by two (1 + 1 + 1), and so we have a point between them at which the two opposites may meet. Here we see a link between this and the third day of the week, Wednesday (ruled by Mercury), because Mercury rules communication, which more often than not is the mediating force that resolves opposition (shown by the number two).

Four

The number four is best understood in the figure of a square, as we can then see its inherent solidity. The foursquare world of this number associates it with the earth and all things that bring security, including money and finance. It also represents the ambition and determination with which this may be achieved and the foundations and victory that then result. All of this can be seen in the traits of Jupiter, who rules the fourth day of the week, Thursday.

Five

The number five can be seen as a figure influencing wedlock, love, and union, and this is because it brings together the masculine two (representing the horned god) with the feminine three (representing the three faces of the lunar goddess). As well as representing union, the coming together of the God and Goddess brings creativity, just as egg and sperm may produce a child. This can be further seen in the fact that five combines the four elements with spirit (4 + 1 = 5), which is the pouring forth of spirit into a physical vessel—the very act of creation. The symbol of five, the pentagram, is considered a protective device, and by correspondence the number five takes on these protective virtues also.

The number five also splits the universe, represented in the dead by the number ten, into two halves, and so five can also be considered as having influence over justice. The last virtue of this figure is seen when we consider that we are adding impulse (the number one) to restriction (symbolised by the walls of four), informing us that five symbolises freedom from bondage and positive outcome through strife.

Six

Six is the most perfect number; it combines the two principles with the first true number (1 + 2 + 3 = 6), and so it comes to bring completion to projects, relationships, and so on. Generation is also seen in six. Whereas in five we had wedlock (3 + 2), in this figure we still combine two with three, but end up with something far greater than the sum of its parts (3 x 2 = 6), meaning that this number represents childbirth, growth, and increase.

The figure of six also signifies harmony, and this can be seen in what many refer to as the "Star of David." This is because it combines two triangles (2 x 3) representing the alchemical figures of fire and water (masculine and feminine) into one symbol. These two have a great enmity between them, so to balance them in harmony makes for a very potent force.

Seven

A sense of fulfillment pervades seven because it brings together the elemental world (four, as in four elements) with the spiritual world (three, as in the God and Goddess issuing forth from the unknowable source of zero). Seven is also the number of the moon and all her feminine mysteries, because 1 + 2 + 3 + 4 + 5 + 6 + 7 equals twenty-eight, the number of days it takes for the moon to complete her cycle, and the number of days in the menstrual cycle.

Seven is also barren like the moon, in that it is not generated (it cannot be created by any figures in the decad, and therefore universe, by multiplication), and doesn't generate anything in the universe (that is, nothing in the decad is made by a number multiplied by seven). Due to its unfruitful nature, the number seven is virginal, clean, and pure, and, furthermore, outside of time; as a result, seven becomes the regent of time itself. The link with time is seen in the week, where after seven days the week is renewed, and in the musical scale, where after seven notes we reach the eighth, which is the same as the first. Both of these examples furnish us with the means by which we may see how seven comes to influence fulfillment, progress, and change.

Eight

We come now to the first number that we are able to split into two even numbers (8 ÷ 2 = 4), and so eight holds sway over justice and fullness. This sense of fullness is again seen in the figure of the lemniscate, an eight on its side, the symbol of eternity. Eight multiplies the power of four, which causes it to be a particularly powerful agent in increasing four attributes, such as physical energy, the aptitude to command and direct, as well as proficiency in manifesting desire.

Eight has a further sense of change about it because it follows seven, just as the eighth note of an octave begins the next. It consequently comes to be that eight represents banishing and destruction; it is the end of the world because it follows seven, the number of time (seven doesn't end or begin, as it isn't generated, and neither does it generate). In this sense it aids in workings to do with binding, restriction, and ending.

Nine

As the last single number, nine is symbolic of the end of a cycle, and consequently holds sway over completion and fulfillment on all levels (physical, mental, emotional, and spiritual). It is also the ultimate feminine principle, as there are three lots of the feminine three, and so especially linked with magic, psychic power, intuition, and all feminine abilities. However, nine is just deficient of perfection (it is one short of ten, the universe), and so we must now move on to the last number of the decad.

Ten

Ten, as the universe, is everything, and it contains an equal number of odd (negative and feminine) and even (positive and masculine) numbers. Furthermore, it is circular in that it returns us to the beginning of the decad, that is, the number one. To illustrate this:

$1 + 0 = 1$

$1 + 2 + 3 + 4 + 5 + 6 + 7 + 8 + 9 + 10 = 55$

$5 + 5 = 10$

$1 + 0 = 1$

This tells us that everything goes back to the source. Just as we saw in the ouroboros, the tail of ten returns to the mouth of one, and completion and beginnings are mystically linked in the scale of number. This can be illustrated by the fact that all water returns to the sea and all bodies will return to the earth from which they came. Ten, therefore, rules transformation, and is the state where ultimate achievement must end in order for us to go on to new and better things.

This ends our appreciation of the power of number, although there are sufficient mysteries still contained in mathematics if one wishes to explore it further. Our attention now turns to the power inherent in colour.

The Power of Colour

There are virtues in colour, just as we have seen that there are inherent forces in the planets and numbers. Here we shall deal only with the basic few.

Red

Red is the colour of Mars and shares many of this planet's attributes. The association of red with blood, which has already been mentioned, tells us of this hue's ability to invoke vitality, power, strength, energy, and liveliness; exposure to it can actually raise one's heart rate. Being the colour of blood additionally affiliates it with grounding; it brings us back to our physical roots. Further to this is the connection with the element of fire, and so red is imbued with the traits of passion, daring, anger, and conflict.

Additionally, when the eye perceives red it has to adjust in such a way that it makes red appear nearer than it actually is, hence its use in warning signs. From this we may understand that red has a sense of immediacy and danger about it, very much like its fiery ruler.

Orange

Orange is a warming colour, but less harsh than red, as is seen by its position in the spectrum. Whilst red conjures the masculine, orange calls upon the feminine in her sensual, amorous form. Orange holds within it all that is warm, comforting, welcoming, cordial, sensual, and abundant. However, orange is very much like the harvest after the summer (and orange is the colour of the sun); you can only enjoy that which you put the effort into. Consequently, this colour has a karmic sense to it.

Yellow

Yellow is the colour of the element of air, and therefore is the hue of the mind and intellect. This considered, yellow helps influence the ability of communication, memory, study, and so on, all of which are mercurial. Yellow may also inspire optimism and a bright spirit, air being the element of inspiration and fresh starts.

Green

Green is at the centre of the spectrum (the seven colours of the rainbow), and so balances the warm, dry, and energetic colours (red, orange, and yellow) with the cooler, moister, and slower colours we shall shortly be looking at (blue, indigo, and violet). This tells us that green acts to bring balance, a trait that is further emphasised when we recall that it is the colour of earth, the element of stability and grounding. This stability and balanced nature is necessary for progression in any area; without it we are merely building towers on sand. Moreover, green as the colour of earth invokes the forces of growth and fertility as well as the resulting material prosperity—all virtues of Venus, with whom this colour is linked.

Blue

Blue is the first colour in the cold half of the spectrum, and is related to the moon and the element of water. This elucidates the reason for the enmity between fire and water, because not only do they act against each other in their natural forms, but their colours are at opposite ends of the spectrum. Just as we can gaze at our reflection in water, so we can use the colour blue to promote reflective qualities, and as we become lost in our musing we can reach our subconscious levels, bringing tranquillity and peace. In this reflective state we are also more open to inspiration from the deep wells of our inner self. For all these reasons this colour is an obvious choice with which to invoke peace, hope, happiness, and calm. Blue also has the ability to slow down and expand, making things seem bigger and farther away, unlike red, which as we saw earlier has immediate impact. It is these traits that give blue its reputation for inducing meditation and devotion.

Indigo

Indigo links the colours of blue and violet and combines the properties of both. It fosters the reflection of blue, but introverts it, leading us into the spirituality of violet. Indigo is the colour of Saturn, and the introversion can be seen in the slow nature of the heavenly body itself. This colour accordingly brings forth the virtues of maturity, wisdom, authority, mastery, and restriction. It also brings things back to a more lingering and ponderous pace.

Violet

Violet is the colour of introversion and spirituality, the complete antithesis of the outward expression denoted by the fiery energies of red, and this is seen in their placement at the opposite ends of the spectrum. However, this is not to say that one is more important than the other, just that they are on opposite poles of the same spectrum, and I believe that by balancing them it opens the way for a more "natural" way of living. We don't want to completely give in to physical pleasures, but neither do we want to turn to an ascetic lifestyle, denying our earthly embodiment—ours is the path of balance, after all! In magic, violet may help to protect from outside energies, just as Jupiter (the planet to whom this colour is ascribed) is the protector of the gods; it may also aid in turning the thoughts inward and opening the self to spiritual insight.

Besides those of the spectrum, we will now also briefly consider a few other useful colours; namely, white, black, silver, and gold.

White

White is one half of the polarity of black and white, the two colours of the element of spirit. It relates to the masculine, positive force, and hence has more to do with the mind than the material form. This may go some way to explaining why white is often considered the colour of purity and chastity, as taken to its extreme this colour can denote mind over matter. Of course, the implication being made here is that only the mind is pure; however, I don't see it as a matter of hierarchy, but of balance. I suggest that white is not the colour of purity, but of the mind. I consequently feel that this colour invokes the visionary inspirational qualities of the mind, and a spiritual awareness. White is technically the presence of all other colours (in terms of light), so it may be used for any general purpose, as it contains all the spectrum vibrations within.

Black

Black is the other half of the masculine/feminine polarity, and accordingly of the element of spirit. This colour is related to the feminine negative force, and is thus affiliated with matter and form. Black is the absorption of colour and the presence of none; with this in mind, it is very easy to see how it relates to the destructive negative force. One only has to think of the black hole pulling everything within, destroying creation. It is important to note that many people are afraid of darkness, destruction, matter, feelings, and so on, and often of the goddesses associated with this feminine polarity, such as Hecate or the Morrigan, but it is plain to see that these functions are essential to life—creation not kept in check is cancerous. From this analysis it may be deduced that black can be used for rest, change, banishing, binding, protection, and obliteration.

Little needs to be said of silver and gold, for they are essentially representative of sun (gold) and moon (silver) energy. As such, they may be used for the purpose of invoking the said planetary energies. This very much concludes our foray into the occult attributes of colour, although there are of course other colours that you may choose to explore.

All of this, although interesting, is without use unless we are able to draw the occult virtue from the said items; however, before we broach this subject it is best to first examine how magic itself works and some of the laws that govern it.

The Art and Science of Magic

To paraphrase Crowley, magic is the ability to affect change in line with will (Crowley, 131), and with this in mind we may immediately deduce a connection between the human mind and its environment, which we are aiming to alter. It is simplistic to imply that our desire manifests change by itself; this change may only occur through the addition of focus and power. A bulb, for example, will not glow without the addition of electricity. In short, one must raise energy and direct it using the will in order to affect the environment.

The first hurdle arises when one tries to define the environment in question. Is it simply the would-be spellweaver's own mind that is being altered, or maybe another's, or can the will affect the physical environment also? The answer comes down to personal opinion and experience, so what follows is merely my perspective on the question.

Ultimately, the energy of spirit and matter come from the same source, it's just that the form is different, so I see no reason why magic power (which is also of this source) should only be able to work upon the non-physical. I feel that this power is capable of altering not only the individual, but also his or her entire world, whether it be corporeal or not. I shall not dwell on this subject because ultimately experimentation will bear out your own opinions. However, a short quote from Crowley adds an interesting elucidation on this point: "Matter is an illusion created by Will through mind, and consequently susceptible of alteration at the behest of its creator" (Crowley, 230).

There are a few basic types of magic with which this work will concern itself, but ultimately the styles of magic I shall be describing come under two headings, and these are referred to by Sir James Frazer in *The Golden Bough* as sympathetic magic and contagious magic.

Sympathetic magic is based upon the Law of Similarity, which says that "like produces like," and implies that the effect will resemble the cause. This type of magic works on the principle that, through symbolic representation, one object can actually "become" the environment one is wishing to affect; for example, a person inserting pins into a wax doll would see himself or herself as inflicting pain on the desired recipient, with the doll acting as a proxy.

Contagious magic works the principles of the Law of Contact, and this says that what is done to a physical object is done to that thing of which it was originally a part. This law has an important part to play in the often-neglected magical link.

The Magical Link

As explained earlier, everything has an occult virtue, which it receives from spirit on the basis of the nature of the vessel. But more than this, it is possible for the virtue of one thing to pass into another when in proximity. This is physically demonstrated by the fact that a magnet will pass its magnetic ability into a piece of iron (albeit for a limited time) when they have been in contact for a while. On a more occult level, a stone that has been present during a miraculous healing may take on the virtue of healing that particular malady, and may be able to bring about this healing in the future via an allegation or contact with the ill person.

Items that have been close to a person will take on the essence of that person, and will to some extent become a part of him or her. These items, which include clothing, favourite pieces of jewellery, hair, nail clippings, spittle, bodily fluids, and so on, consequently become linked to the person, providing a magical "cable" along which power may travel. If one were conceiving a healing spell and the person could not be present, then there would not be the means for the power raised to reach the destination; however, a photo of the person or a piece of the person's clothing could symbolically represent him or her, providing the magic link between the person and the spell.

It is now time to leave this aside in order to examine how all of this information may enhance one's practice of magic.

The Goal

The first step in any magic is the assumption of a goal, and this needs to be strongly desired so that the all-important emotional connection to the outcome is present. The goal can be anything from the wish for basic physical needs to be met (home, money, security, and so on) to the banishing of bad habits to the ability to do certain things. Whatever the goal is, it needs to be condensed into a short phrase that describes exactly what is wanted with no room for error. One of the laws of magic is that it takes the shortest, easiest route to fulfilling wishes, so if you are looking for time off work it is best to add "with harm to none" at the end of your desire to rule out the possibility of your time off being sick leave.

Planning the Physical Operation

With the goal in mind, one must set about deciding which elemental and planetary rulership the goal is under in order to choose appropriate items for the spell. It would be no good utilising fiery martial objects in a spell for peace, for example, and similarly one would be unlikely to increase his or her passion for life with docile earth. Once the rulership is determined you should have some idea of the types of tools appropriate to the working; for example, you might use incense and feathers in air spells, candles and red threads in fire spells, blue crystals and fluids when the spell concerns water or stones, and plants when of earth. The list is endless.

Another important consideration when choosing the tools of the spell is similarity to the goal. The basis of most magic is that the physical operation follows the Law of Similarity (that is, "shows the power what to do"). This is an extension of the "as above, so below" maxim, for by enacting the goal on the physical plane we affect the energies on the higher plane. If one wanted to encourage some rain during a particularly dry period, for example, then the obvious thing to do for the physical operation would be to throw some water in the air to mimic the rain and "show the power what to do."

If you cast your mind back you may remember the concepts of friendship and enmity. Basically, friendships between forces or items indicate that they will attract each other, whereas enmities will repel each other, so we may not only work with those friendships and enmities of an elemental nature, but also with those easily observed in the natural world—an occult drawing and repelling based upon symbolism. For example, not only does the cat repel mice when living, but also the image of a cat will repel mice from a building due to the law of correspondence. Likewise, a piece of rose quartz may draw love, with which it has obvious associations (being pink and related to the rose), into a person's life.

A few more words are here necessary on the subject of "sympathetic magic." It must be remembered that it is not the symbolic enactment itself that causes the change to happen, any more than it is the mere desire to obtain the goal that grants our wishes. This much should be obvious. I have thrown water in the air many a time without being surprised with a shower, and I have deeply desired the ability to make my dishes wash themselves, yet that ability still eludes me. It is the *will* of the person for the desire to be made manifest, combined with magic power, that brings the results in.

The physical operation has a dual purpose, and the most obvious is that it focuses the mind of the witch upon the goal, so it lessens the chance of the mind wavering, which would decrease the likelihood of the spell succeeding. The second purpose is that the items themselves act as a base for the magical manifestation; that is, they provide a link between one's desire, the power, and the outcome.

I shall now present a few ideas for spells. These are not intended to be templates for future spells, but examples in which you can see the above ideas in action. Furthermore, I am not dealing with ethics in this work, this being a matter of personal concern, so to some individuals the following examples might seem repugnant. I accept that those with different codes of behaviour may consider some of these magics unethical, but I ask that it be remembered that they are merely here to illustrate the mechanics; they are not here as incentives to try them out.

If the goal of the witch was to procure revenge against an enemy, then he or she might make a wax figure of the person, perhaps loading it with a hair of the victim or a piece of cotton soaked with some of his or her bodily fluids (by "loading" I am referring to the practice of hollowing out a part of the doll and inserting the item into it). The witch might then vent his or her pique by the insertion of eight saturnine blackthorn spines into the figure, on principle that Saturn aids workings that have a baneful element, and eight is a number of destruction. Inscribing the name of the intended victim upon the doll may further enhance the magical link.

The same situation could be remedied by wrapping a piece of paper with the victim's name upon it around a martial onion, in order for the occult virtue of the onion to pass to the person via the magical link (the name on the paper). The goal in this case, rather than revenge, would be the seeking of defence from an enemy, and this charm could be further embellished by pinning the magic link to the onion using red (martial) or black (protective and absorbing) pins.

It may be that a witch would use a charm to draw upon lunar influences in order to aid magical workings. In this case one might take a piece of silver cloth, place within it various lunar items (herbs, crystals, and symbols) and maybe other items symbolising the goal, and then gather it up like a pouch, tying it with silver thread. This could then be worn about the person when engaged in magical workings, allowing the occult power to pass from the charm to the person directly, negating the need for a magical link.

When an item comes into contact with the body it makes what is called an *allegation* with it, and when such a charm as the one described above is made for wearing around the neck or on the body, it is known as a *suspension*. Other suspensions might include wrapping dried berries in a raspberry leaf and then tying the leaf with a piece of green cord in order to implore Venus to bestow greater friendships upon the wearer. Suspensions are most powerful when they include living matter, by which we mean vegetative or bodily items, as well as natural things such as cotton, silks, wax, and so on. In fact, it is worth bearing in mind that magic always manifests most potently in bases that have a "living" component, and by "living" I am not alluding to living animals but rather organic matter.

Another common method of magic utilises the candle. In this operation one might take a candle of the proper colour for the working and etch upon it the appropriate sigils for the working (such as the planetary symbol under which the working comes, as well as any other befitting markings). The candle can be loaded with the magical link by scooping out some of the wax at the base of the candle in order to produce a cavity.

The material making up the magical link can be placed into the cavity and sealed in by placing the wax back over the opening, and the candle can then be burned for a number of hours determined by number symbolism, for a quantity of days befitting the working.

A charm can also be as simple as binding the magical link to something that will bring the desired effect. People who consider themselves gossipers might tie something of themselves to a symbol of earth, on principle that earth has an enmity with air, which is the ruler of communication (gossiping being communication in excess). Conversely, if people want to inflame their otherwise dull lives with passion, they could bind their magical link to the martial ruby, a supreme object of fire virtue.

Along similar lines, one might also tie a magical link to an amulet of some such description so that the occult power acts against the magical link. An example of this could be tying a bird feather to a hag stone (a holed stone that acts as a protective amulet) in order to protect berries from bird damage. The reasoning behind this is that the protective device works against the object to which it is bound.

There are numerous other techniques, and some ideas might include tying magic into items with knots (this can include knotting pliable twigs on trees, cord, or ribbon, utilising number and colour), placing items into boxes as concealed charms (boxes "shut" the magic in), writing wishes upon coloured paper using coloured inks (perhaps again placing into a box or pouch with well-suited herbs), burning apropos herbs in order to release their powers, making necklaces of strung berries, incorporating suitable herbs and spices into foods, and numerous other methodologies. The limiting factors are your own imagination and your ability to believe in the power of your own constructs.

By this point one should have both a goal in mind and the method by which it may be physically demonstrated. It is now fitting to consider the timing of the operation.

Timing the Magical Operation

Timing an operation can be as simple or complicated as required, and often the immediacy of the need plays a large part in how appropriate timing can be incorporated. Obviously one shouldn't wait for an opportune time when the need is immediate, as this would be foolish, but neither should one be surprised when a working for increase fails at a time when nature's tide is destructive.

The largest cycle of timing is that of the seasons, and although this is a huge subject in itself, it is enough to say that spring is ruled by air and is readying, summer is commanded by fire and is fulfilling, autumn's regent is water and is concerned with harvesting, whereas winter is under earth's dominion and is consequently completing. Other associations can be made with the elemental qualities and a cursory understanding of the waxing and waning of the year. Obviously one cannot always wait for spring to come around when trying to get a project off of the ground, but when possible this can be a propitious way of timing magics.

Earth energies are also affected by the moon's tides, and with the moon ruling hidden forces such as magic this planet is a great indicator as to what the energies are doing at specific times. The moon's phases were mentioned in brief earlier, but here we shall look at them in a bit more detail.

When the moon shows her waxing face we may know that the hidden tides are increasing in nature; this can be seen in the fact that the illuminated crescent is on the masculine right-hand side, thus informing us of positive growing energies. A full moon tells us that the forces of nature are fulfilling at this time; the forces manifest the desire of the waxing phase. This is embodied in the fullness of the moon, where both left- and right-hand sides of the orb are illuminated, thus symbolising the creation that occurs when sperm and egg come together. The darkening of the right side as the left side brightens heralds the waning moon, and this advises us that the hidden powers are negative and destructive at this time.

There is a fourth face of the moon, and that is the phase at which it is completely unlit, and consequently unseen to the naked eye. This hidden aspect of the moon is an indicator that the tides are especially propitious to workings that concern transformation—as this phase is symbolic of the transition between death and rebirth—as well as those that aspire to reveal hidden information. It is the case that most workings can be altered to fit the moon phases, and so health may be procured through the increasing of vitality at the waxing moon, or the banishing of disease at the waning moon, or even the manifestation of health at the full moon.

One may also carry out the working on a day ruled by the appropriate planet using the following correspondences:

- Sunday is ruled by the resplendent sun
- Monday has the watery moon as its regent
- Tuesday is commanded by the aggression of Mars
- Wednesday is claimed by the hermaphroditic Mercury
- Thursday is under the dominion of benevolent Jupiter
- Friday is impelled by the empress Venus
- Saturday is under the reign of masterful Saturn

Further, to daily rulers, the planets also rule hours, and these can additionally be taken into account. A chart of these hours follows. The chart is used by commencing magical operations at the hour ruled by the correct planet for the goal, but, again, this isn't a die-hard rule, although utilising it will put the chances of success further in your favour.

	Sun	Mon	Tues	Wed	Thurs	Fri	Sat
1 a.m.	Sun	Moon	Mars	Mercury	Jupiter	Venus	Saturn
2 a.m.	Venus	Saturn	Sun	Moon	Mars	Mercury	Jupiter
3 a.m.	Mercury	Jupiter	Venus	Saturn	Sun	Moon	Mars
4 a.m.	Moon	Mars	Mercury	Jupiter	Venus	Saturn	Sun
5 a.m.	Saturn	Sun	Moon	Mars	Mercury	Jupiter	Venus
6 a.m.	Jupiter	Venus	Saturn	Sun	Moon	Mars	Mercury
7 a.m.	Mars	Mercury	Jupiter	Venus	Saturn	Sun	Moon
8 a.m.	Sun	Moon	Mars	Mercury	Jupiter	Venus	Saturn
9 a.m.	Venus	Saturn	Sun	Moon	Mars	Mercury	Jupiter
10 a.m.	Mercury	Jupiter	Venus	Saturn	Sun	Moon	Mars
11 a.m.	Moon	Mars	Mercury	Jupiter	Venus	Saturn	Sun
12 p.m.	Saturn	Sun	Moon	Mars	Mercury	Jupiter	Venus
1 p.m.	Jupiter	Venus	Saturn	Sun	Moon	Mars	Mercury
2 p.m.	Mars	Mercury	Jupiter	Venus	Saturn	Sun	Moon
3 p.m.	Sun	Moon	Mars	Mercury	Jupiter	Venus	Saturn
4 p.m.	Venus	Saturn	Sun	Moon	Mars	Mercury	Jupiter
5 p.m.	Mercury	Jupiter	Venus	Saturn	Sun	Moon	Mars
6 p.m.	Moon	Mars	Mercury	Jupiter	Venus	Saturn	Sun
7 p.m.	Saturn	Sun	Moon	Mars	Mercury	Jupiter	Venus
8 p.m.	Jupiter	Venus	Saturn	Sun	Moon	Mars	Mercury
9 p.m.	Mars	Mercury	Jupiter	Venus	Saturn	Sun	Moon
10 p.m.	Sun	Moon	Mars	Mercury	Jupiter	Venus	Saturn
11 p.m.	Venus	Saturn	Sun	Moon	Mars	Mercury	Jupiter
12 a.m.	Mercury	Jupiter	Venus	Saturn	Sun	Moon	Mars

In the example of a candle spell, one may time it to begin on an appropriate day and then light it sequentially for a suitable number of days. If the spell was for a job that would bring security, then it would be correct to begin it on Thursday, as patriarchal Jupiter rules it, and it would be wise to burn the candle for four days. If the spell was to control one's fiery rage, then one would utilise water, the enemy of fire, and therefore the moon would be used to temper passionate Mars. In this case it would be suitable to light a blue candle on a Monday, and light it for a number of hours on each of six or seven days (six for harmony between fire and water, or seven for the moon).

This concludes the subject of timing so far as the basics go, but you may also choose to time your workings with specific weather types (rain, thunderstorms, or snow) as well as other celestial phenomena (including occultations of the sun, traversing comets, and so on).

With all of the aforementioned things considered and planned, we must now spend some time contemplating the actual magic operation itself.

The Magic Operation

This section is going to be based upon a ritualistic method of magic, and implicit in this are certain ceremonial techniques. However, I am not implying that this is the only way magic can be worked; there are of course freeform styles of magic that can be employed, many of which I use myself. That said, it is far easier for you to discard items from the following method than to add missing components, and, furthermore, an involved method better illustrates the many ways that occult philosophy can be added to magic.

The first step is the preparation of the space and your own self. You should gather everything that is needed and take it to the place where you plan to carry out the ritual, which should be somewhere quiet, secluded, and where you are unlikely to be disturbed. Many people find that a shower or bath puts them in the proper mood; this also cleanses the body of negative energy, which is important when the body is to act as a conduit for magic power. To further strengthen the working, you may decide to use herbs or oils in the bath; these herbs or oils should have a connection with the working that you are going to carry out.

Before you start the magical act it is provident to announce the purpose, this in order to set the goal in your own mind and to declare your will to the astral planes. This can be as simple as, "I come here to bring about _____ by magic rites," followed by a number of claps or bell peals, which should be a number appropriate to the working. These knells can be performed at various points in the rite, perhaps at the start of the rite, after the circle is formed, and at the end, so that the raised power is intensely focused on the goal.

The next step is the creation of space set aside from the physical world, and for this we utilise the circle. The reasons for a circle are many; some are related to its symbolic value and some are for practical reasons. The main three practical reasons are as follows:

Protection

A circle protects the witch from negative energy/spirit. It seems to be assumed in some circles that every spirit in nature has come straight out of some Victorian dreamscape, despite the fact that in many mythologies (for that, should we read "past experience"?) fairies and the like seem to be indifferent at best, and more often than not quite openly hostile. When working rites one should always allow for protection from spirits attracted to the energy being raised, and the circle is a way of achieving this. These entities include malevolent earth spirits, trapped souls of a negative persuasion, and also passersby!

Container

The circle may be utilised to contain the energy that is raised. I liken it to pressure-cooking; you can raise and concentrate more energy in a closed, hermetically sealed crucible than you can in an open container. It is this quality that is responsible for the charged atmosphere that one experiences in the circle.

Preserver

As well as containing the energies that one raises, the circle also prevents them from dissipating during workings. This means that the raised energy is there to be used when one carries out the working, and is not dissipated into the ether.

In terms of symbolism, the various qualities of the circle inform us of the following truths in our workings:

- All points on the circumference being equidistant from the centre symbolises a balance in workings.
- The circle symbolises belief in the eternal nature of life.
- Working in a circle symbolises that we are restrained and guided in our actions by our beliefs.
- By having a masculine symbol in the centre of the circle, such as a solar cross (equal-armed cross) or altar, the two symbolise the union of the God and Goddess, masculine and feminine; thus, the witch is at the centre of creativity when in the circle.

The circle is drawn clockwise starting in the eastern quarter, and symbolises the path of the sun from the rising in the east to the setting in the west. The sun plunges into darkness in the north, where its fertile energies turn inward, thus entering a transient point between its death (it's not visible to us) and its rebirth (even though we can't see the sun its light is still shining, fertilising the dark earth).

However, one not only draws the circle east to east to illustrate the path of the sun, but also to symbolise the process of creation. East/air is the initial inspiration, south/fire is putting the idea into action, then west/water is the nurturing and reflection of the idea's progress, and north/earth is the idea completely manifested, laying the foundations for future growth. Furthermore, it shows the elements solidifying from the desire of air to the material embodiment of earth, and consequently informs our workings with the power to manifest the will ("as above, so below").

Prior to drawing the circle one should sweep it in a widdershins (anti-clockwise) fashion to banish any residual negative energy attached to the space. Following that, markers should be placed at each quarter. You could use coloured candles, stones, or even suitable elemental symbols (incense in the east, a candle in the south, a bowl of water in the west, and a stone in the north). It may be helpful at this point to lay out a length of cord to delineate the edge of the circle, which will make it easier to cast the circle and guard you from accidentally stepping over its boundary.

The next step is for the witch to "draw" a circle from east to east in a deosil (clockwise) direction. It may be befitting to draw the circle more than once, perhaps utilising number correspondence in order to choose a figure that vibrates with the goal. The casting can be executed using an athame, wand, or outstretched finger to project a line of energy, which will then form the circle on the astral levels. The correct action is to will the energy and the circle into existence whilst physically "drawing" it, or else you will have accomplished nothing more than a bit of exercise.

The wand represents the will, on virtue that it takes the desire and projects it into being, and this is why one may use it to cast the circle. A wand of course could be nothing more than a length of wood that measures a cubit (elbow crease to fingertip), but it may also be decorative, perhaps being tipped with a phallic symbol (for example, an acorn or pine cone) to further associate it with the masculine force of creation in line with will.

Appropriate words may be used whilst setting up the sacred space, and in fact to accompany any action. Sound is vibrational energy and as such is a part of spirit. It can therefore both create and destroy. Words themselves utilise sound energy and carry the will upon them. With this in mind it is far more appropriate that the words come from the self rather than a book, or else they will not be perfectly conveying one's own desire. However, in order to give some general idea, words as simple as "I cast this circle as a meeting place, to protect, preserve, and contain the energies that I raise within" will suffice.

With the circle cast, it is appropriate to call the elemental spirits to aid the work. This can be achieved by standing at their appropriate quarters, envisioning their qualities, and then inviting them with words such as "I call upon you elemental air, guardian of the east, to attend my rite and guard this circle." The calling can even be by symbolic action, for example, lighting incense for air, lighting a candle for fire, sprinkling water for water, and scattering earth or salt for earth. Once this is done one might choose to call upon personal deities or guardians to attend the rite, but this is not strictly necessary.

With the temple formed it remains to raise the energy that will empower the magic. There are numerous methods that can achieve this, and here I will present a couple of the most common. The first is sound, and this includes steady drumming, shaking a rattle, and chanting.

If chanting is chosen, it should be rhythmical, and can be formed of rhyming couplets or even just vowel sounds, so long as the chant is something repetitive that requires little thought. Additionally, rocking backward and forward is often found to aid the rhythm of the chant.

Another method of raising energy is to use circumambulation. This is the term used to denote the action of walking around the circle, and Aleister Crowley describes it faultlessly in the following quote: "This tread should be light and stealthy, almost furtive, and yet very purposeful. It is the pace of the tiger who stalks the deer" (Crowley, 208).

The exact number of circumambulations is again determined by number correspondence, with it borne in mind that deosil is creative and widdershins is banishing. Therefore, eight circumambulations in a widdershins fashion would not be appropriate for a working that proposed to enhance one's sense of freedom, for example.

Whilst raising energy the mind should be focused on what is being done, not lost in thoughts of household chores or worry over being discovered; this type of wandering will dissipate the energy and lessen the likelihood of a successful outcome.

With the energy raised one can now carry out the actual working that has been planned. One might choose to face the direction most closely associated with the purpose; for example, facing west when the spell involves cleansing, on principle of the connection with water. Whilst carrying out the act, the witch should inhale the energy of the circle, breathing rhythmically and deeply, feeling the body tingle with the infused power. Once the action is complete the witch needs to transfer the energy to the charm.

The transference of energy should be done to activate the charm, enabling it to begin the manifestation of the desire. This is where the importance of the correct objects is significant, for the power manifested in the charm will work to the vibration of its host. This means that power infused in a saturnine herb, for example, will not aid the impelling of abundance. In the case of a candle spell the power should be transferred before lighting the candle, as igniting the wick begins the spell, and the burning releases its energy. In most cases the power should be transferred as soon as the charm or physical operation is concluded and complete.

Transference of power can be achieved by either spitting on the object, blowing upon it, or holding it and envisioning the energy flowing into it as one proclaims a keyword to represent the goal. In the first method the power and purpose are transferred via spittle, thus acting as a magic link. In the second example the charm is given the "breath of life," and as air carries the will of a person, the charm becomes imbued with both purpose and power. In the third example the withheld power is released instantly, and so flows into the object, and the keyword is uttered to clarify the purpose, such as "abundance."

This concludes the magical working. The next step is to ground any energy left, which is done by placing one's hands on the ground and letting any excess drain from the body into the ground where it may be earthed and dissipated. Following that, one simply thanks the quarters for their attendance and, walking widdershins around the circle from east to east, draws the circle back into the athame, wand, or finger, and ultimately back into the body. It is appropriate at this point to finalise the operation with words such as "The rite is concluded," demarking the end of the spell.

Although the working itself has ended there are still things that must be addressed, such as the correct manner to maintain after the spell. It is not sound practice to constantly reflect upon the magic you have carried out, and neither is it helpful to talk about the working. Reflection on whether or not it has worked yet, or idle speculation on whether or not it will, reflects a poorly trained will, and as it is the will that directs the power, you would be merely defocusing the spell and adding negative energy to it. By refusing to keep silent about the operation you will be constantly dissipating the energy that is concentrated through silence, hence lessening the chance of a favourable outcome. Chatter will also allow others to discover the act, and if they are opposed to your goal then their negative thoughts may further influence the outcome.

If the desire has not manifested within a reasonable time then it may be necessary to repeat the spell, although one must always remember to remain patient when dealing with magic. The decision of whether or not to repeat a spell should be judged by the size of the change required; for example, a spell to heal a swollen tongue will probably produce results more quickly than a spell that aims to bring a long-term project to fruition. A spell may be repeated two or three times if necessary, but first ensure that you have composed the spell correctly. It may be that the operation is in some way imperfect.

It must also be remembered that a spell should be backed up in the physical world; no amount of rose quartz will draw love when one locks himself or herself away, and if the spell requires a job it may be provident to look in job columns in order to allow the perfect job to come into your life. One must always work toward the goal in the mundane world if the goal is truly desired. Magic impels—it does not compel.

This completes our appreciation of some of the many ways in which occult philosophy can help us to understand the world around us, and how it may subsequently be integrated into magical living. This is by no means a complete study of the subject, and those interested should research the subjects deeper and allow for their own ideas to be considered, for the applications are limited only by human ingenuity.

Bibliography

Agrippa, Henry Cornelius. *Three Books of Occult Philosophy.* Edited by Donald Tyson. St. Paul, MN: Llewellyn Publications, 2000.

Bardon, Franz. *Initiation Into Hermetics.* Wuppertal, Germany: Dieter Rüggeberg, 1971.

Crowley, Aleister. *Magick.* London: Guild Publishing, 1986.

Culpeper, Nicholas. *Culpeper's Complete Herbal.* Hertfordshire, UK: Wordsworth Editions, 1995.

Farrar, Stewart. *What Witches Do.* Custer, WA: Phoenix Publishing Co., 1983.

Frazer, Sir James George. *The Golden Bough.* Hertfordshire, UK: Wordsworth Editions, 1993.

Kozminsky, Isidore. *Numbers: Their Meaning & Magic.* London: Rider & Company, 1972.

Levi, Eliphas. *Transcendental Magic.* Translated by A. E. Waite. London: George Redway, 1896.

Regardie, Israel. *The Golden Dawn.* St. Paul, MN: Llewellyn Publications, 1989.

———. *The Tree of Life.* Edited by Chic Cicero and Sandra Tabatha Cicero. St. Paul, MN: Llewellyn Publications, 2001.

Valiente, Doreen. *Witchcraft for Tomorrow.* London: Robert Hale, 1978.

The Eightfold Ways of Magic

ANNA FRANKLIN

There are more books on Wicca and paganism today than there have ever been. There are even TV shows with witches as the heroines. With a flick of the fingers or the muttering of a spell, people can fix all their problems and get whatever they want. Not surprisingly, this has led to a great increase in the numbers of wannabe witches and people calling them-selves Wiccans. But is that really how magic works? Can you really get something for nothing in this way? Sorry, but the short answer is no.

When a person uses magic, he or she invokes the deep, primal forces that lie at the mysterious heart of creation. These forces have untold power, but no morality, and no reasoning ability. Magic is neither black nor white, neither good nor evil, but can be used all of these ways. Forces invoked by magic will take their task literally. They will fulfil the request by the shortest route.

Say that you want £1000 to buy a designer coat—you don't need it, you just want it—and perform a spell to get it. You don't think about the chain of events that might bring this about. A few weeks later a cheque for £1000 drops through your letterbox. So what's the problem? The force of magic, remember, has no morality. Perhaps your aunt is killed by a runaway bus and leaves you £1000. Do you feel guilty? After all, you didn't take a knife and murder her, did you? You just asked for £1000, and you weren't bothered at the time about how it would be delivered.

Well, maybe you feel sorry, but it's all over now, isn't it? No, it is far from over. Nothing happens in a vacuum, and the aftereffects of your spell continue to have consequences. Your aunt had a daughter who is now left motherless. Perhaps your aunt was a doctor who was destined to save many lives or discover the cure for cancer. Can you estimate all those possible future lives and destinies that will never be fulfilled, and all those children who will never be born, and all because you stirred the forces of the universe to get yourself a designer coat? Still not guilty? You might be responsible for the deaths of more people than Hitler, but it doesn't count if it was only by magic, does it? Oh, but it does. Everything has a price, everything costs, and those things you achieve by magic will be paid for threefold. Do you now wish you'd just saved up for that coat?

Hopefully I've frightened you into some sense of responsibility when it comes to the use of magic. However, magic is an intrinsic part of Wicca. All cultures, worldwide, have recognised and practised magic. Even Western society has, as part of its inheritance, folklore tales of magicians who were capable of harnessing invisible powers and of understanding occult laws. The tribal shaman, village wise woman, or cunning man served the community by healing the sick and mediating with the spirits for the benefit of the people. But spells are a tiny part of Wicca and a tiny part of magic—some experienced high priests and priestesses do not use them at all. A common mistake that people make is to assume that spells are the only way of making magic. This is far from true, and Wicca recognises eight ways of making magic, and these are called the Eightfold Ways (see page 141).

Wicca is a religion, it is not a game or a tool that you use to get something for nothing (oops—remember that coat?). The worldview of the pagan is essentially different from the normally accepted materialistic view of Western society. Real Wiccans hold that all life is sacred, that all life contains spirit, a living force within it—this includes people, animals, plants, and the earth itself. Wiccans believe that the divine spirit is not separate from creation, but is contained within it and within each of us.

In other words, deity is manifest within nature, is imminent, present—we can go out and touch God.

This part of the divine within everyone and everything is connected by a series of fibres and forms a web of being, a net of power that links and gives life to the cosmos. The shamanic view of the world is that everything is connected. The life force is the force that we work with, and via the web we mediate between the world of spirits and the world of mankind. Any vibration on the web eventually reverberates everywhere else, like ripples moving out from a stone thrown into a pond. The witch can integrate and communicate with the web, and through its fibres, perform his or her magic. As our understanding and consciousness grows, we become aware of the working of the web and its more subtle realms. We are part of the web, can attune to its various energies, and magically vibrate the web with full knowledge of the outcome. Because there is a part of the divine in everyone and everything, there is a connection between all things. Because magic touches the sacred, it should only be put to sacred use.

Wiccans believe that there is a natural balance in the world, a harmony that recognises the perfect balance of male and female, day and night, summer and winter, light and darkness, life and death, god and goddess. One cannot exist without its opposite. One is not good and the other bad, but both are equally necessary, like the two sides of a coin. This harmony is symbolised in the ancient Chinese yin/yang symbol. The symbol is a circle, which represents wholeness. It is divided into two interlocking halves, one white and one black. Within each half is the germ of the other, represented by the dots of opposite colour. It stands for the two opposites that form one perfect whole.

When balance and harmony are lost, then negativity, depression, illness, or conflict results. When a body is out of balance, for example, a person becomes ill. Wiccans always try to maintain the natural balance, and this is sometimes achieved by using magic. The village wise woman or witch was the first person to whom someone in trouble would turn, as the witch would understand what had happened to disturb the natural balance, and could see what had to be done to put it right. Witches were the healers—not just of human bodies, but of the whole natural balance.

This maintenance of balance gives the witch his or her code of honour and rules of conduct. Wicca has its own laws; just two basic rules that encompass everything. The first is the Law of Threefold Return. In its easiest form, for everything you do, you will get three times as much back, for good or ill, but not always in the same form. This concept of the threefold return is akin to the idea of *karma,* a philosophy accepted by a large percentage of the world's population. The doctrine of karma differs from that of sin in that every deed is thought to contain the seeds of its own punishment or reward. In magic, like attracts like, so positive deeds and generous thoughts attract good things back, while negative thoughts and selfish or evil deeds attract bad things back. A witch must keep the balance and understand the consequences of actions. This is why witches were called "wise women" or "cunning men." If you perform magic and cast spells, then the Threefold Law is called into action, which is why we are so careful only to perform magic that is necessary. Witches must consider the consequences of any action, especially when it comes to casting spells. Is your intention good? Have you thought about the consequences? Sometimes an act that seems beneficial can have a knock-on effect that will harm another, and you can be sure that the Threefold Law will swing into action. Nobody will be asking whether you meant to cause the damage.

In the past, people have described magic as white and black. Magic is neither good nor evil, but a force that can be wielded. I was always taught that unselfish, helpful, sacred magic is called white, while selfish or evil magic is called black. Because magic uses the sacred part of ourselves, it is sacrilege to use it for anything other than sacred purposes. Magic is a real and powerful force that taps into the deepest forces at the heart of the cosmos. If you alter one thing then a whole cascade effect is caused. Using magic is an honour and a great responsibility. The workings of the cosmos should not be shifted because you want a pair of designer shoes. This is black magic and could cause untold suffering.

The other witches' law is the Wiccan Rede:

> *Eight words the Wiccan rede fulfil—*
> *An' it harm none, do what ye will.*

Sounds easy, doesn't it? Do what you will—unless it harms another. This means that magic should not harm any other being, the earth, or yourself. Wiccans believe that all life deserves respect: people, animals, plants, and Mother Earth herself, most of all. The Wiccan must learn this and live by it. Consider what it means. Do you hurt people by your words or actions? Are you polluting the planet?

So what kind of magic do real witches use? Like the ancient Celts, Wiccans believe that there is an unseen Otherworld overlapping our own, inhabited by gods and goddesses, nature spirits, elementals, and wildfolk. These are honoured and sought for their guidance and help. This knowledge is far more exciting and fulfilling than the use of black magic to gain material *things*. The real magic is concerned with transforming the witch into an enlightened being who can know the Otherworld. The English occultist Dion Fortune said that magic is the art of changing consciousness at will. To accomplish this we use the Eightfold Ways.

Eight is a magical number, encompassing the four elements and the four directions. It is the number of solar increase, giving us the number of solar festivals within the Craft year—Samhain, Yule, Imbolc, Ostara, Beltane, Coamhain, Lughnasa, and Herfest. The musical scale is based on the octave; the periodic table is based on multiples of eight. In numerology, eight is the number of balance, of dualism, reflected on the way it is drawn, one circle topping another: 8. The sign of infinity is an eight on its side. In spiritual terms, eight represents new growth and new life. The Eightfold Ways, as given in Gardnerian Books of Shadows, are as follows:

1. Concentration, activated by the certain knowledge that you can and will succeed

2. Trance states: using focus and control

3. Herbal knowledge

4. Performing rites with a purpose

5. Dance

6. Chants and spells

7. Body control

8. Total involvement in worship

All of the above can be, and are, used as individual paths to expanded consciousness by different practitioners. In the Craft, we seek to explore and combine them all to a greater or lesser extent, depending on the abilities and predilections of the individual witch. Some mastery of each of the paths is required, though each person will eventually come to specialise in one particular aspect.

We are used to experiencing the world through our five senses alone, and our interpretation of reality is derived from them, our responses based on them. By our memory and experiences, we recognise the shape of the world as it superficially appears. The Wiccan learns to expand his or her consciousness and understanding to take into account other, more subtle realms. From childhood, we are taught to suppress this ability— our instincts, intuition, and clairvoyant powers. When people enter the Craft they must be taught to recover these other senses, to unlearn thought structures that have been instilled as they grew. The Eightfold Ways are the steps to liberation from earthly existence into a new consciousness. Steps that help us cross to the spiritual plane. Each step teaches us how to expand the consciousness, to reveal what is hidden. This is the *real* magic.

In my own tradition, we consider the Eightfold Ways to be eight distinctive paths of magic:

1. Concentration: The Path of the Hunter

2. Trance states: The Path of the Shaman

3. Herbal knowledge: The Path of the Wise Woman

4. Ritual: The Path of the Priest/Priestess

5. Dance: The Path of the Sacred Dancer

6. Sound: The Path of the Bard

7. Body control: The Path of the Warrior

8. Total involvement in worship: The Path of the Witch

Let's look at each path in turn.

The Path of the Hunter: Concentration

Concentration rates as the first of the Eightfold Ways. It is a fundamental quality that must be developed by anyone seeking spiritual progress or anyone seeking to work magic. We call this the Path of the Hunter, but we do not hunt or kill animals—the object of the hunt is the soul of the witch.

The Hunters seek to develop those qualities within themselves that will further their spiritual growth: unwavering concentration on the object in hand, attention to detail, and single-mindedness, all of which are developed through a programme of exercises and meditations based on hunting magic.

Hunting magic is perhaps one of the oldest kinds of magic in existence. Cave paintings show hunters and animals, and one of the oldest representations of a god (or shaman dressed as a god) dates from round 12,000 BCE: the "sorcerer" of Les Trois Frères, shown with the horns of a stag. Gods continued to have horns for hundreds of years, and the Celts worshipped several horned gods. The stag is inextricably linked with gods and goddesses of the hunt. A sculpture from the sanctuary of Le Donon in the Vosges shows a god who is both hunter and protector of the forest and its creatures. He stands carrying pine cones, nuts, and acorns in an open bag under his arm. He wears a wolf pelt cloak and boots ornamented with animal heads, and carries a hunting knife, axe, and spear. He rests his hand on the antlers of his companion, a stag. Other hunter gods have the same ambivalent position in relation to their prey. They are the protectors of the herd, but also the hunter who culls them in season.

Cernunnos, often called the God of the Witches, is portrayed on the Gundestrup Cauldron, dating from 300 BCE, as a seated figure with antlers growing from his head. He holds a snake in one hand and a torque in the other, showing that he is a god of winter and summer, sky and underworld, death and resurrection. He is surrounded by the animals of the forest. A secondary illustration shows him as Lord of the Animals, holding aloft a stag in either hand. Cernunnos was an intermediary between the animal kingdom and man, a guardian of the gateway to the Otherworld. The stag god is at the same time the divine huntsman, the Lord of the Animals, and the god of the dead and keeper of souls. It is for this reason that he is sought by those on the Path of the Hunter.

Remnants of the ancient stag cult may also be discerned in the legend of Herne the Hunter, possibly a British stag god equivalent to the Gaulish Cernunnos. Herne the Hunter haunts Windsor Great Park and rides out with the Wild Hunt at the midwinter solstice. He is described as a mighty, bearded figure with a huge pair of stag horns on his head. He wears chains, carries a hunting horn, and rides out on a black horse with a pack of ferocious hunting hounds. Many British witches call upon Herne as their patron deity.

Folk tales and legends give us clues as to the occult significance of the stag hunt. King Arthur's knights took part in a yearly hunt of the white stag, and its head would be presented to the fairest lady in the land. This may be a seasonal tale in which the white solar beast is killed. It was once thought that the king stag, the leader of the herd, should be ritually hunted and killed every year to ensure the return of summer. The king or royal stag was a beast with twelve or fourteen points on his horns (a stag would have to be seven years old to have twelve points). In Celtic myth, the stag or hind often symbolises the soul, usually the soul of a king or hero.

Stags, especially white ones, frequently appear as fairy animals that entice heroes to the Otherworld. Pwyll, Prince of Dyfed, was out hunting one day when he chanced to meet Arawn, the Lord of the Underworld, who was hunting a stag. He failed to give way, which was a breach of hunting etiquette. He apologised and offered to make amends. Arawn agreed that he should swap places with him for a year, and at the end of it fight his enemy Hafgan (summer) for him. So Pwyll ruled the Underworld for a year. The tale is plainly one of the solar forces of summer in yearly conflict with the chthonic forces of winter. The stag that Arawn was hunting was Pwyll's soul.

What is it that the hunter hunts? The answer is his or her own self. He or she works with hunting deities such as Cernunnos, Herne, Diana, and Artemis. Finally, the hunter pursues a quest for the truth and seeks the courage to pursue his or her quarry, knowing what that quarry *is*. These skills are of prime importance, though many people go into the Craft without considering them, and without them will get nowhere. Initial training programmes, by reputable groups, usually seek to get the candidate to explore these questions before going any further. These skills develop alongside other disciplines, and continue to be honed throughout life. They should constantly be reexamined and practised.

The Path of the Shaman: Trance States

The word "shaman" is thought to derive from the Tunguso-Manchurian word "saman," derived from the verb *sa,* which means "to know"; so, a shaman is "one who knows." The word is correctly pronounced "sham-an" rather than the Anglicised "shay-man" or the Americanised "shar-man." The term "shaman" is properly applied only to the neo-Siberian practitioners of the nineteenth century and early twentieth century, though the term is more broadly used in anthropology to categorise the phenomenon of the "shamanic crisis" and practice in many cultures.

The experience of the shaman is a constant, from Norway to Alaska. In all parts of the world the dawning of the shaman's enlightenment begins with a "shamanic crisis," often in adolescence but sometimes much later. This is an illness or breakdown that actually threatens his or her life. The shaman then recognises that the world is alive and connected (a concept that anthropologists call *animism*). I experienced this myself during a period of serious illness, and I can tell you that it is a path that no one would seek willingly. Rather, it is a path that chooses you.

The shaman recognises that we are surrounded by spirit, and when the shaman interacts with the world of spirit, he or she is practising shamanism. The powers of the shaman are drawn from the energies of the earth and the stars, from the sun and the moon, from sacred places, from crystals and stones, from plants and from animals.

You don't have to buy all the trappings of a Native American medicine man or African witch doctor. In the past twenty years I have studied shamanic paths and have been struck by how similar the practices of shamans in Siberia, Africa, and North America are to those I learned as a traditional witch. I was taught that the witch works with the spirits of land and place, plants and animals, as well as gods and goddesses, and that this knowledge is only gained by journeying into the Otherworld in a trance state. The shaman lets go of his or her conscious ego, allowing his or her soul to be released into an ecstatic spirit flight into the Otherworld.

At the deepest levels of pagan teaching the practitioner or magician travels at various realms of consciousness in order to gain knowledge and personal teaching from Otherworldly beings and Innerworld teachers that inhabit these places. When the student comes into contact with these teachers the real gaining of knowledge begins. In everyday life, we rely on the evidence of our five senses to gauge our waking reality. For the shaman, this reality, this level of consciousness, is only one of an infinite number of realities and levels of consciousness.

This necessitates a change of consciousness to a world of nonordinary reality, beyond everyday consciousness. Sometimes glimpses of this realm and its possibilities are beheld through visions, miracles, and clairvoyant experiences, but the shaman trains himself or herself to access

146

these realms at will. The primary method of being able to enter into other levels of consciousness, to access other realms, is the method of being able to shift into trance states, to turn off ordinary consciousness and enter nonordinary reality. Part of Craft training is to learn to be able to attain trance states of consciousness through certain exercises such as meditation, drumming, dancing, and the use of herbs and incenses. Tribal shamans also used more extreme methods such as sleep deprivation, pain, drugs, and subjecting the body to extremes.

The shaman heals through journeys into the Otherworld, where he or she might find the cause or cure of an illness, or through banishing negativity that centres on the patient. The shaman communicates with spirits for the good of the society he or she lives in, maintaining the balance between human and spirit world, making the proper offerings, rituals, and prayers.

Shamans often have animal helpers or allies. Working with animal powers formed part of my early magical training over twenty years ago and has been an essential part of my work ever since. Shamans and traditional witches all over the world work with animal spirits. These spirits often represent a species as a whole: not a bear, but Bear. Through this connection, the shaman can call upon the strength of the bear, the swiftness of the horse, the courage of the boar, or the far sight of the eagle, and so on. Witches call these spirit animals *familiars*. The word *totem* is slightly different and implies a blood relationship or kinship between a person, a family, or tribe, and an animal. Those so related would be forbidden to hunt or kill their totem, or to marry a person with an inimical totem.

You may have a spirit animal helper that stays with you throughout your life, or, more often, the animal will change as you change. Some stay for years, others only a few weeks. You might have more than one familiar. It is usually necessary to make a deliberate effort to contact your familiar, though you may have an idea of what it is and connections sometimes occur spontaneously. In addition to familiars, witches and shamans also strive to forge relationships with animal and plant allies who will help them when there is need.

Many claim that it is not possible for modern Westerners to experience the same mystical relationship with the Otherworld as a tribal shaman. Some writers imply that those striving to realise a relationship with the cosmos today, through exploring their relationship with the Otherworld, should be treated with contempt. This is to deny that the modern human being is capable of recognising and honouring spirit, or perhaps to deny that we have any kind of spirit or soul at all. The human body and brain have changed little since the time of the cave shamans, and the experience of shamans today remains the same as it was then, the same inner flight, which Mircea Eliade describes as "the archaic techniques of ecstasy" in his book *Shamanism: Archaic Techniques of Ecstasy*. Different cultural overlays seem to have not affected this mystical experience at all, except perhaps in its interpretation. The knowledge is part of the human makeup; it comes from within and cannot be given by other people.

The Path of the Wise Woman: Herbal Knowledge

The path of the wise woman involves the use of herbs. It is my own particular speciality within the Craft. Every society from the dawn of mankind has used herbs. They have been used to heal the body and spirit, in religious ceremonies, and to communicate with the gods.

Wiccans recognise the principle of divine consciousness manifest in nature; all of creation is sacred and valuable. We are of the earth: she gives us life, sustains us, nourishes us, teaches us. She gives us food and herbs in their correct season to heal and sustain us. When we prepare food for the festivals we like to make some attempt to use the wild food that grows around us; this gives us a greater sense of the gifts that the Goddess gives us all year round as opposed to buying our feast from the supermarket. We also like to make our own wine; the wine we make at one Imbolc is ready for drinking at the next, giving a continuity in the cycle. Even if you live in town, it is possible to find altar decorations in the park and hedgerows or to spend a day in the countryside before the festivals to attune to what is happening in nature, and gather some of the Lady's gifts.

However, the craft of the wise woman is primarily concerned with the use of herbs. Strictly speaking, an herb is a nonwoody plant that dies down after flowering, but the term is more generally applied to any medicinal plant, including trees. It has been said that plants are the link between animal and mineral kingdoms, as plants absorb minerals from the earth. When the plants are eaten, the minerals are assimilated by animals. From red plants, we get iron, from sea plants, iodine, and so on. All the chemical components of our blood and tissues are available from plants: natural chemical factories and energy powerhouses. Some plants produce complex chemicals that appear to have no part in a plant's own metabolism but have a profound effect on the humans and animals that ingest them. This can be no accident. It is the reinforcing of Mother Nature's web, which links us all together in a complex, interdependent ecosystem. The chemicals contained in plants can be synthesised or isolated and used in a conventional allopathic way. This is to ignore the benefits of the whole plant, which contains a range of chemicals. For example, a diuretic normally robs the body of potassium, whereas the dandelion is one of nature's best diuretics and also a rich source of potassium. (Sadly, herbal remedy manufacturers are now issuing "standardised" herbs, which means that everything but the active ingredient has been stripped out, depriving us of this benefit.) Particular herbs seem to treat particular parts of the body; for example, forget-me-not treats the lower left lung, barberry works on the liver, birch works on the urinary system, lime on the muscles of the eyes, and so on.

In herbalism, different parts of a plant may be used—the root, stem, rhizome, bulb, leaf, bark, flower, or fruit. In annual plants the healing properties reside mostly in the seeds; in perennials, the roots.

I gather many of my herbs from the wild, but I grow most of the herbs I use. I rarely buy any that I can grow myself. Even if you only have a window box or a kitchen windowsill, it is still worthwhile to grow some of your own. Traditionally, the wise woman's garden contained plants for healing, plants to attract and feed familiars, plants to contact the spirits, plants for divination and spells, and trees like rowan and holly for protection. Work with the ebb and flow of the earth's energy, and with the moon. All herbs are infused with the energy of the moon. As she waxes and wanes, pulling with her the tides of the sea, she influences all that is living. As the moon waxes the energy flows upward into the leaves and stalks of the plant; as she wanes the virtue travels to the roots. Plants to be harvested for their roots should be planted and gathered at the waning moon, and plants required for their flowers, leaves, and fruits should be planted and gathered at the waxing moon. Take time to know and understand the requirements of your herbs. Pennyroyal, violets, and thyme are quite happy to grow between cracks in paving slabs. Feverfew, pellitory, houseleeks, and wall germanders will grow next to a wall. Some plants like shade, including alexanders, angelica, chervil, and woodruff. A clay soil supports foxglove, mint, and parsley, while broom, lavender, and thyme will be happier on a sandy soil.

Few Western magicians today understand or work with the Old Knowledge concerning plants. So-called "magical herbals" give instructions on how to collect a plant by drawing a circle around it, telling it a little rhyme before hacking it about, and leaving it a coin or pinch of tobacco in recompense for its trauma. What good these are to it remains a mystery. Some books will tell you that you must ask a tree or plant for its favours—walk round it three times and ask, "Can I have a bit?" How many people know when they have an answer? Is the plant even listening? You might as well buy an herb off the shelf in the supermarket, or pick up a dead twig from the forest floor. These instructions are based on folklore, a debased and half-forgotten form of the true knowledge. Plants and trees must be approached as individuals and respected as living, spiritual entities. No two oak trees have the same personality, no two yarrows have the same qualities. Some plants will give willingly, some must be courted, some hunted with stealth, others fought. Some will never give you anything.

Trees and herbs are not really "used" magically. When properly approached they may share something of their life force, their spirit. True magical herbalism is not really a case of following a kind of cookbook approach, a pinch of this and a pinch of that. Individual herbs and plants can be befriended as allies to enable the practitioner to travel to Other-worldly places, and to become in tune with different energies. The craft of the magical herbalist takes many years and absolute self-discipline to master. The plant itself is always the teacher. Each plant must be correctly approached and harvested in perfect condition. It must always be respected as a living being: its life force is the essence of its power. This force is harnessed by taking the plant internally, fresh, or as an infusion, by smoking it or employing it in an incense or bathing herb, by using it as a magical condenser, and so on. (Note: Any plant used in this capacity should be extensively researched.)

If the herb is approached with love and trust, its force will harmonise with the witch and share its secrets. If the plant is taken with the wrong motives, if it is mistreated or misused, it may cause discomfort, mislead, or seek to gain control of the witch. If an enemy is made of the plant spirit, it can destroy. It is a common misconception that a plant needs to have hallucinogenic properties to facilitate expansion of consciousness. Only a small number of power plants are psychedelic, and these plant spirits are the most difficult to deal with and easily overcome the weak will of anyone stupid enough to use them for recreational purposes. Every plant, from the common daisy to the mighty oak, has its own power and vibration, and by taking time to gain the trust of the plant spirit, these can be shared.

The Path of the Priest/Priestess: Ritual

Within Wicca, every initiate becomes a consecrated priest or priestess, capable of performing ritual and permitted to invoke the God or Goddess. Everyone knows that witches employ ritual, dancing in magic circles under the moonlight. But how many people really understand what a ritual is, or what its purpose might be?

The Concise Oxford Dictionary defines "ritual" as "a ceremonial act or series of acts, a prescribed method of procedure." By this definition, the Japanese tea ceremony is a ritual, dancing the tango is a ritual, making the tea and toast in the morning can be a ritual.

Pagans have many forms of ritual. We meet together to drum, to sing, dance, feast, tell stories, or share a sweat lodge. Individually, we might meditate, cast spells, practice herb craft, and so on. As working groups, we aspire to the casting of the circle, the calling in of the powers, and the invocation of the gods: the manifestation of the divine consciousness on the earthly plane. By a loose definition, all these things might be considered magical rituals, that is, something that changes the consciousness of the performer.

The Fluffy Bunny School of Magic would have us believe that magic is all about nice little ceremonies praising pretty goddesses who spend their spare time posing for Vogue. This kind of New Age nonsense is alien to practising pagans who embrace the whole of the wheel—light and dark, life and death, growth and dissolution, Beltane and Samhain. One half doesn't go away because we don't like to—or are afraid to—acknowledge it. Both sides of the coin are necessary: there can be nothing without the balance of the two. Without night there is no day, without death no rebirth, without dissolution no room for new growth. We must seek to understand both sides of the mystery.

Every place, not just a "sacred site," has its own resident wildfolk, deities, and magic. If we are to work in any place we must seek to know the wildfolk, to show them our respect, ask their permission, and demonstrate serious intent. This trust, of necessity, must be built up over a period of time. We can't descend on a place and demand the cooperation of its spirits and energies. Many sites I have revisited over recent years have been closing down, withdrawing, to protect themselves from the inept efforts and childish demands of some so-called "pagans."

All places have their own attendant energies, often their own guardians. It is these entities we must seek to know and work with. The gods are real and tremendous forces; when they honour us with their presence we are privileged indeed. They are not simple spirits for us to command to do our bidding, however worthy we might think our cause might be.

In the practical use of ritual, there are Five Essentials to ensure the results are both effective and beneficial. Five is a key number: there are five senses, five magical elements (earth, air, fire, water, and spirit), five magical directions (north, south, east, west, and centre). The pentacle worn by witches symbolises this. It is the sacred number of the Goddess. In ancient Greece, the five points were used to represent mankind. If these steps are followed, then ritual becomes a transcendent experience rather than the embarrassed muttering of a few words found in a book, and this is the real purpose of ritual. A trained priestess and coven can blend together, aided by the Five Essentials, to reach Otherworldy consciousness at the same time, and the ultimate aim of the ritual is to bring this divine consciousness into the world. They are as follows.

Intention

This is the first step, knowing what you want your magic to achieve. Intention also means having the absolute will to succeed and the determination to win against all obstacles. The intentions of a ritual can be several. Ritual may be used to raise magical power, or may be a seasonal ceremony during which we attune to the season, the changes in the power of the earth, reenacting the cosmic drama to turn the Wheel of the Year. Spiritually, we aim to raise our consciousness to the level that this can act upon us and transform our understanding. To do this we must have the determination and discipline to concentrate the mind on the purpose at hand, the season, and the ritual.

The body must also be concentrated, the eyes must look on the visible evidence of the season, and everything in the ritual must visibly represent it—decorations, robes, or candles, for example. The ears must be attuned, so listen to the wind, the animals, the movement of the plants, the music you play. Every word spoken in the ritual must be in keeping—the invocations, chants, and so on. They must act on the sense of hearing to raise the consciousness. Even the sense of taste helps us—taste the wind, the smoke from the fire, the earth in the wine and the cakes. Smell the scents of life around you; the incense must be correct. Touch the earth, your tools, your robe; use touching with intent. When you take the hands of your companions, you should be aware of what it is you are sharing. Every bodily act performed in the ritual must be performed with intent.

Preparation

We must prepare ourselves mentally and physically for the ritual. The body should be prepared by being cleansed and purified. Abstain from meat and dairy produce for two to seven days before the rite. They ground you and clog the psychic channels. On the day of the rite you should fast all day to cleanse the system and raise the body's vibrations.

The next step is to gather everything that will be needed for the work ahead—robes, flowers, props, and tools. Magical tools should be cared for properly and kept in a constant state of readiness. Neglected tools lose their power and become ineffective. They should be kept clean and charged.

Yet the operation goes far beyond the readiness of the tools. Choosing the correct time for magic is essential—the phase of the moon, the position of the planets, the ripeness of the season when energies come into or leave the world, the time of day. All become part of the magic to be performed.

Coming up to the rite, meditate on your intent. For a seasonal rite, read about the season, go for walks, and see what is happening. Read about the doings of the gods and goddesses at this time. The mind should be fully prepared.

Many people do not have the luxury of a temple room, or even an altar permanently set up, therefore the place of ritual must be prepared in a fastidious way. Creating the environment will be aided by incense, oils, decorations, coloured candles, and so on. They should be chosen with care. Before the rite commences everything must be in a state of readiness. Anything needed for the rite should be at hand and in its proper place. Anything that should not be in the circle must be removed. If you have forgotten anything when the circle is cast you will not be able to go out and get it.

Purification

When we enter the circle, it is necessary to suspend the thoughts and concerns of everyday life. We must be free of malice, hate, envy, and negativity, or this will warp the ritual. It is difficult, but possible. Magic comes from within, and what we think is what we are. If positive magic is to result, then positive thoughts are needed to create it.

The physical and auric bodies are purified. This is begun with abstinence and fasting. Meditation is used to clear the mind for the purpose at hand. Before the time of the ritual, a purification bath is taken with suitable cleansing oils and herbs, and any negativity is allowed to drain into the water. As the robes are donned, the everyday self is left behind and the magical identity assumed.

Consecration

The tools used should have been properly prepared and consecrated, or blessed, dedicated to the Lord and Lady. The robes should be special clothes you use only in the circle, and set aside from everyday use. Anything taken into the circle should be consecrated or blessed.

The place set aside for magic, usually the circle, as well as the tools, must be consecrated. The circle is cast with the athame or magical knife. Where the point of the athame touches is the boundary of the circle. This cannot be stressed too much.

All of these things take time and effort. There are no shortcuts in magic, and the series of steps exists to reinforce the power to be raised and channelled. Once cast, the circle becomes a doorway between the dimensions, and is consecrated with earth, air, fire, and water, usually by carrying the elements round the boundary of the circle.

Invocation

The first step in invoking the circle is creating the *axis mundi* through the centre of the circle, which connects it to all Three Realms. Then the elements are invoked, creating the fourfold balance.

The Mighty Ones must be invoked. The manner in which this is done varies in different traditions and groups. The most important thing is not the words used, but the visualisation of and reverence for those invoked. To see them in your thoughts, to feel their presence, helps create the right vibration to draw them to you. This visualisation requires sustained effort.

Often the God and Goddess are invoked into the bodies of the celebrating priest and priestess. They become the deities for the duration of the ritual, and what they do and say for that time are the words and actions of the deities. They should be addressed with the names of the God and Goddess for the duration of the ritual, without confusion and with intent.

If the invocations are not successful, they must be pursued until they are, or the ritual must be abandoned.

All places are sacred to the Lord and Lady. Every place has its own energies and is connected to some person, animal, plant, or spirit. However, the creation of the circle is the building of the sacred ceremonial space to gather the energies of elements, spirits, allies, the Three Realms, and the Lord and Lady. Through ritual we honour our connection to the spinning Wheel of Life, celebrate, and give thanks.

When the circle is drawn it is aligned to the cardinal points of the compass: north, south, east, and west. It is not symbolic, and the east of the circle should be aligned with the real east, and so on. The flow of earth power is north to south. The North Star stands still at the north of the circle. To the Celts it was Caer Arianrhod, the castle of the silver wheel, the entrance to the Otherworld and the place of death and rebirth. The circle must be oriented with the energies of the cosmos.

The Path of the Sacred Dancer: Dance

It is said that dance is the original form of sacred worship. All over the world, dance is an essential part of sacred ceremony, an expression of joy or sorrow, marking birth, marriage, death, and the passing of the seasons. Dances were used to plead with the gods for rain, for sunshine, or to provide good harvests. Sadly, dance was largely frowned upon by the Christian church, and we have lost this meaningful aspect of dance in Western society, where it has lost its sacred character, though it still remains part of the mating ritual.

Pagan temples often employed sacred dancers who lived within the holy precincts and were considered married to the God. Their dances celebrated and articulated this relationship. Amongst goddess-worshipping cultures, dance played a predominant role, with the Goddess portrayed by a dancer who expressed the changing pattern of the seasons and the cycles of life. In some temples, the dance went on for centuries without cease, with one dancer taking the place of another. These dancers kept the Sacred Time, the patterns created by the universe as it repeats the cycles of the seasons, life, death, and rebirth in an endless dance.

For the sacred dancer, movement becomes an expression of worship and celebration, a means of meditation and empowerment. However, the path is not an easy one, and involves a great deal of discipline and hard work. Only when the steps are mastered can the dancer surrender to the ecstasy of movement and become one with the dance, experiencing its transformative energies.

One of the most commonly used dances in the Craft is the Circle Dance, where everyone holds hands and revolves around the edge of the circle, all dancing in time, in the same direction, using the same steps.

When everyone takes hands, it symbolises the completion of the circle, the attaining of oneness and harmony. Energy flows around the circle from one person to another, round and round in a continuous exchange of energy. This brings about a unity and cohesion among the participants, moving toward a common goal. Everyone is connected with each other, with the dance, with the circle, and through it, with the Three Realms and with the Gods. This dance symbolises the turning of the Wheel of the Year, and the movement of the sun through the sky each day, or through the zodiac throughout the year. It is used to raise power.

The Spiral Dance is led by the high priestess or maiden, and circles inward to the centre of the circle, where all times and places meet. It symbolises the yearning of the spirit toward wholeness, and the heart at the centre of the group. It raises tremendous energy at the centre of a circle. The spiral is one of the basic geometric forms of nature, repeated over and over again in the shape of shells, plant growth, and even the human inner ear.

The spiral path is seen in another of the best known Craft dances of British Traditional Wicca, the dance of the labyrinth, a perennial favourite at pagan gatherings. The labyrinth represents the life journey, treading the spiral path inward to death and initiation, and outward again to rebirth.

These are just three of the many dances we use, but Craft dances come in many varieties, from simple to complex, from gentle and slow to fast and aggressive. The most important thing is to allow the spirit to take over and guide the performance, letting go of the self and all thoughts of past and future to be present in the eternal now, which is a powerful form of meditation. To live is to move, to progress from what was to what is to be, as we exist in the eternal present, eternally in transition between the two.

Dance moves energy and may allow healing to take place. It facilitates transformation in touching the ecstasy of spirit, each step taking the dancer nearer to that goal. It changes consciousness. Dance expresses the unity of mind, body, and spirit. The steps of the dance can form a complex spiritual language that expresses the patterns of the universe, geometric patterns expressed in form, light, colour, and sound, repeated throughout the cosmos, and connected by a web of energy.

Dance is to movement what poetry is to language.

The Path of the Bard: Sound

In our tradition the Path of the Bard is not the role of a mere storyteller or keeper of lore, but of an adept who deals with the magical vibration of sound—one of the ways to access, attune to, and vibrate the web.

The witch believes that everything contains a life force, which vibrates to the pulse of the earth itself. Everything vibrates, both matter and energy. Every kind of energy has its own wavelength, whether it be colour, light, or sound. It is well known that sound affects matter. Scatter some sand on a metal disc and subject it to various musical notes, and the sand will form a variety of patterns, depending on the note. A French engineer, Professor Gavraud, discovered the impact of low-frequency sound when he built a six-foot version of a police whistle, powered by compressed air. The technician who tested it died instantly, his internal organs destroyed by the low-frequency sound.

Japanese Samurai warriors were reputed to be able to kill a man by uttering a single note. In many religions, it is believed that it is the energy of vibration that causes chaos to coalesce into organised form. The Australian Aborigines believe that the manifest world was brought into being by song, while others believe that creation was effected by "the word" of God.

The Hindu chant "Om" is said to be the vibration of the universe, encompassing everything. Interestingly, if it is chanted into a tonoscope (a device that renders sound into visual representation), a circle, or *O,* is produced, which is filled with concentric squares or triangles. In Western magic, "the squaring of the circle" represents the integration of spirit and matter. Sound vibrations and symbolism may be used to awaken the harmony within.

In magical and sacred languages, words or tones spoken correctly can affect other realities and encompass concepts that everyday language does not.

Each person has his or her own vibration or pitch; the sonic field that resonates from the human body is as distinctive as a fingerprint. This is the origin of the secret or magical name, which, each time it is spoken, serves to retune the consciousness of the initiate to a new vibrationary level, resonating within to awaken new levels of consciousness. The giving or choosing of a magical name is not a purely symbolic act; it retunes the individual resonance to be more in harmony with his or her new way of life. In many cultures there is a fear of revealing this secret name, since it contains the true essence of a person, and the frequency might be used by an enemy to cause harm or even death.

It can be said that music resides within all things, whether animate or inanimate; for example, all crystals and stones have particular vibrationary rates. Knowledge of vibration is important within ritual. Sounds, colours, shapes, and numbers echo each other to create the correct vibrationary pitch to reach the desired level of consciousness. Any disharmony will throw the ritual off course and the required results will not be achieved. In general, low vibrationary sounds facilitate Underworld contact, whilst high vibrationary sound facilitates Overworld contact.

Chants and drumming may be used to induce a light trance. It is the persistent, monotonous nature of the beat that makes this possible. Shamans refer to their drums as their "magical steeds" or "canoes." It is this that transports them into magical reality and sustains them on their journeys. Drumming effects changes in the central nervous system, affecting sensory and motor areas in the brain ordinarily not stimulated. The beat of the drum contains many frequencies, mainly low, and can induce the deep theta level of trance. The EEG frequency range of theta waves is four to seven cycles per second, and the drum can be played at this vibration.

The rattle provides a higher frequency than the level of the drum, and the two played together produce a more complete harmonic effect. The rattle is played at 180 times per minute. It stimulates the higher frequency pathways in the brain, reinforcing the effect of the drumbeats to the brain. The player regulates the tempo, for only he or she can feel its appropriateness. Sometimes, instead of a rattle, tinkling ornaments may be worn on the costume, and the tempo is set by dancing.

Each person has his or her own power song, given to him or her in a vision, that can be sung to induce trance and to enter into new levels of consciousness. The songs are usually monotonous, and increase in tempo as the practitioner approaches the required level of consciousness.

All religions use chants and liturgies to affect the consciousness of the congregations. The most effective chants are repetitive and quite monotonous. Chanting obviously affects the breathing, in a manner similar to yogic breathing. The words of the song or chant should reinforce the purpose and relate to the practitioner's symbolic system to reinforce the power. Some chants are nonsensical, used for the effect of the sound and rhythm alone; this offers the benefit of concentrating on the chant rather than on the meaning of its words.

For a group working together, the dance and chant are used to raise the cone of power. By moving and chanting together, an attuned group can enter a new realm of consciousness as a *group mind* and work together within the magical reality.

One further province of the bard is the spell. The ancient Celtic bards were feared for their powerful spoken spells, which could rob a warrior of his courage or a king of his dignity.

Remember that spells are to be used only when needed and with good heart. There is a temptation to cast a spell for someone if we think that the person needs our help, but take great care. What might look like a terrible situation to you might actually be somebody else's idea of happiness. You should never interfere with someone else's life without asking for his or her permission—you might be doing more harm than good, and what you think is right for someone may not be what he or she wants at all!

There is an old saying: Be careful what you wish for, as you may get it. You must think very carefully about using a spell, what its aim is, and how you word it. Do you remember all those tales of people who got three wishes and ended up worse off because they were not careful?

Accuracy and focused intent are vital or the spell might not have the effect you wish it to have; it might go awry and do all sorts of strange things. This is why you have to record every detail in your Book of Shadows, including all ingredients with details of quantities and any special instructions for gathering, such as season, time of day, and so on. There should be clear instructions for working the spell, including any deities or powers to be called upon and words of power to be included.

Magic is energy and energy is never destroyed. There is no time limit on a spell unless you put one on it. A spell cast will not just last for three weeks, then fizzle out—if you say "forever," it will last forever unless broken in a magical way. No spell should have an ending that includes the word *forever,* or any similar expression.

Timing is important in magic. Every day of the week and every moon phase—even the time of the year—will affect the energies of the ingredients. Certain times provide the right energies for specific types of magic.

Witches often cast their spells according to the phases of the moon. The time of the waxing moon is best for spells of protection, love, money drawing, studying, fertility, friendship, creativity, relationships, and healing. The energies are expansive and growing, so any spell you cast now should be concerned with things growing and flourishing. A healing spell cast now would be concerned with growing health (as opposed to a diminishing-disease spell cast at the waning moon). The energies of the full moon are best used for scrying and divination, love magic, fertility, developing psychic abilities, clairvoyance, and healing. The time of the waning moon is best for spells of purification, cleansing, and banishing. It is a time when the moon and its energies are diminishing, so it is used for spells to diminish something, whether this be an illness, a bad habit, a negative energy, the effects of a bad spell, ending relationships, and so on. The days of the dark moon have their own magic that is best used for deep meditation and inner journeying, though magicians have been known to use the time for casting curses.

In addition to the energies of the moon, the planets also affect magical work. Each day is ruled by a planet, which in turn governs certain areas of magical work. Sunday is ruled by the sun and is the best day for spells concerning work, employment, friendship, and healing. Monday is ruled by the moon and suits spells concerned with gardens, agriculture, psychic ability, the home, and medicine. Tuesday is ruled by Mars and is the best day for spells concerned with competition, debates, and gaining courage. Wednesday is ruled by Mercury and is the day for spells concerning study, teaching, divination, messages, and communications. Thursday is ruled by the planet Jupiter and governs material things such as money, property, and luck. You might cast a spell today to change your luck. Friday is ruled by Venus and governs love, art, music, incense, and perfume making. Saturday is ruled by Saturn and concerns magic that has to do with the elderly, death, reincarnation, wills, and endings (ending relationships, for example).

Spells do not have to be complicated or contain a large number of ingredients—remember, they are there to focus your intent and the magical energy you raise. However, everything you use has energy of its own, and you can use this to reinforce the energy of the spell. Conversely, if you use many things with unsuitable energies they can diffuse the spell before it has even started, so it is worthwhile to prepare your ingredients carefully.

After this you might compose a verse to chant while you mix and empower your spell. It doesn't have to rhyme, but rhyming is traditional. These words help to focus the magic. Some books offer spells that invoke a god or goddess to help, but remember, these are awesome beings and might not want to be disturbed. They are not your servants, and may not be interested in your whims. You really would not want to annoy a god.

The Path of the Warrior: Body Control

The Path of the Warrior concerns the psychic warrior, whose weapons are his or her body, mind, and spirit. These must be trained to work in harmony. The warriors face their own fears, develop their spiritual courage, hone their will. Will is not impulse or desire; it is the unwavering strength that seeks the personal truth and path.

There are many methods that seek to harmonise the mind, body, and spirit—yoga, the martial arts, and so on. It may help to pursue one of these for at least a time, to learn how the mind affects the body and how the body affects the spirit.

We are all subject to many fears, and it is the warrior's purpose to seek them out and defeat them. It must be recognised that the body has its own fears—fear of injury, fear of physical danger. These are natural and proper. Without these fears we would put our hands in the fire, crash our cars, jump off cliffs. The body has an in-built mechanism of self-preservation. I didn't fully realise this until I had a near-death experience a few years ago. My mind and my spirit were quite calm and resigned, willing to depart from my body, but my body, quite independently, was panicking. It clings to life; that's its job. The warrior may decide to face many of his or her physical fears to develop will and courage—to get on an aeroplane when he or she has a fear of flying, for example. Fear facilitates a change in consciousness, to conquer a fear facilitates the development of the will. To do something so dangerous that it may result in injury or death, however, is no part of the warrior's path; it is self-indulgence.

The warriors may subject themselves to physical extremes to force their will and consciousness beyond the ordinary. Religious sects around the world have subjected neophytes to extended fasting, heat, cold, isolation, and so on. My personal view is that these methods simply weaken the candidates and make them more susceptible to indoctrination. They are the techniques of brainwashing. If anybody tries to do this to you, run a mile! Your spirituality is your own quest, and you must find your own truth. You can, however, test and push yourself, run that extra mile, swim the extra two lengths, dig the extra few yards. You can do much more than you imagine, break your self-imposed limits. Anyone who has ever taken part in fire walking will realise just how far the mind and the will can overcome what you think is possible.

The deepest fears lie within the mind itself; they arise from childhood and adult experiences and conditioning. Such fears limit us and prevent our development. At some point the warrior must confront them, one by one, and deal with them.

The Path of the Witch: Total Involvement in Worship

It is the goal of every witch to combine all of the previous paths into a greater one. Central to this is a relationship with the land, in a real, not symbolic manner—to observe and celebrate the Wheel of the Seasons and become part of their ebb and flow. The spirits of the land are sought for their teachings and honoured for their work. The Gods and Goddesses are honoured as the powerful beings that they are.

Wicca is a religious impulse rather than a religious dogma. It recognises the principle of divine consciousness manifest in nature. The Tradition is also a complete magical system. Magic is a very misunderstood principle. Many people see it as a shortcut to getting what they want, be it material goods, friends, lovers, or control. Magic is no shortcut to anything. The path of the magician is the hardest one of all to follow; it exposes all your weaknesses and shortcomings. For anyone to embark on a path of magical study without first coming to terms with himself or herself, the light and the shadow, is an extremely dangerous business. If you meet people who tell you otherwise you can be sure they are ignorant or charlatans. In over thirty years of study, I have come across many people who thought they could use the Universal Principles for trivial purposes. Most became bewildered by the "bad luck" that followed them around, others scared themselves silly, and one or two went mad.

The primary business of the magician is the transformation of the magician. Magic is a constantly expanding state of consciousness, an

165

awareness of the subtle workings of the universe. You are not an initiate because someone in a long frock anoints you with oil and tells you that you are. You are not an initiate when you have learned all the words and phrases in a book. You are an initiate when you have reached that level of consciousness. Initiation is not a matter of collecting degrees as you would Boy Scout badges; it doesn't come because you have served for a year and a day, or for that matter for twenty years and a day. In the Old Ways, people often had to serve for at least ten years before they were even considered for initiation into the Tradition. It is a continuous journey of discovery, a lifetime commitment, and more.

It is not to walk the path; it is to become the path.

Bibliography

Eliade, Mircea. *Shamanism: Archaic Techniques of Ecstasy.* Translated by Willard P. Trask. New York: Pantheon Books, 1964.

The Concise Oxford Dictionary. London: BCA, 1977.

Wild Enchantments

POPPY PALIN

Wild enchantment is rooted in the inherent wisdom of the earth and echoes her heartbeat; it is a magical way of enhancing everyday life that comes from flowing with her natural tides. It is a blend of inspiration and application, discipline and spiritual autonomy. It blends an appreciation of, and an interaction with, the cycles of life and a solid grounding in the practical aspects of spellcrafting. Wild enchantment is all about a weaving of celebration, invocation, visualisation, and our heartfelt intent into our familiar practices, while respecting and recognising the spirit inherent in each part of creation. It is a magical way for the sylvan-spirited, for those willing to be affected by spirit-voices that rise on the wind, calling to us from brook and rock alike. It is both nurturing and enabling.

To practice such spellcraft we may consider ourselves to be wildwitches.

A wildwitch can create formal spells in a controlled way, but chooses to do so not as an isolated, occasional act but rather as a part of an integrated magical life in which every thought or deed can become an act of devotion or enchantment. Wildwitches consider the Craft to be part of them, not only something that they do but something that they *are*. It is lived minute by minute on a daily basis, enlivening and enriching mundane experiences, elevating them beyond meaningless chores and routines and filling them with purpose and pleasure. It gives meaning to all acts so that there are no dull moments but instead a seamless merging of magic into life.

Enchantment is at the heart of wild witchcraft, just as magic is the very core essence of life. We do not *use* it, just as we should refrain from using (exploiting) the earth and all her children. Enchantment is, rather, something to be worked *with*; it is a natural condition of the universe that modern life can make us oblivious to. It is that which animates the green, curling caterpillar and brings about the transformation from leaf-munching creature to inert dun-brown chrysalis to a glorious winged being. Magic is Fey and Otherworldly, yes, but it is also in the food we eat, the words we speak, the love we make. It is immanent.

For those who walk the way of wild enchantment the veils of separation begin to lift and everything becomes alive with possibility. This way is animistic and holistic: it gives reverence and relevance to all energetic beings, seen and unseen, making it both earthy and ethereal . . . a beautiful, burgeoning blend.

It is true that spellcraft can be practiced under a full moon in robes, but it can also be worked whilst baking bread, shelling peas, watering plants, combing hair, or painting a room. The word *craft* that is used here in wild spellcraft is about translating the magical spark into grounded and ordinary tasks. Magic is ubiquitous. It is only for us to remember that and to apply ourselves fully, with a prayerful intent and with respect to certain natural laws. Whether we act spontaneously or whether we plan a more formal rite, the magic exists just the same. The key is to see each moment as magical and each act as a prayer, in potentiality.

The wildness gives our practice an unpredictable element, making sure we are ready even in the midst of the most tedious aspects of life (like doing the laundry or cleaning) to interact with our surroundings magically. The craft of it ensures that we have the skill, regarding knowing how magic works and what is safe procedure, as well as a knowledge of the energies, the spiritual attributes, and the seasonal meanings of all that we choose to work with. When we work magic we *weave* these energies into our manifest practices. The "witchy-ness" comes into the equation by means of our starlight vision, our ability—and our *will*—to perceive these energies, that which is of mystery, and connect with that which is considered hidden.

What do we need to know before we begin to bring this green-spirited way to bear in our own lives? How do we go about integrating such wild enchantment into our daily existence? And what sort of magics may we practice, and why?

To begin we need to look at a sort of equation, a magical mixture necessary for the practice of wild witchcraft. This is:

Protection plus Guidance plus Tides plus Focus equals Magical Change.

The first two aspects of this equation, protection and guidance, refer to the "unseen" or spiritual aspects of our work. The second two, tides and focus, refer to the practical manifest things we can do to support the first two in order that the result is achieved. All magical work is a blend of the eternal and the corporeal. There are many other incidental factors that will come into play as we follow these guidelines, but here we have the basic stages and formula. We will look at each stage separately so that we may follow the process through.

We must first root ourselves firmly in the Earth Mother like a great oak so that we may touch the stars with our branches. Without roots the tree would be unstable, disconnected, unable to draw in energy. Like the tree we too need to be "bound free," tethered yet able to reach upward, to spiritually fly. We act as the "living wood" that makes the link between the land and the *beyond,* and so must have a strong and secure foundation in order that our "will and wish," our focused potent life force energy, may travel through us. Our energetic sap filters through the rich loam of our earth-magic into the wider world.

Wild enchantment relies on spoken affirmation and repetitive rhyme (hence the "chant" in enchantment, which means using verbal incantation for magical purposes); therefore, throughout this chapter there will be adages in quotation marks that may help us to focus on and reaffirm the magical process. The first of these, which sums up what we have talked about above, is "Grounded we must be, to let the dream fly free."

Trees crop up again and again in the wildwitch's work, as they are our special teachers, much beloved by those who seek to walk a magical path that veers off the beaten track and into the ancient greenwood. Like the trees, we have a resinous inner knowing at a deep cellular level and they help us to remember and reconnect with it. These wise beings are the mainstay of our world in more ways than one. Not only are trees the primary life-givers of oxygen and the representatives of a totally balanced way of being, but they are analogous to how we make our connections as spellweavers between earth and sky, the manifest and the spiritual. They allow us to experience the interconnectedness of all creation with ourselves as a valuable (although not superior) part of it. Hence we employ the tree visualisation to assist us on our magical journey.

Stage One: Protection and Connection

The tree visualisation we are about to look at has two purposes: to ground us (connect us to the earth-level while we open up to external, *spiritual,* energies) and to protect us. If we are not connected or rooted in the current manifest reality, then our magic has no root, and like a fluffy seed head blown loose from the mother plant it may be deliciously free but is also at the mercy of the wind or any other influence. As our work is about spiritual unseen energies, as well as nature and the earth, we may be leaving ourselves anchorless at the whims of other forces if we do not connect ourselves to this physical reality.

We also need to psychically protect ourselves using a visualisation every time we open up to that which is an external unseen influence. Protection is essential before any spellwork because in order to do successful magic we need to be open to spiritual guidance and seasonal energetic tides. We need to be *attuned.* We may work as solitary practitioners of wild enchantment but we have to work with other energies outside of ourselves for the work to be potent and pertinent. When we are focused on our spellworkings and directing energy into them, we are like an attractive light on the astral levels. If we are not protected in some way then this light becomes a focal point for miscellaneous drifting astral energies—entities and beings that may be unscrupulous. It is well to be sensibly aware but not scared by this. Just as there are butterflies and dormice in the manifest world, there are also sharks and vipers, and consequently there are the equivalent of these beings "in spirit."

This is summed up as "as above, so below," meaning "as we can see it, so is it reflected in the unseen."

The sharks and vipers of the unseen levels may not mean us direct harm, but by their very nature cannot help but be troublesome to us. The universe is not human-centric nor even necessarily human-friendly, just as the manifest earth-level is not entirely so. Suffice it to say that it is common sense to take sensible precautions, protecting ourselves in the jungle and ditto when traveling spiritually for magical purposes.

If we have a magical act planned in advance, say, based on seasonal celebrations, then the tree visualisation is recommended before we begin. Even if our magic is of the more informal, spontaneous kind (in a cafe or on a train), then some form of protection is always appropriate. Even if we are doing a simple act of wild enchantment at home, like making a healing soup for a friend, we are still tuning in to external energies and we need to cover ourselves energetically. Therefore, we will look at the tree visualisation as something to engage with before a more lengthy magical act, and follow it with a truncated version (pardon the pun), which we can apply "on the hop." We need to be fully conversant with the tree visualisation to understand the quick method.

The Tree Visualisation

We must firstly position the body in a way that is appropriate to suggest connection. Remember, we are conduits (channels for raw elemental life-force energy) in the great tradition of the trees, and therefore the most appropriate positions are those that allow us to have a firm contact, with our feet on the ground and our spines upright and erect. The aim is to let the energy flow around your body while you connect to both the ground and the energies above or around you. This means no tense areas and a broad-base connection to the earth or a solid object. Although standing seems like the logical position (as trees stand upright), being seated on the ground (preferably directly on the earth herself) with a straight back and feet firmly planted on the floor is more suitable, as it is our spine that acts as our trunk, not our legs.

It would be wrong to assume that all wildwitches are physically able, and some postures may be hard for some people with physical difficulties, in which case you can adapt them at this stage to a simple lying-down position, or sitting up supported in a high-backed (yet comfortable) armchair—whatever feels that it connects you to the earth, to the solid manifest realms, while relaxing you.

If you are able, sit with your spine as straight as possible and have your knees bent and your feet resting squarely on the floor. You may of course lean back against a wall, chair, or even a tree (take care here—the tree must be asked; it is not an inanimate object to be used at your will) to help you keep your back straight. Either have the hands on the floor, palms down, or have them resting on your knees similarly, thus connecting you further to terra firma, making that solid bond.

Alternatively, have your feet squarely on the floor but the palms of your hands resting on your knees and facing upward, symbolically open to the energies around you. If you find your own comfortable variation on the theme, then consider the symbology of what you do with your body carefully and let it echo the spiritual intent. Symbolism is important to this work.

Try to avoid crossing limbs, as it does not symbolise free-flowing energy but rather crossed wires. Keep thinking of your whole being as an uncluttered circuit.

Because we are working as wildwitches it is highly appropriate to make up a small rhyme of affirmation as a piece of enchantment that really emphasizes our intent. It is well to get into the habit of such chants to back up all that we do magically. It certainly helps when we have to protect ourselves in a hurry in an unfamiliar place. A piece of word-magic can get us into the required frame of mind very quickly and remind us of our focus. Obviously we don't have to say or sing the words out loud. Repeating the verse up to three times can really set it firmly as reality. An example of what we may say at this juncture may be:

Like the tree I bond with soil,
beneath my feet the root is strong,
and up my spine the power goes,
and through the trunk the life force flows,
up through the heartwood, to the crown,
up to the leaves and then back down.

Now close your eyes and aim to have a clear mind; let any extraneous thoughts drift across your awareness and evaporate away.

Take several (three minimum) slow, deep breaths. What constitutes a deep breath? The sort of breathing advocated in yoga is the one to apply here. If you are not familiar with this, then breathe in through the nose while inflating the abdomen (to practice, place the hands on the belly and feel it physically inflate like a balloon; in fact, visualize it expanding like a balloon filled with air). Hold this for a few seconds, whatever is physically comfortable, then release the breath for as long as you are able through the mouth (or nose if it feels more comfortable), making a drawn-out *pfhhh* sound, and let the belly deflate inward. Pause for as long as is comfortable before taking another deep breath, and so on.

Put your hands to your belly and feel the concave effect it makes as it deflates completely, again imagining the balloon, only this time watching as it deflates slowly. This may seem like the very opposite of what "normal" breathing feels like to you. It is common to associate the "in breath" with somehow pulling inward, and the convex, puffing out motion with exhaling. This exercise can take a lot of practice; therefore, do not feel downhearted if it takes a while to get into the rhythm.

The sound that the rhythmic breathing cycle makes is like the sea. If you are able to tune in to this rushing/whooshing sound of the sea coming in and being drawn back, then it can be a great aid to relaxation and help you with your own body's drawing in and expelling of life-giving air. The breathing both takes us deeper into a relaxed state and tunes us in to our body's inherent way of taking in the life-nourishing oxygen and releasing waste in the form of carbon dioxide. We seldom breathe properly whilst engaged in human worldly pursuits, ending up with a shallow and unsatisfactory way of inhaling and exhaling. This exercise will help us enormously, centring us in the body's processes while letting us experience the alchemical action of sucking in all that living energy, transmuting it, and releasing it again.

The tree's vital connection to our life-breath is obvious and should always be honoured. The way the complex branchings of our own lungs echo their root/limb systems is a further sign of our connection.

Enjoy the sensation of breathing steadily and deeply. Keep the mind clear, and do not become tense trying to do this. Just let any invasive thoughts float on past, as they are unimportant at this time. Your conscious human aspect will get impatient and want to distract you with all manner of mental trivia, and will no doubt tell you that you have an itchy big toe, need to feed the fish, and so forth. Just focus entirely on the breathing rhythm and let such thoughts waft away like smoke. The breathing is all that matters, so become absorbed in it, slow it right down. Have a full awareness of your breath.

If we find relaxation hard at first, as so many of us do, then breathing can be accompanied by clenching and relaxing each muscle group in turn. This makes us aware, beginning with the toes and moving up the calves and upward, that we do have tension in each part of our human selves and that we need to release it before we can focus on our breath. Mentally talk to the area concerned, telling it what you are doing; inform your body that you are clenching that area and let all tension recede from it. Remember to keep the deep rhythmic breathing going at the same time.

Now that we are positioned comfortably and correctly and have found our rhythm of breathing, we can concentrate on both connecting to the sustaining ground beneath us and linking in to spirit "above." Spirit is, of course, not in one place, like a biblical "heaven in the sky," but all around us. For the purpose of this exercise we simply express spirit/unseen energies as being in the "above" position as we are acting as the conduit to transmit and transmute energy between two levels of existence—the manifest and the ethereal. As we can literally feel the manifest below us, then we can easily relate to the spiritual realms as being above. There are no such divisions as above and below in terms of spiritual value judgments; here we speak symbolically for the purpose of creating an effective dynamic.

As we root ourselves in our "now" reality of being incarnate, we also draw our awareness up to the eternal spiritual essence, opening ourselves to a wider universal energy than our own, and because of this we must now engage our protective process.

The best way to do these three things at once (ground manifestly, breathe rhythmically, connect universally) is to imagine that our human host body is a tree. Relate your own spine to a tree's trunk, and think of it carrying energy and information to the brain, which has many complex nerve endings that branch out like a tree's canopy. Similarly, witness your spine continuing down, as if it still had its prehensile tail, pushing into the earth like a great tap root seeking sustenance. Now see all the nerve endings coming from this central spine point and twisting and twining their way into the soil beneath you like subsidiary roots. Roots may also sprout from the soles of the feet. Visualise them pushing the dark earth aside as they wriggle to find better purchase. Imagine the gentle scuffling sound as they stretch and find their place of security amongst small stones and carapaced creatures.

Do not worry if you haven't literally got the ground beneath you; for instance, if you live in a second-story apartment. Remember, our work here is all about visualisation, symbolism, and intent. Remember also that it is very beneficial to get out into the landscape and actually feel the soil directly beneath us as often as possible.

As you breathe in, feel your sap/energy rising up to your leafy boughs, out around your head, stretching up toward the light. Now feel and see this light strongly above and all around you, and feel the roots of your hair straining upward with the irresistible urge to reach the light. You are being pulled up toward it, growing closer to its warming, illuminating source, yet your position is firm and rooted. The light that enfolds you, nurtures you, and urges you to spread your great branches out and upward is clear, bright, and golden yellow. It shimmers, seeming to contain tiny reflective fragments like glitter or infinitesimal pieces of mirror caught in its glow. It is like sunlight, but this is the brightest, purest light that you have ever witnessed. It is warm, strong, and, above all, protective. It is *alive*.

As you breathe out, feel the energy pull down into your tap root and push deep into the ground beneath you. Pull the golden light of protection down into you and all around you, and then let it rise again as you breathe in. This golden, sparkling light should keep spreading around your vast branch system above (that which extends from you and travels off, connecting you into the universal energies), and should surround your root system that reflects the shape and size of your branches above. You become a mirror image of yourself, above and below the earth's surface, surrounded by this protective dancing light. Again this reflects the magical maxim "as above, so below"; both realities are real and mirror each other to some degree. Keep breathing steadily, deeply, and see your beautiful, glowing yellow light pulse and swell as you inhale and exhale. Slow your breathing if you can, and just keep imagining your glowing, protective aura that advances and recedes with your breath, an organic cloak of shining light that envelops your trunk as it rains down from above. Feel your roots searching for water in the loam beneath you.

You are completely surrounded, above and below, by glittering golden light. You are anchored into the earth-level and yet open to the spiritual realms.

You may like to accompany this visualisation with an affirmation, something like:

I surround myself by protective golden light.
Each time I breathe in, it swells,
each time I breathe out, it recedes.
I am in the light; it is part of me.
I am rooted like the greatest tree.
I am protected, so may it be!

It is worth noting here that the protective glow you "see" around your person, or know to be there, does not mean that you see the world through a golden mist. No, it means that it exists on a profound level as an energetic shield, not a literal cloak. We are in the realm of subtle energies. Your visualised/perceived protective layer will fade away if it is not replenished; if you spent time making it strong and bright then it will not fade until long after you have completed the work.

To be protected instantly in a situation, understand that focused visualisation plus a statement of intent equals change. If you state and actually "see" with the mind's eye/imagination that something is so (that is, you are protected above and below), then it is so astrally. You have affected a change on the unseen level, where the energies are pliable. Such is the basis of all our magic, and so may we be protected almost instantly if we truly focus on what we wish to achieve. The meeting of spirit and earthed reality combines effectively, and the more we practice our protection during longer meditations, or in more suitable settings, then the more faith we will have and the quicker off the mark we will be on the hop. It will be our second nature, like putting on clothes before we leave the house.

Similarly, asking spirits directly for assistance is effective if approached in a reverent (and appropriately worded) way. Even if, at this stage, we do not know who our companion (guiding) spirits are, we can still ask them for help by acknowledging their existence. Whether we perceive them yet or not, they exist. When we know their names and have a good working friendship established with them, all the better, but for now we could send out a prayer such as:

> *Spirits who come for my highest good, hear me.*
> *Companions who guide me, I ask you to shield me.*
> *Spirits who come for my greatest good, heed me.*
> *Protect me with love as I ask you to help me!*

Such pleas to those in spirit who have pledged to help us should also become second nature. We are never truly solitary on the wildwitch's path.

You will not always have time to do this formal protective act, and there are a number of quicker protective fixes that can be used when you need an instant way to attune to an energy or situation. Sometimes you will need to act in the moment, and there will be no time for sitting in silence. Such an instance may be when you are walking back from the shops at dusk and see a great flock of birds begin wheeling and spinning in one fluid motion as they go to roost. You may want to perform a quick invocation that links with their energy, as you have been doing a lot of magical work on home, family, or community, and it fits in perfectly. So what to do?

Well, you could hardly sit down in the street and perform the full tree visualisation, as this is highly impractical, not to mention hazardous in terms of both traffic and the less obvious energetic intrusions of passersby. Therefore, as a quick fix, simply affirm your connection to the earth beneath your feet and feel the power of your own energies running up and down your spine. Make the connection firmly in your mind and feel that strength the connection gives to you instantly. The more we practice this aspect of protection, the more the sensing of this connection will become a reflex.

We could then take three measured deep breaths and envision the cloak or bubble of light around us. Ask the companion spirits to draw near. State calmly and clearly (speaking to ourselves in our heads is as valid as proclaiming out loud) that we are now rooted, connected, and protected.

It is vital to ground yourself fully again after any magical work, no matter how quickly the work is achieved, but we shall come to this after our next section.

Stage Two: Guidance from Companion Spirits

This is the second ethereal aspect of the work.

For the witch, the companion (guiding) spirits we have communion with are often known as *familiars*. This may conjure up images of animals and imps, but it simply means that they are the spirits that are closest to us, most familiar, and walk with us much like our closest manifest friends and companions do. The only difference is that they are unseen. They are once removed from human affairs and can see our situations more clearly from a less physically dense, more spiritually connected per-spective. They can see the webs of fate that link us all, incarnate or in spirit, and can have a much better idea of how our well-intentioned green magics can affect others around us inadvertently.

Are these beings our deities? Well, we can have a profound respect and love for the universal energies, earthly powers, spirit companions, and archetypal beings we encounter, but we do not *need* to deify them, nor do we need to be overly deferential or sycophantic in their presence. To be awe-inspired and fired with a passion that is not sexual but still burns down deep in the very root of us is to encounter such spirits in an honest, earthy way. A genuine companion spirit would never seek your obeisance, only your genuine positive regard. Companion spirits are nei-ther servants nor gods.

Is there a deity to be acknowledged in wild witchery? Yes, but not in the sense of a human image. The universe is not, as we have already sug-gested, human-centric; indeed, how can it be? Therefore, why should the Creator/Deity be humanoid? The universal Creator is unknowable to our human minds yet omnipresent in terms of our human lives today, being expressed in all creation. We can reveal our appreciation of this when we respond joyfully to each of the Creator's gifts, born of the sacred source energy. These gifts are found both within us and within our fellow travellers, seen and unseen, on the winding road of life. And this is how we may measure our relationship with the divine; not in terms of religious rites but in terms of how much praise and acknowledgment we find within us at any given moment. It is a spontaneous and immediate response, an integral part of our craft.

The wild craft we are discussing here is not Wicca, which is often taken as the only form of modern witchcraft. In Wicca there are god and goddess forms to be worshipped. It is possible to witness these beings as spiritual representatives of certain energetic principles, and it is perfectly valid (and valuable) to call upon them when working enchantment. However, there are no direct references to gods and goddesses in wild witchcraft.

So what of our companion spirits? They are also commonly known as spirit *guides,* as they give guidance as opposed to laying down the law and controlling us. Guidance gives us the chance to weigh the pros and cons of our magical work as well as to understand the energies involved more clearly. Our companions may help us talk through a proposed enchantment or life decision just as a true human friend would—with the added advantage of that far-sighted detachment of vision that gives them a little more scope. Yet they are still close to our earth-level (or else would not be able to talk with us at all), and so are not infallible, just more able. They are those who have chosen, usually because of soul-links or long-lasting spiritual kinship with us, to assist our incarnate learning process. This is not just for our own good, but so we have a better chance of walking the earth in a harmonious way, for the good of the All.

There is not enough space in one chapter to discuss types of companions or the attributes of spirits in general. However, it must be said that not all of our companions are humanoid. Some may appear as animals, birds, or representatives of the Faery way, including elves, pixies, and so on. What is important is to state that everyone, but *everyone*, has spiritual companions on his or her life-journey, and so, using a combination of psychic protection and meditative (trance) journeying, we can all contact and maintain a relationship with them in a safe and effective way.

What do they get from this relationship? Well, they get our promise, as fellow beings, that we will express their wisdom in the world. We are incarnate and they are not. We can make manifest change while they are not able to express themselves in a way that is considered substantial. It is a mutually beneficial friendship.

Journey to Meet Your Companion

If you already know your companion spirit(s), then you can either skip this stage or follow it through to become better acquainted with it. Use it as an opportunity to experience a "pathworking," that is, a magical prescribed journey to achieve a specific outcome in a light trance state. Incidentally, "trance" here isn't meant to suggest the out-of-control state that is attributed to the "victims" of stage hypnosis. Here it signifies entering a relaxed state in which Otherworldly contact can be made. Full awareness, albeit in an altered state of consciousness, is necessary to this process.

What follows is the pathworking. It may help to read it several times over and make an audiotaped version that you can play to yourself to guide you as you travel. If you worry that you will forget what the directions were, then you are clearly not going to relax deeply enough and it would therefore be preferable to have a guiding voice on tape to listen to. If you choose this option, do make sure that you pause at significant junctures to allow yourself to fully partake in the experience. For instance, if it says "cross the stream by stepping stones," then give yourself time to do this in trance, knowing that you will be observing the colours, scents, and sounds as if the experience were very real—which it is, of course! Alternatively, you could get a friend to read it and guide you through the journey.

Ensure that you are connected, positioned comfortably, breathing deeply, and well protected as per the tree visualisation. Now follow the instructions below, written as directions to yourself.

(Note: These instructions can be adapted to suit the individual. Do be creative with them as long as they follow the same pattern and remain within the journey's framework; that is, do cross water, go under and over things at the same juncture, but feel free to change the environs and the means by which you do these things. And make certain that you use the same structure for meeting the companion spirits.)

I enter my safe astral space by means of a gate into a meadow. By climbing over this simple wooden gate I have symbolically made the transition from my conscious human state into the spiritual realms of my trance-journey. I pause for a moment, feeling my bare feet on the sun-warmed ground, the grass tickling my toes as it moves in the gentle summer breeze. Above me the sky is cornflower blue, flecked only with insubstantial wispy white clouds, and the sun is high.

I survey the land before me. To my left the meadow slopes down to meet fields that lead away as far as my eye can see. Some fields are golden with wheat, others green with tall sweet corn plants, while still others reveal their rich, dark soil. To my right I am aware of hills that I have not yet explored, and behind me lies the gateway over which I came. In front of me I follow the winding badger track through the grass with my eager inner vision. I know that I am ready to travel along it.

I walk on slowly, noting the wild scarlet poppies that nod their delicate heads at me and hearing the plaintive cry of a buzzard as it circles way above me, nearly out of my sight. Tall buttercups and ox-eye daisies line the shallow track, and all around are forget-me-nots and dandelions, some in flower, some as seed-clocks. The air is full of butterflies of all hues and bees laden with pollen. I follow the track to the edge of a wood, standing still at its edge in order to catch a glimpse of the deer that I know reside within its cool green shade. I see a fawn, its eyes wide with surprise, skip off after its disappearing mother. A hare hops out, its loping stride making me smile. It accompanies me as I leave the bright sunlight and step into this dappled world, the greenwood of my heart.

The badger track leads me deep. I sense all of the changes in my environment, hearing the "coo" of wood pigeons now and the song of the blackbird filtering down to me from the dense leaf canopy above my head. Occasionally a squirrel bounds from tree to tree. The air is pleasantly cool and smells of secret places, verdant and damp, and my hands reach out instinctively to touch the smooth bark of beech trees, feet brushing through ferns as my toes feel springy damp moss between them as the track peters out. Late bluebells cluster around the base of tree trunks and I stoop to hold one in my hand briefly, admiring the shape and shade of this tiny flower. Sunlight shafts through into the glade, illuminating fallen tree limbs wreathed in ground ivy. My fellow traveller the hare lopes away and I bid him farewell, for now.

I pause, for I am at the hollow oak. This I must pass through in order to feel myself going deeper into my spiritual awareness. It is another symbol (rather like a bridge between the worlds) that means that I am leaving the manifest realms behind. I always ask the tree if I may pass through its dark interior. I wait for response, which, as with all voices in this realm, I hear in my mind. Sometimes this tree, which I know is named Melerai, allows me only to pass around its girth, not through. Some days I am not allowed to pass at all and must turn back. Today, however, I am granted safe passage through the heart of the oak, and once inside I pause to appreciate the chill, the scent of loam, and the feel of living bark surrounding me. I hear the tiny scurryings of bark creatures, insects feeding on the soft interior. I feel the sap travelling through the remaining bark skin, keeping the tree strong even though the inner wood is beginning to die a little now.

Passing through, back into the green and gold world of the wood, soaking up its leafy mysteries, I give my thanks to the tree and continue. I walk down a small bare slope of earth lined with briars and brambles, and see that the trees are thinning now, letting more light in. I have reached an area of open ground where the grass is glistening and luxuriant again, and I see one of the most beautiful of all sights on my journey, the bubbling stream. I hear its musical voice greet me as it rushes joyfully over the pebbles, its crystal clear waters washing them smooth. I move forward and peer hopefully into these bright waters, hoping to glimpse a tiny silver fish or two. I scoop the deliciously cold essence of the stream up in my cupped hands and bring it to my lips. I taste minerals, the collective distillation of all beings that live here, a cleanness and freshness that refreshes my very soul. I ask that such clarity be granted to me to energise my own creative being. I then thank the stream for its gift and ask if I may cross it.

The stream is bridged by three broad, flat slate-grey stones that look slightly pink as the water passes over them. This is another symbolic passage between manifest being and spiritual understanding. Granted permission, I step boldly onto the first stone, aware of its slipperiness and its unyielding but not unpleasant chill. I pause on the second, looking down at the tiny insects who dart around the surface of the water or skate and skim over it. I step onto the third, which is a slightly irregular shape, and then I step onto the bank with gratitude.

Before me there is a high hillock obscuring my view of whatever may be ahead. It is relatively steep and a good few heads taller than me. In order to reach whatever lies on the other side I must climb it with care, engaging fully in the activity, feeling my toes gain purchase in the soil and my fingers clutching at clumps of grass. This is my final barrier between the human manifest level and this place of spirit. I pull myself up to the top.

On the other side of this bank there is a plain. On this plain I may journey to wherever I wish, seeking meetings with spirit guides and mentors, or looking for adventures to broaden my horizons and understanding. Today I stand and, using my will and wish, I visualise a circle of flickering blue-gold flame around my feet. It is a magically protective fire—*I deem it to be so*—bright but cold. It cannot harm me, its creator. A comfortable distance in front of me I imagine a second circle of flickering yet constant flame, like that of many fiercely burning candles, on the ground. It is big enough for a figure to appear in when I am ready to bid them to do so.

I invoke for my true companion spirit, the one who walks with me at this present time, to appear in this circle. I know that I am addressing a friend, not a servant or a god, and so I could say something like:

> *You who are wise and generous.*
> *You who walk with me, ever faithful and gentle.*
> *Please join me now for my highest good!*
> *I have prepared a space for you and you alone.*
> *If it is your will as it is mine then come!*

Then I point a finger at the space and wait.

Whatever spirit appears, no matter how it looks to me, must then be "checked" for authenticity. The most aesthetically appealing spirit can be a trickster donning a disguise. I point, and a thin beam of luminous blue-gold light, like the protective flame directed at the figure who has appeared, travels from my fingertip to the spirit. It represents my directed will. As it is my sacred land the spirit has come to, it must adhere to my rules. I can, if I wish, also hold a mirror up to the spirit, in which it must be reflected truly. I speak with authority:

Show yourself truly, spirit!

And it must be revealed to me as it truly is. Any "impostor" spirit will vanish, not wishing to be unmasked. Any true spirit will stay and be revealed. If on the first try I somehow get an intruder, then the procedure should be calmly and carefully repeated until the true guide appears for me.

When it does appear, I spend time getting to know it. The spirit's appearance may be dazzling or disconcerting, although if it is my true companion it will wish to blend with my inherent energies, not distract me totally! It will probably have chosen a guise pleasing to my soul type and interests. I will try not to dwell too heavily on its apparel, but more on how it *feels*. I must remember to ask the spirit its name, and if I may call on it when I do magics. I should ask if there is anything that I should know at this time. I should ask if any planned enchantments are appropriate. I should not ask too many questions on the first meeting (three is adequate), as I will simply forget by the time I return to manifest reality.

I thank my companion for turning up and take my leave of it for now.

I return down the bank and retrace my steps. The bonding with my safe place is done, and I have met one of my spirit mentors and friends. I am strengthening my link with it and with my sacred space, and thus strengthening its astral, or etheric, reality. I go down the bank, across the stream, through the hollow tree, out of the wood, and across the meadow. When I climb over the gate I am ready to return to the manifest realm again.

And on returning to the present manifest reality we must become grounded; that is, establish that we are fully back in our manifest circumstances, including our physical body! We can easily get "carried away" on an involved or affecting spirit-journey, so grounding is essential. One of the very best ways to do this is to immediately write down what you can recall of your journey. A witch usually has a magical journal in which to do this, and it can be anything from a sumptuous engraved Book of Shadows and Light to a simple spiral-bound notepad enhanced with lovingly drawn symbols or green-themed imagery.

We could also have a cup of tea and a biscuit. If outside, we could stamp our feet or clap our hands.

Now you have a way of protecting yourself, and a guiding spirit to call on for advice and help.

Stage Three: Solar, Lunar, and Daily Tides

When we are immersed fully in the magic of life it is impossible to escape the gently spiralling, cyclical nature of existence. But how to do this, how to shake ourselves free of the remaining fetters that come with the modern Western frame of reference and truly look beyond that first understanding of nature's roundness, of her meandering rotations?

Well, firstly we can set ourselves the task of trying to find any evidence of straight lines in nature! We can lie on our bellies, looking at tiny shells, pebbles, petals, beetles . . . or we can lie on our backs and see the cumulus clouds, the birds of prey riding thermal currents, the flitting passage of a tiny blue butterfly. We can observe leaf litter caught in a whirl of wind or concentric ripples spreading slowly out after the fish has leapt. We can study the stars, look at cells under a microscope, witness the beauty of fractals. We can compare all this to that which is hard-edged, linear, and manmade.

When we are passionately experiencing on a daily basis what it means to be a part of this swirling motion, the wheeling and spinning, then it is impossible to say that we are not affected by it or that we have not within ourselves many reflections of it. The maxim "as within, so without" is relevant here, as it means that what we find to be true and valid within the microcosm of our own lives is inevitably reflected as a universal principle, and vice versa, with beautiful simple symmetry.

Much has been written about the importance of magically working with the seasonal cycle, as well as the subtle yet potent effects of lunar waxing and waning, but not so much has been mentioned about the daily flux and flow of energy. Therefore, as it is seldom focused on, the emphasis in this chapter will be more on daily rhythms and their relation to enchantment in our lives. We clearly need to understand, and have a deep personal experience of, solar and lunar rhythms, so it is important to summarise, in a poetic way that suits our lyrical craftings, the key points relating to each, as well.

As the Earth Mother spins gracefully around her great companion, the sun, he keeps up a steady stream of supportive yet intense energy. This energy encourages her to turn a personal pirouette (which moves her into light from darkness and round again), and also allows her to experience fruition to dying back and on to germination once more. He himself performs his own sedate yet sensual dance of rotation. The sun's time of performing an entire turn is approximately one earth month. As he is a ball of gas and not a solid being, and because he is so vast, his central area moves faster than his pole regions. Therefore, his entire revolution is between the twenty-six and thirty-four day mark.

We can experience that which the Earth Mother experiences as we move through the Wheel of the Year and through the lesser cycles of her own daily personal revolutions. We can feel within ourselves, through our deepening spiritual connection and profound observations, the fluctuations in energy that occur in any period of twenty-four hours. There are clearly certain times within this ebb and flow when it is pertinent to connect with the energies for magical purposes.

For example, at noon, when the sun is at its zenith, we may want to release a charm for increased creativity or invoke passion in our lives through a wild dance on a sun-blessed hilltop. At midday we are simply echoing the sun and earth in their positions and are working with full-bodied, peak-powered magic concerning physical strength, endurance, desire, personal performance, and optimum self-expression. It is obvious that doing a sombre banishing spell would not fit in with the fiery positive pulse of the moment, yet a green-spirited magical act based in an ardent artistic or amorous energy would.

Midday is clearly a time of full-on, upfront power. As such, it sits opposite on the wheel of the daily earth-dance to night's hidden but no less potent vibration. The two other main daily emanations, dawn and twilight, are more subtle; they are also opposites yet are connected by their wafting melodies. Midday has the hot and thrusting power, night the deep, mystical influence. Both are aromatic times. Dawn has the air of renewal and growth, and twilight has the atmosphere of reflection. Both are fragrant times.

Regarding the energies of sunrise, it is appropriate to feel the dew on our skin at dawn and watch the daisy petals gently unfurling at first light if we are thinking about renewal in a less vibrant and urgent way than at midday. Sunrise, and the opposite waning energy of twilight, are certainly inspiring and evocative times, but not the ones imbued with the most magical "oomph." To lie on the cool wet grass and gaze up at the rain-washed sky as a watery sun emerges, a sun that turns a stream to a rill of gold as the birds thrill the spirit with their sweet, rising voices, clearly suits the more gentle magical touch. It is restorative to experience the earth's turning and the sun's blessing from the unique perspective of magical rebirth at dawn.

Playing a simple wind instrument like a penny whistle could be a wonderful way of piping in the new day with the birds at sunrise, as could singing a melodious enchantment about the return of love into your life as an accompaniment to their joyful vocalisation. We are never simply humans sitting in the landscape performing our set piece; we can interact, observe, and be spontaneous enough to let go of previous expectations, going with the flow of the moment, feeling it authentically, and letting it be translated through us.

We are a part of nature and can get involved!

Whatever we find at midday in the brightest rays (even when it is overcast we still experience the blessing of that heightened energy), we have as a more pale and lucent reflection at dawn . . . passion is muted to love, creativity to inspiration, desire to wistful dreaming. The energy of the sunrise is about returns and is ideal for prayers around the theme of the Greening—the verdant resurgence for the Earth Mother and all her children. Other magical themes include the further merging of magic into the mundane, the reemergence of the Fey into the manifest, the revival of an earth-honouring culture, and the resurgence of love and kinship with all nature. A very simple prayer for the dawn could be:

As the light grows the stronger,
so shall my love grow the brighter in the world.
And in my love may all love be found,
Burgeoning in the light of a new day.
As the lark ascends and the blackbird gives voice to new joy,
So may it be!

We are dealing with magic as soul-poetry here, and each time of day must evoke a certain response in us in order for us to align the energy with it effectively. Whether we are wide-eyed in wonder or moved to the core, we must *feel* whatever we do.

We see here that dawn and midday have their correspondences in our work and to each other, relating as they do to love and desire, renewal and a vital resurgence. So it is that twilight and nightfall are also silvered reflections of one another—night being the time of deep magic, profound insight, and twilight being the misty-eyed and soulful moment of yearning and remembering. Dusk is full of Fey magic, powerful but ethereal, while the midnight blackness enfolds and surrounds, taking us down into the real depths of experience, beyond that which is human or even Fey, but of eternal mystery.

Dusk is veiled and full of whispered secrets and sighs, and nightfall is shrouded and silent, pulsing with primal power, the revealed firmament glittering and beguiling us to forget what is trivial and of human concern but to focus on what is all-encompassing and cosmic. For this reason it is possible to experience profound night-terrors in the darkness—where there is fear there is real power—while at twilight we may simply feel mildly disturbing shivers of anticipation, thrills of the unknown, and possibly unsettling pleasure.

As the burned apricot skies of twilight pass away into the indigo darkness, the one segues into the other; subtle enchantments of dusk's meditative energy move with a fluid motion into more hidden mysteries, more intense experiences, more deeply felt interactions. Therefore, nightfall is the time when we may commune with our spiritual companions for the purpose of gaining insights that are universal; that is to say, guidance that does not relate to the personal but to the wider consciousness, the great eternal spiritual questions. On a practical level, night is the time when most of humanity sleeps, and so the extraneous buzz of human activity, voices, and electronic gadgets is lessened, and a more pure and resonant level of communication may be reached.

Night is a time of invoking for the moon-blessed power of sight and for starlight vision, to heighten the perception we have beyond our current limited human facilities, for the good of the All. It is a time for journeying into deep inner space and making soul prayers for bright night blessings. We may intone a night prayer that has this resonance:

As the light grows the dimmer,
and darkness creeps into the hidden recesses of my soul,
may I turn from the lights of temporary human life,
and look within to that which is dark and eternal,
to the ancient well within me, that which reflects star patterns,
and so may my fear be dispersed in that void.
As my fear recedes so shall my vision flare brightly,
as my fear is swallowed by velvet night so shall I know myself more fully.
As my vision expands so shall I see what it is I must do.
In truth, revealed, so shall my fear fade.
In truth, revealed, so shall my fear recede!
By that which is luminous, held by that which is endless.
So may it be!

Nighttime is the time to use the magic of candle flame to full effect, to reclaim the lost power of the witch who works hidden by her flickering tallow torch. It is a time for leaping shadows and lanterns, for swirling incense smoke wreathing wavering reflections in dark mirrors, for all the wonderful "props" that enhance the mood of mystery.

Twilight is a marvellous time for the wildwitch who desires to strengthen his or her Otherworldly connections and gain deeper understandings into the ways of earth's more secretive denizens. Spirit conversations held at this time could focus around the need for a more profound level of understanding of the hidden aspects of being. We may contact the Fey and speak with the night creatures who inhabit a shadowy nonhuman world. We may use poetry to cast green magics relating to inspiration as twilight suits flowing lyrical invocations. We could express this as something like:

> O Shining Ones who slip between the realms,
> clad in your mantles of mist and wreathed in moon-berry mystery,
> hear me now as I call to you in the voice of the lone hawthorn,
> hung with tinkling silver bells, shrouded by the veils that separate us.
> Children of the amaranthine, dancing ones of the white apples,
> hear me and draw closer, for I wish to hear your poetry.
> I long for your inspiration in my life,
> and to feel your timeless beauty in my own Fey soul.
> Hear me now if it pleases you and dance closer!
> By elder blossom at midsummer and the tears of the weeping willow,
> by your grace and by my fascination, I ask that this may be!

(Note: The Fey will not be commanded and will probably get quite irate, if not very troublesome, if we choose to be as foolhardy as to summon them in such a way. A prettily worded and polite request would be far more pleasing to them.)

Twilight is the time of the weaver of fate who sits on the edge of the worlds whilst being connected to the rhythms of life and all the beings. To be a walker between the worlds at this time is to work with the energies of the day. Of course, some of us may feel the need to practice our communing with spiritual companions at any convenient time of day. We may only ever practice spells at night when we have the required level of privacy. We may consider it to be suitable, or convenient, only to use poem, prayer, and chanting in the middle of the afternoon when walking the dog in the woods. It is absolutely fine to have these feelings and requirements as long as they do not become habitual and without meaning. From time to time it may be good to try something new, to tune into a different time of day or to break with routine and do your meditation in the evening, just to ensure that you haven't become stuck in your ways.

As the sun, that dynamic, explosive, vibrant body of energy, that living being of fire, interacts with the Earth Mother on a daily basis (as she turns her face away and reveals it again), so does the dance continue on a greater level, that of the seasonal cycle. That endless procession leads the beings of earth and the earth's living body through the sacred round of death and rebirth, transformation and dissolution.

It may be important to note here that climate change, wrought by a combination of our human thoughtlessness and the Mother's own desire for change (which she experiences at intervals through her own incarnatory process), can affect how we feel/perceive the seasons, and therefore can affect how we practice the craft of the wild. The feeling of a "seasonless" world has been a common one in England of late, with one long experience of grey, wet, and mild conditions predominating. However the climate feels to us at present, we may still honour the energies behind the weather we experience, as the earth is still orbiting the grand body of the sun, whether that is obvious to us or not.

Weather fluctuations aside, we will now look at the core energies of the seasonal festivals as we process with the earth around the sun in the age-old annual dance. Here it seems appropriate to use specific dates, as it helps us align to the point when the energy is most concentrated. The dates give us the traditionally observed agricultural festival or holy day (holiday), and act as guidelines. The dates are flexible markers in that intuition tells us the best moment to celebrate a culmination of the appropriate seasonal energy, which may last for a period rather than just a day. The energy of a season may be felt to peak at a particular point, but we will only feel this, as we are sensing, experiencing, and in some way acting out magically the energies involved.

The Inherent Energies of the Earth-Dance?

October 31: The Time of Mists and Sighs

All things have a season, and this is the wildwitch's hour and the time most sacred to those who walk the way of green enchantment.

Known as All Hallows' Eve, Halloween, or Samhain (the Celtic New Year), this marks the end of autumn and the coming of winter in a slow season of wood smoke and drifting low cloud. It is a festival of that which is past, of going within and travelling through the veils of separation between the worlds to access lost wisdoms, gain ancestral blessings, and feel the ghosts in our lives shifting and settling.

We can banish our own fears at this time, sending them to ground symbolically, to be transformed into new hope in the spring after they have been transmuted by the power of the dying year's mystery and purified by winter's chill touch. Suitable wild magic would be, for example, writing what we wish to see recede from our lives on a piece of recycled unbleached paper in the dark juice of old blackberries, then hiding it inside a hollow tree so that it may rot down and be swallowed up by the energies of the dying year, by the sodden and leaf-littered soil. Perhaps in spring an offering of thanks for swallowing up what was outworn in your life could be made to the tree. To ask the permission of both blackberry bush and tree is of course vital, and, in the case of the offering, a dialogue could be established over the dark months of winter to ascertain what the tree would like as a gift.

December 21: The Time of the Glittering Ground

Also known as winter solstice, Yuletide, midwinter.

This date marks "the longest night," when daylight hours are scarce and darkness is the better friend of our waking hours. But even as we mark this we observe the pattern shifting as the Wheel of Life turns steadily, inexorably onward. After this day the balance will shift and the sun will reclaim a little of his territory every passing day. Thus, many on a green-spirited wild path may choose to rise early to witness a chilly dawn and hail the still weak but ever-victorious energy of the sun as he tips the balance from darkness into light within the pattern of our days.

We may make magical wreaths to remember this, binding the shining green and red of the holly and their berries with bright ribbon, symbolic of the light we seek in the darkest days, an acknowledgment of its sure return.

We, like the little creatures, huddle close to loved ones, counting our blessings and drowsily dwelling on what we have. It is an excellent time to offer prayers of thanks for an abundance in our lives. We could raise our voices in a spirit-song of heartfelt prayer, asking that as we are fed and sustained by Mother Nature's generous bounty in the darkest hours, so may those who are less fortunate find sustenance, comfort, and joy. We may light candles as a symbolic act, asking for the brightly flaring return of a certain energy into our own lives, or to wish for a particular glowing blessing for the earth in the coming cycle—preferably both, entwined.

February 2: The Time of the Quickening Pulse

Also known as Imbolc or Candlemas.

This marks a seasonal celebration of the earth's first stirrings. Here and there the shock of the first tenacious, supple shoots that push up through the cold, hard ground begin to flower, and delicate snowdrops bloom against a backdrop of purest white and darkest brown, the bare earth glimpsed under its frosted mantle.

The snowdrops are a sign of inspiration. The shoots and buds that may appear at this time are signs to us that anything is possible, that we too can create new and fresh ideas, images, or practices. How may we take our own pale and pure hope, as complex as a snowflake and surely as delicate and unique, and fashion it into a spell for the future? By thinking of seeds growing restless in the deep hidden places we can attune to what it is that we need to do.

We could decide what the theme for this year will be and meditate on how it will be expressed magically and physically; that is, the theme could be living without cruelty, and this could involve adopting an animal from a shelter, changing our diet to exclude animal products, giving money to antivivisection charities, and so on, combined with spells that take our personal commitment out into the world.

March 21: The Time of the Hatching Dream

Also known as Oestara/Eostre after the ancient goddess of fertility (hence Easter eggs), and as the Spring Equinox, when day and night are of equal lengths before the sun wins out again. It is recognised as the first day of spring as well as the time of Jesus's apparent resurrection.

Now we actually witness the earth rising, refreshed and renewed. We can spin and play like the creatures on the hillsides and in the woodland, newly emerged; we can test out new ways of being, thoughts, songs, creations. We can plan which seeds to plant, both in our lives and in the land. We can rededicate ourselves to a path that has been revealed again, after the long, grey days and snowy embrace of winter, and renew any promises made. It is a time to take that which was incubating over winter, a spirit-seed, a piece of comfort in the cold and barren times, and really give it life, filling it with all the real delight of a green resurgence.

May 1: The Time of the Blossoming Blood

This festival is also known as Beltane in the Celtic tradition. It is May Day, a holy day, for it is the celebration of a strengthened sun and longer days are upon us!

The essence of this time is romance and loving union, of wild blood surging and passionate relationships blossoming. Thus the season is about creation, not only in partnerships but also in individual ways, referring to lovingly created projects, ideas, and so on. It is about being wildly enthusiastic about something or someone. And how can it not be when the creatures around us are mating, building homes, feasting on lush grass, and singing out their pleasure?

As bud-clad branch becomes leafy bough, so it is that we experience a real thriving, a spurt of impetus, inspiration, and magical purpose. Mind, body, and spirit are married in a bright burst of briar rose, and hawthorn petals spill and spin around us like confetti. Our marriage is of the worldly with the Otherworldly, of enchantment and action. We fall in love with what we do, with who we are, as well as with each other.

We may undertake trance journeys to align ourselves with the resurgent energies and travel to meet the Fey ones as they dance their own untamed reel within the ancient boundaries of a stone ring on a high moor.

June 21: *The Time of the Deep Green Kiss*

This is the Summer Solstice, midsummer, the longest day of the year. It can also be called Litha. It marks, as with the winter equivalent, a point after which there will be a change in the energetic tide. With the summer solstice we observe a peak, the opposite of winter's trough, and we know that from this point on there will be a waning. Therefore, it is a good opportunity to celebrate what is given to us, the bounty of sun-kissed summer life, at the moment of climax as the sun reaches its annual and daily zenith at midday.

Seasonal wild magic should concern living life to the fullest and being thankful for all that fulfills us. Therefore, simple green-spirited spells could be performed while focusing on the energy, golden like the sun, at the centre of a wild (dog) rose as we visualise ourselves as fully opened, vital, beautiful, and fully realised, untamed beings. We can eat wild strawberries, dedicated to experiencing the sweet, red, wild heart of being. Or we could gather hedgerow (not roadside) elderflowers (with a prayerful intent, as always asking permission of the tree), and make a light, sparkling cordial with sugar, lemon, and white wine vinegar. As we stir and tend the brew we can sing praise to it for our gladness, our delight at being a part of something so utterly magnificent as nature in full bloom. We can bottle it up in green bottles marked with swirls of bright energy and share the resulting drink with friends in weeks to come as a celebration of life, friendship, and kinship with nature.

August 2: The Time of the Abundant Promise

This is also known as Lammas, which derives from a Saxon word and relates to the loaves we associate with the harvested grain of the season, and the feast of Lugh (Lughnassadh), who was a Celtic fire god who gave his life in sacrifice at this time to ensure a continued good harvest.

The first fruits of our year's harvest are showing in our lives just as the blackberries appear on twisted bramble limbs in the busy hedgerows, still reddish but swelling to ripening. Even as the sun begins to decline in strength gradually, we see the rich jewel-like beauty of the rosehips, sloes, elderberries, and haws coming into being. Nature is still active, but slowing her pace; butterflies still fly, alighting on privet flowers, sending the heady scent of vanilla wafting out to hang heavy in the air down country lanes.

It is a time to join hands and give thanks for what we have managed to bring to bear so far, knowing that there is one last phase before the energy truly begins to wane, and that we may use the last of this sun-blessed vibrant summer energy to push our dreams and projects one step further.

As an act of natural enchantment it would be fitting to make a small pouch from recycled fabric in a rich, subtle colour that is suitable for such a mellow, ripened season. Into this pouch we could place anything we feel to be symbolic of the first fruits of our year's journey, symbols of any project we are involved in, or any creative idea or work. Along with this we could add some of the first hedgerow fruits that we see, dried and dedicated to the union of our wildwitch's work and the natural, fruitful progression of the land. We could make a woven tie from tall meadow grass to close it, and as we weave we could pour all the warm, lingering dynamism of the time of year into our hands, ensuring that the work we do, and our link with the land, is blessed by this magical energy. We could wear this around our necks, or about our person, until the seasonal wheel turns again.

September 21: The Time of Changeling Winds

This is the second harvest festival, the autumn equinox that speaks of days of equal length, to nights of divine balance, of waiting, of hanging, of being centred and poised before the energy shifts and wanes. It is also known as Mabon.

Here we experience a gathering in of gifts both physical and spiritual, a reaping of what has been sown in the fields, in our lives. There is nothing obvious or blatant about this season. There is a bronzing of the land as leaves, grasses, and petals all experience the touch that turns them from amber to russet, sapping their strength and making them drift away, curl up, retreat back.

And what has grown and what is to wane in our lives? Our enchantment banishes that which we wish to wane and gathers our achievements to us. Like a squirrel with its precious nuts, discarding the empty or useless ones and secretly storing those that are sound and wholesome for the lean times ahead, we can use found windfallen nuts to magically represent our own needs and wants.

Spiritual Flow: Moon Dance

The moon, as we are about to discuss in poetic terms, is a witch's energetic guide. She is our patron.

And why is she a "she," and not an "it"?

Just as we see the sun as being male, we see the moon as either a cold, dead lump of rock that just happens to orbit the earth, or as a living being who inspires the human female menstrual cycle with the influence over the water of earth. Her effect is felt on all the watery, emotional, female aspects of earthly existence, and so she is referred to in the feminine. With her blessing we may see a moon-washed world of infinite and overwhelming beauty, and consequently our practice then becomes celestial, Otherworldly, fantastical. We have crossed the boundaries of fantasy and reality, and she offers us her luminosity so that we may have the clarity to work wonders. She may induce madness with her beauty, or invoke the most stunning poetry, music like waves, outpourings onto paper and canvas, encounters with strings and keyboards.

Just as some people find driving rain exhilarating whilst it renders others miserable and moody, so do the moon's phases have markedly different resonances on us as individuals. There are obvious symbolic qualities associated with each phase, and we will all find them more or less energetically compatible with us. There is no correct way to feel influenced by a full moon, although the energies that are involved are constant. In order to express the cycle we can journey through the three main phases, realising that within this fluid motion there are many lesser phases, and that this is an ongoing round that flows continually with no real beginning or end.

New Moon: Rising Tide, Waxing

From the first bright fingernail of light to appear in a velvet sky it is the time of beginnings and renewal. Because of this the new moon has a strong resonance with the period of February 1 to March 21. The same quickening energy applies—as it does at dawn within the daily dance of sun and earth. The whole feeling is of budding, beginning, and moving toward a blossoming and bursting forth as the waxing of the moon continues.

Spells for new beginnings find a perfect expression at new moon in February or March, when the balance of physical and spiritual renewal is appropriate.

Full Moon: Neap Tide, Peaking

As the new moon waxes so does the energy concerned symbolically rise through the seasons from April to May. This full moon energy aligns with the time of the Summer Solstice; it represents the zenith, a culmination. Therefore, the most powerful time of the year to make magic concerned with completion, success, and fertility would be the full moon in June. The correspondent time to full moon, in terms of the earth-dance, would be midday/early afternoon—the time of high-powered and positive celebratory magic.

A full moon is wonderful for praying for a heartfelt desire, and, if the desire is altruistic, then all the better for the energy to flow through us and onward. We become enhanced as we channel the power and send it in a new direction. The lovely, full, luminous face of Lady Luna so eloquently says that we should focus on that which requires illumination, that which needs to be brought to fruition and fullness, and that which is of full-bodied love and beauty.

Dark Moon: Ebbing Tide, Waning

Here is the season of sorcery. Dark moon is a real wildwitch's time, as although it has not the obvious beauty of the full moon, it holds a great deal of wild power. It belongs to the waning time of October 31, and sees its culmination at Winter Solstice in the time between times. Because the moon is hidden from us (although obviously still present), it is a time of delving into the "occult" side of being, diving for pearls of wisdom in the inky blackness of ourselves.

Just as we practice transformative dark magic (not in the sense of evil, only in the sense of mysterious, shrouded) at the waning time of year, so may we work now to cleanse ourselves. As ever, moon magic is more concerned with the nebulous and ethereal, and so thoughts and feelings can be transmuted by means of inner work. In the act of spiritual self-exploration we may employ trance vision to go on journeys to find answers, and may work with other visionary techniques and divination tools to gain further deep insights.

Stage Four: Focus, the Will, and the Wish

With the environmental adage "Think globally, act locally" in mind, we can acknowledge how we can affect the wider world with our homespun gifts of green magic. It all begins with us and our simple, yet potent, gestures. The stronger our belief in our connection to the All, the more we are able to influence it. This faith in the connected nature of the universe makes us strong, too—how can it not when we are directly linked, by sharing the same life-force energy, to vast and enigmatic planets, cascading waterfalls, and lions bringing down their prey on sun-baked savannahs? We acknowledge their elemental power, and therefore that of our own wild self.

Acknowledging the wildwitch's ability to bring about manifest magical change is a liberating experience, but also a responsibility to be taken very seriously, as it could easily be misused. "For the good of the All" (the All being all-encompassing, all that is) must always be our primary motivation when we are considering weaving spells and enchantments. In a spiritual way, with no absolutes in terms of tenets, that one heartfelt plea serves as well as any as a principle to work by. To understand what may be for the good of the All we need to consult with our companion spirits in the safe astral space we have created. They can give us the overview so that we may make an informed decision on what to use our will and wish for. Willing and wishing, focusing our intent and directing our energies in an appropriate way, is fundamental to spellcraft.

Another way of stating this honourable aspiration when considering enchantment is "and it harm none." There is something to be said about this latter phrase. Although its intentions are perfectly valid, it is sometimes inevitable that someone will consider himself or herself hurt in the process of change that is for a greater good. The whole ethos is never to deliberately hurt anyone or anything, but perhaps it is realistic to acknowledge that to work for the highest benefit of creation we must sometimes put a few noses out of joint—just never with a malicious intent. It is perfectly possible that an oil company could consider itself doomed if we all switched to using bicycles and wood-burning stoves tomorrow, yet our intention would be to help Mother Earth, not harm the individuals associated with that company. As we are all connected, some repercussions may be considered inescapable.

How do we actually build a spell? We know that we work with protection, with our companion spirits, with the tides of life, and our unique, individual cycles of being. Then, having checked that it is appropriate, we employ a magical threefold plan.

1. The Promise (The Purpose)

The promise is that which is unseen, a piece of word-magic in which we have faith, a green-spirited wish. It is that which flies our aspirations, our dreams, and our prayerful bidding up to the stars. It is something that is spoken or chanted with spirit and filled with our heart's desire. It is the ethereal aspect of our wildwitchery.

2. The Token (The Representative)

The token is a manifest (or "seen") object that reflects the purpose—a symbolic item that corresponds to the energy of the enchantment. This is our focus in the physical world. It is something that can be worn, buried, kept hidden, and so on, like a feather, a piece of wood, or a ring. It is a physical way to recall the wish, and the way to ground the magic in our current reality, an "earthing" device.

3. The Intent (Our Sacred Energy)

This binds the aspects together by wish and will. The intent is the will. In this example it is a way of focusing the energy of the promise into the object. It also is a way of projecting that energy (outside of both human wish and manifest object) into the universal whole. It is both a binding and a releasing agent. Why? Because you intend it to be so. You need your spell to be "bound free," something that exists both in you and outside of you at the same time. We employ our intent by focusing on the object and releasing our wish/promise in a safe space.

What safe space? Well, when we ourselves are psychically protected then we can work anywhere, which means we can practice our spell-craft at the kitchen sink or in the park. To do this, we can use the same technique we used in our meditative journey and imagine a circle of blue-gold flame around ourselves. Wherever we are we can stand or sit in a circle of protective astral fire.

It is an excellent idea to be in a particularly elemental place for weaving enchantments. Elemental places have a surplus of green life-force energy and connect us further to the heartbeat of nature. We can think about the whole idea of wild magic and all its verdant possibility—its wind-whipped and briar-tangled mystery, its sun-kissed, moon-bathed delights—and pick an appropriate spot, but one not too "highly peopled," as it is best to avoid extraneous human energy if at all possible.

We can also deliberately set up a space at home that is appropriate to our wild enchantment by ensuring that there are "representatives" of the season and of the natural world all around us, perhaps fallen green branches or blossoms, nuts or seeds, even homegrown fruit or vegetables, if possible. In the wild craft, it is not always appropriate to cut flowers or living branches, so do try to find windfalls if possible until you feel you can communicate fully with the essence of the plant and ask permission to take its blossom or leaves. Having some physical manifestation of the energy of the wild around us is essential if we are to make a spell of green-spirited authenticity.

Try to pander to your newly opened senses and get as many good smells—warm earth, cool, wet local rock, wild hedgerow herbs—in your vicinity as is feasible. We can then place these representatives around us at the compass points, with earth corresponding to north, fire to south, air to east, and water to west. The energetic correspondences for the elements are:

- Earth: manifest reality, matters to do with the physical and practical—home, work, money, security, and so on.

- Fire: vitality, passion, activity, including what drives and motivates us, our spirit, the "fire in the belly."

- Air: inspiration, ideas, and all things that are in the mental/intellectual sphere. Air relates to communication as well as problem solving and study.

- Water: emotions, intuition, and creativity; matters pertaining to relationships, artistic pursuits, home life and family, and psychism.

There are many books that may be useful in broadening an understanding of the elements, as they elaborate on these attributes in relation to the tarot and astrology. For the sake of wild witchcraft, it is well to both meditate on and physically witness each energetic quality to gain our own insights and experiences. Further, we can call on the spiritual representatives of each element to join us in our workings if it is appropriate. This should be done with the utmost respect and care, making sure to thank them and asking them to leave afterward, as it is clear that being rash with elemental forces is not advisable!

Stage Five: Magical Results in an Enchanted Life

In spellweaving we have a formula:

> *We say our piece, we represent our piece,*
> *and we send, yet keep, our piece.*
> *Then we keep our peace!*

This last line reminds us that power is held in silence—to discuss what we have done is to weaken the energy it has been given; it leaks away every time we link into it to discuss it. The work is primarily about energy and energy transference, after all. Our energy of personal intent makes our spellwork live; it weaves it into the universal energy matrix.

Because magic is brightly woven, not executed by means of hammer and chisel, it may not always be immediate in its results. It integrates itself into the web of life as is appropriate, depending on the seasonal tide, the amount of energy put into it, the rightness of the request, and so on. We can see a "magical turnover," which is either next week or next year, and it is well to remember when working an enchantment and asking for spiritual guidance that spirit-time is "Faery-time," and could turn out to be next decade! So be specific in a lyrical, energetic sense, stating that you would like to see the spell come to being when the frost is on the ground or the apples are on the tree. Coming into being sometimes means a drip-drip effect, and other times means an absolutely stunning response. We are dealing with wild energy, and part of its beauty is that we always get what we need—it just may not present itself in the most obvious way!

It is worth reiterating here the relevance of working with companion spirits. If we do not know the consequences of any request we blindly make, then we don't know how this will affect others adversely, no matter how nicely we word it or how good our intention is. To be forewarned of any consequence to our actions is to be wise and considerate. Regret is a terrible thing, especially when it could have been avoided by asking, "What will happen if I do this spell at this time?" Sometimes we aren't meant to ask for certain things, as life has other things in store for us on our path, and it is good to know this, too. The spirits will tell us this if we ask them directly.

And of course there is the "payback" we may receive if we dabble in such "tempting" fare as curses and hexes. If we truly believe in "as above, so below" and "as within, so without," and if we understand our energies to be connected to all other energies on the web of life, then how can we intentionally do harm when we understand it will be mirrored back at us on some level, sometime, somewhere? If we are practising wild enchantment, then the well-being of the earth and all her children is paramount. When we harm one on the web of life, we harm all by connection. The energy of harm is sent into the world. It is that simple.

We are free to take the risks if we know the consequences.

Examples

Wild witchcraft is not prescriptive, but is based on the individual's daily relationship with nature and the unseen. Therefore, to offer "prepackaged" spells is not appropriate, but to state when magic may be used, and to give symbolic ideas for how to approach it, is to provide a starting point. What follows are some suggestions of how enchantment may fit into daily life. Only by practising that which we have previously discussed in this chapter may we bring our spells alive. As unique beings, with a part to play in the unfolding dance of life, we must add our own energy into the equation.

Once you have a need to weave enchantment into your life, and have a suitable idea, then don't forget to follow the given route, with your own choice of diversions. You can make the magical journey as scenic as you wish as long as you travel from A to B to C, and so on.

- State your intention
- Root into manifest reality
- Breathe deeply to relax on all levels
- Protect yourself from energetic intrusion
- Affirm all of the above
- Connect above and below, and let the energy travel through you
- Consult with the familiars/companion spirits on the feasibility or appropriateness of your proposed act of magic
- Decide what you are willing to give in return for the spell working, what can you offer in energetic exchange if your wish is granted (for example, dedicating yourself to a charity if you gain wealth)
- Consider the symbology of your enchantment; its inherent energy or theme
- Observe the seasonal tides, lunar cycle, and consider the right time of day
- Respectfully acknowledge the elemental forces you will be calling on for assistance
- Ask permission from any being, place, or object you may wish to work with or for
- Gather any symbolic objects for focusing on, and keep them apart from external energetic influence
- Consider where the work will be done and make the space sacred in an appropriate way

- Dedicate your enchantment to a spiritual being or to an overall purpose (for example, "As this spell for my healing is begun, so do I dedicate it to the healing of all beings; may my journey be for everyone. As within, so without.")

- Do the practical work (light a candle, sew a symbol on cloth, and so on) while focusing the spiritual intent on the enchantment

- Ground yourself after the magic is undertaken, and write notes

- Speak to no one about what you have undertaken until the spell comes to bear fruit in the world

To conclude, here are two samples of when to do wild magic and how to think of the symbology to use.

When Seeking a New Home

Consider the element of earth. Work with symbology appropriate to putting down roots or seeking shelter. For example, plant a tree seed in the area you wish to live in, or bond with a tree already there, take it a suitably nurturing organic gift, and ask for its roots to be as yours. Make a snail-shell talisman to wear, breathe your wish into it, and seal it up. Undertake a walk with the sacred intent of "going home" to where you wish to be, then carry a token from your current home and leave it at your intended destination. Paint a picture, weave a rug, or make something that you envision being with you in your new home. Consider the fact that every being has its natural place—badger to set, bird to nest— and so have you.

When Seeking Better Health/Healing

Tune in to fire for both vitality and burning away that which is not beneficial, and tune in to earth for physical strength. Work with the symbology of regeneration/rejuvenation . . . of dandelions pushing up through concrete paving, of shoots pushing up through frosted ground, of the sun returning at midwinter/dawn. Nurture a seed as if it were the sick person; plant it outdoors at midsummer. Work with the connection between the sun and the "atomic suns" that fuel our own bodies. Steep a shiny round pebble (to represent our cells and our wholeness overall) in an infusion of marigolds or sunflowers. Remove it and paint a vibrant symbol upon it, then keep it close to you. Make a healing soup to be eaten over three days so that the condition improves daily. To banish the ill health, ask that as the sun grows weaker in the day/year, so may the illness fade away. Bury a burned-down black candle stump or a piece of rotten bark into which all the sensations of ill health have been poured.

You now have a recipe for wild enchantment and the basis for creating your own meaningful green-spirited spells. The emphasis here has been on that eternal blend of safe practice that does not stifle and freedom that does not turn into recklessness. The profound poetic flow of a verdant magical life has been established, and hopefully has inspired the reader to end his or her own estrangement from the enchantment inherent in being incarnate on a generous, living planet. More than this, the union between the manifest realm and that of the unseen has been stressed, with us as their link. The starlit strands that bind free that which is hidden and that which is visible, the ephemeral and the tangible, have been shown to weave straight through our daily lives and onward.

If we take responsibility, following the threads we ourselves weave as they spin outward from our being, as we work with a heart full of rhyme and a good dose of balancing reason, then we have a hope of bringing back that which is considered departed.

Of bringing the magic back to life.

Seeking Magickal Advice

MORGANA SIDHERAVEN

In the previous six chapters, my fellow Collective members have detailed their various methods for constructing and creating personal spells. With this chapter, I have included information I felt would be helpful in further enhancing your spellcasting abilities.

As a magickal shop owner, I get many questions relating to various subjects and situations. What I have included here is information that is not easily found within writings on magickal subjects.

Seeking Magickal Advice

All of us, at some point or another, have sought magickal advice. Knowing where to go, who to speak to, and what to expect can make quite a difference. What follows is some guidance that will help you find an outlet for ethical advice.

Why Seek Advice Elsewhere?

Ultimately, you know best what you should do when it comes to personal spell work, but we all have times in our lives when we are perhaps too close to a situation to see clearly. In a case like this, someone removed from the situation can often be more objective. I can think of many situations where our thought processes are so wrapped up in what we are going through that we can't see the forest for the trees. Love, career, money, and health matters are all areas of life that lie close to our hearts, and can confound us on occasion. Getting some trusted advice or perhaps another perspective can give us the breath of fresh air needed to show us where the path lies.

Where Do You Go?

There are three categories of places you could go to seek magickal advice:

- Psychic or tarot readers
- Magickal supply shops (also called New Age, Occult, or Pagan/Wiccan shops)
- The Internet

Psychic or Tarot Readers

These are the most visibly accessible, found nearly anywhere in the United States. They are "psychic," "tarot," or "palm" readers. I have seen them in tiny little towns and villages in the middle of nowhere, and major cities are rife with them. They can be in tumbledown shacks, middle-income neighborhoods, or with the most exclusive of addresses, in posh highrises or homes in the neighborhoods of the rich and famous. You will find readers in storefront shops, working out of their homes, on call-in telephone lines, or on the Internet.

Most of these places make their money by getting you to part with *your* money! The scenario goes a little like this: you go for a five-dollar psychic, tarot, or palm reading. You are given a slight bit of information that is possibly correct. Eventually you will be told that you have had a curse cast on you. The curse could have been cast directly on you or your family, and will continue to plague you, your family members, and your descendants. The reader will say that he or she is very skilled with the removal of such a curse, and will tell you exactly what the removal involves, including the price for removing the curse. I've heard variations on what the removal entails. Sometimes the reader makes a bath for you to take home and use, or creates a candle for you to light. Sometimes things get more elaborate, and you may be told that you need a full chakra cleansing, perhaps done in the reader's back room. I have even heard of one reader who told a client that she needed to cleanse all of her money and asked the client to bring it in to her! After it was brought in, the money was switched and the client was told not to open the box for a certain period of time. Guess what was in the box? Clue: it wasn't her money! I heard of another story where the reader said she needed to go to Jamaica to consult with a healer there in order to facilitate the removal of the curse. The client was asked to pay all expenses, which included luxury hotel reservations. Consider that this took place during the winter in New York City and you get an even clearer picture of the reader's ethics.

In another scheme, a reader will tell a client that he or she has a black aura that needs to be cleaned immediately or else the client will be plagued with bad luck forever. This scam is similar to the one outlined above. The client is charged according to how much the reader thinks he or she can pay.

The previous situations will also change if a client says he or she cannot pay an exorbitant amount of money. Immediately the price goes down a good deal, and the reader offers a different, less expensive option that supposedly works just as well. (But not as effectively as if you had the big bucks, I'm sure!)

This type of reader is very good at judging a person based on his or her appearance. The reader will observe the client's body language, clothing, jewelry, and note how the client reacts to certain questions as well as the type of questions the client asks. The reader will always ask a lot of questions to try to get more information out of the client. Sometimes the reader may actually have a psychic gift, and this type of reader is even more dangerous, as he or she can pick up on the client's fears and insecurities. Ninety-nine percent of the time, this type of reader is not a legitimate psychic, and is merely running a confidence game. Many do indeed get charged with fraud, and spend time in jail. However, there are many who have done this for years, and because the victims are too embarrassed to go to the police, the readers never get caught and continue to bilk people out of their life savings. Their neon signs luring you in with the prospect of an inexpensive reading will easily clue you in to this type of reader, as will the advertisements promising "FREE psychic reading, call NOW!"

Magickal Supply Shops

The next type of place to seek magickal advice is a magickal supply shop. Most magickal/occult supply shops have readers on hand, or you can book a reading by appointment. As a general rule, the going rate for readings in a magickal shop is one to two dollars a minute, with a minimum reading of fifteen minutes. Usually, fifteen-minute readings cost slightly more per minute than half-hour readings. The readers are usually screened, and generally the setting is very relaxed and private. A bit later I will explain what you can expect from this type of reading.

Magickal supply shops often hold psychic fairs, where you can choose from a variety of readers. Most shops also offer spell-related services such as consultations, readings, hand-carved candles, or even hand-blended charm bags.

The benefit of going to a magickal shop is that the employees are generally very knowledgeable, and their expertise can help guide you to information on just about any topic. The service is more personalized, and you may get some great guidance from a magickal practitioner.

If you have a magickal shop nearby, try to visit first to get an idea of the type of services it offers. Unfortunately, magickal shops are not all run by magickal practitioners, so a little legwork may be required to find a good resource.

The Internet

Regarding the Internet, the best advice I can give is to be wary. The Internet offers some fabulous resources, but also some complete drivel. Unfortunately, it does not provide you with a face-to-face encounter, and there are too many predators out there with hidden agendas.

I ran a search for "spell work" and found close to four thousand websites. Upon further investigation, I realized that most offered plagiarized spells that were taken from popular witchcraft books. There were loads of spell kits to purchase, and I also found many negative spells that entailed controlling people and forcing them to do things against their will. And there were also sites that were set up by people trying to be "authorities" on magick, but in my opinion they didn't seem to have much of a clue!

Try to back up any information found on the Internet with a friend, magickal shop, or book information. Many authors have their own websites that contain wonderful resources for further study, so that would also be a good avenue for advice.

What to Expect

When you go to a legitimate reader, expect to be treated professionally. This isn't to say your reader won't have a sense of humor, sensitivity, or warmth about him or her. Each reader will have his or her own personality and style, but should always be professional.

Never expect to pay more than the amount that was agreed upon. While tips are usually much appreciated, they are optional. If you like the reading, please feel free to offer a tip, but don't feel obligated. In addition, don't feel slighted if the tip is refused. If you are confused about whether to offer a tip, ask the shop owner or manager if it is appropriate. The only case where you should expect to pay more is when you have asked for a longer reading than what was originally agreed upon.

An ethical reader will offer you *guidance*; he or she will never say that something is set in stone and will definitely happen. You always have free will and can change the course your life is taking, and a good reader will point that out. The reader should be positive and show you avenues for change should there be blocks or negativity in your life. An ethical reader will often point out that readings are "for entertainment purposes only," as he or she knows that you have already changed the course your life is taking by sitting down and having a reading! This isn't to say that the reading is a fake; it is to help you understand that you have the choice to change the direction of any course your life may be taking.

Most readers will not offer to do magick for you, but may suggest magickal techniques that could enhance your life, depending upon the situation. The exception to this is a reader who offers a service such as candle carving or making charm bags. The reader may offer to make something for you to use magickally. In that case, he or she will make the item and give it to you with instructions for use. There will be a set price (usually a small amount—where I live, the going rate for hand-carved candles is twenty to forty dollars for a large, seven-day candle), and you are under no obligation to purchase the item.

In a magickal shop, expect similar treatment. The atmosphere is usually pretty relaxed, and the salespeople are friendly. Of course, there are exceptions, and if you don't feel comfortable in a shop, don't patronize it! Always listen to your intuition, and if it doesn't feel right, leave.

Look for salespeople who are informed and helpful. They should be able to help you with the stock by showing you how to use various items, or where you might find the information you are looking for. Ask if they offer any services such as spell consultations, readings, classes, special book searches, and so on. If you like the shop, ask to be added to their mailing list so you can be informed of services, events, or special sales.

Ask for references wherever you go for magickal advice. Usually readers are happy to provide you with a list of places they have worked, or happy customers. In magickal shops, ask the readers where they got their training. I would be wary if they were not willing to provide this information. Keep in mind that they may be very general, as it is not always possible to name names when it comes to many oath-bound traditions.

Expect to pay a cancellation fee if you do not show up for a scheduled reading. The fee will vary from place to place, so be sure to ask in advance what the charges will be. If you wish to reschedule, ask if your fee can be used as a credit toward the new appointment.

Do not expect every reader to be spot on for you. Having a psychic reading is a very personal thing, and some readers will not "click" with you. If you get a very confused reading, or it seems completely off, then chalk it up to experience and try someone else next time.

There are also times when it is difficult for a reader to read a person. Sometimes this is due to the seeker closing off from the reader, because he or she thinks the reader should see and know all. In other cases, it can be too much confusion, and perhaps the seeker is not focused properly.

Do expect a good reader to ask questions for clarification purposes. The reader should not be firing off questions without giving you information as well. Readers will usually preface a question with information they see, but are not clear on. They should not be probing into your personal life by asking embarrassing, intimate questions.

Always follow up any health advice with a health care professional! In addition, a reading should not be used as a therapy session. A reading can be therapeutic (I personally know several professional therapists who use tarot as a therapy tool), but should never take the place of professional therapy.

If you have a terrible experience, complain! If you were treated poorly or the reader behaved in an unethical manner, speak to the owner or manager of the establishment and voice your feelings. If no one is available, send a letter or e-mail, and be sure to mention exactly why your experience was so awful.

Lastly, readers are human and they can be wrong. Take advice from a reader just as you would from anyone else, by weighing out the options and taking a hard look at what was offered to you as advice.

Etiquette

What? Yes, there is definitely etiquette to follow when seeking magickal advice. There are a few things that are considered poor taste, and the following is to give you some general guidance.

Asking someone else to do magick for you is largely considered a great big no-no. Magickal responsibility dictates that any repercussions will fall back on the practitioner as well as the person who asked for the magick to be done. I don't know many people who are willing to take that responsibility for someone they don't know. We'd do it for our nearest and dearest, but for a stranger, no way. I think most of us feel we have enough on our plates, and do not need to add possible negative repercussions! Unless you are involved in the situation, there is simply no way to know all of the factors at play.

Please notice that I said this is *largely* considered bad form. There are also plenty of people who do not have a problem doing magick for others. Personally, I don't want someone else messing with my life, and I would rather take care of things myself. I prefer to empower myself by taking charge, perhaps learning a new magickal technique to aid me in my spell work. Besides, I think most of us would agree that we can mess up our lives fairly well on our own, and don't need additional help in that particular area!

If someone does offer to do magick for you, I honestly would be suspect. If it's a friend or family member, that is fine, but a total stranger is another thing. There are unethical people who would love nothing more than to have power over another person, and this is a perfect opportunity for them to take control. Perhaps you might try looking instead for someone who offers classes in magickal techniques so you can make your own choices.

If you are seeking advice in a magickal shop, please try not to take up too much time. While a magickal shop is there to serve the community, and should be willing to discuss techniques, the shop is also a business and needs to attend to business matters. If you are seeking advice via a reading, then this does not apply since you are paying for the reading—you are essentially paying for the reader's time.

Spell Consultations

Many shops are now offering a service called a "spell consultation." To be perfectly honest, this was developed by shop owners who got tired of people who sought advice but never patronized the shop.

There are people who seek advice from magickal shops, take up large chunks of time, and then walk out the door without purchasing anything or even saying thanks. They sometimes go back to tell how wonderful the advice was, then go on to say, "And, by the way, could you help me with . . . ?" Then, again, they walk out empty-handed! E-mail is another avenue these people like to use.

The problem has escalated to a point where some practitioners feel taken advantage of and abused. In ancient times you were expected to bring some sort of payment when you sought the advice of the local wise woman or cunning man, or you would be asked for something in return for seeking his or her help. If you call your doctor with a medical question, you would surely be told to make an appointment to come in and discuss it, and would be charged for the medical advice.

Experienced magickal practitioners have spent a good deal of time and money educating themselves about various magickal techniques, and their guidance can be invaluable. Many of them now feel that there needs to be an equal energy exchange, and in our modern times, this equals a monetary fee. The interesting thing to note is that while this service was developed to dissuade inconsiderate people, it has actually turned into a viable option for the serious seeker.

Spell consultations work like this: You are charged a fee to consult with a magickal practitioner on spell work specific to your situation. You will be asked in advance what you need help with, and when you arrive for your consultation the practitioner will provide you with a custom-made spell. He or she may ask for additional information to clarify the situation, so be sure to mention any preferences, such as a specific pantheon you work with. You will be given specific directions and a list of items that will be needed to carry out the spell. Your practitioner may also offer alternative spell work you may wish to try, and ways to boost the energy of the spell. This is a great way to get magickal advice customized to your situation by an experienced practitioner.

Try to be considerate. If you sought advice in a magickal shop and were treated nicely and given great guidance, then show your appreciation by purchasing a few things. Patronizing your local shops keeps the money flowing within the community and allows them to continue helping you and others.

As you can see, a little common sense will go a long way in assisting you to find magickal advice. Remember: the best advice you can follow is what you find in your heart. Your instinct will never lead you astray!

Banishing or Binding?

There seems to be much confusion on when and how to use these two types of magick. Let's have a look at what each type of magick is, and how both are best employed in order to understand better the appropriate times for their specific usage.

Banishing

What is a "banishing" spell? A banishing is used when you wish to repel or send something away from you. This type of spell can be brought into play when you wish to get rid of something. I don't mean in a negative way, like getting rid of your boss, but rather in a positive manner, such as doing away with the negativity that exists between you and your boss so that your working relationship may be more pleasant and productive. Bad habits, toxic people and situations, or conditions such as ill health and poverty all work favorably with a banishing spell. You can also utilize a banishing spell to send away unwanted entities such as troublesome ghosts.

How to Create a Banishing Spell

The foundation of a banishing spell is to remove something harmful from your life. So, to begin, you need to focus on your intention.

- Analyze the situation from all angles to be certain that this is the correct course of action. Is there perhaps another type of magick that might be more fitting, such as healing?

- Why do you feel a need to remove this from your life? Are you feeling angry, hurt, victimized? It's always a good idea to institute a cooling-off period after experiencing something that brings on such strong emotions.

- Have you taken any mundane steps to try to rectify the situation? Sometimes the most effective step to take is not magickal at all, but very ordinary.

- Is there any possibility that you are acting in haste and may wish to reverse the spell somewhere down the line? If so, save yourself a lot of annoyance and rethink your strategy.

Now we get to the "meat" part of the spell. What magickal action do you wish to perform? Candle spell? Petition magick? Water magick? Decide what best suits the situation and collect the items (if any) you will need.

The next step would be to envision your life completely devoid of whatever it is you wish to banish. It is important to focus on the end result, as if it has already manifested. Do not feed any negativity into the situation by focusing on that which you would like to banish. The theory behind envisioning your goal as completely manifested comes from quantum physics. The very basic context of this theory is that all time is happening now, and if we tune ourselves in we can "plug into" various planes of existence. Therefore, on a different plane, your goal has already manifested itself.

Once you have your spell planned out, look at the moon and astrological phases. Banishings are best worked when the moon is in the waning phase. Envision the energy flowing away from you as the moon grows smaller in the sky. The dark moon is also an excellent time for banishing magick. Envision the energy completely removed from your life, as the moon appears to have disappeared from the sky.

Sample Banishing Spell

A sample banishing to rid yourself of an unhealthy habit may go like this:

- Write the habit on a piece of paper.
- Write the intention in a positive affirmation, as if it has already manifested.
- Light a candle.
- Focus and meditate on the affirmation while you visualize yourself healthy and free of the unhealthy habit.
- When you feel you are ready to release the energy to the universe, light the paper with the candle flame while stating your affirmation out loud.
- A final statement or affirmation, such as "So mote it be!" can follow.
- Place burning paper in a fireproof cauldron or dish, and allow it to burn out completely.

I have noted an interesting occurrence the few times I have banished toxic people from my life. They show up one last time! It seems to me that when you do a banishing spell on a person, he or she somehow "feels" the magick, and has a need to come and collect the rest of his or her energy! This is the case with people who are magickal practitioners as well as those who aren't. So be prepared for one last encounter, and protect yourself.

Binding

Binding spells are used when you wish to bind a situation, person, or thing to you. There seems to be some confusion about when to do a binding spell, so let me explain my experiences with them.

When you do a binding spell, you bind the energy of the person, thing, or situation to you until you break the bond. I like to think of it as a sort of magickal superglue. Once stuck, it is next to impossible to break that bond. Therefore, if you do a binding to keep a person from doing harm to you, you will be stuck with the troublesome person until you break the bond. Yes, the person will stop doing harm to you, but are you sure you want a tie to him or her? Once you form a bond, it may be quite challenging to break it.

An example of binding magick in a positive form is a Wiccan handfasting ceremony. During the ceremony, the couple's hands are bound together to symbolize their commitment to each other. If they decide to end the relationship, a handparting ceremony is performed. During this ritual, the binding is cut so that the symbolic bond between them that was created during the handfasting is also broken.

Many people argue that bindings are beneficial to stop negative behaviors. Their reasoning is that you simply untie any cords, or dismantle the material used, burn it, and the spell is broken. It is never quite that easy to break the bond of a binding spell; it takes much countermagick to balance things out once again. In my opinion, I think it is wiser to be sure whether or not a binding is precisely the type of magick that needs doing.

A parent may feel a need to do a binding with a child who has a behavioral or health problem in order to keep the parent from being harmed while helping the child with the problem. Or a spouse may feel the need to do the same with his or her significant other, under similar circumstances. In any case, when a binding is employed, it is important to understand that you *must* be willing to see the situation through to the end, and be prepared to do an unbinding spell when the time is right.

To bind a criminal is a popular binding spell. I see things a bit differently, and prefer to create a spell to ensure that the proper authorities catch the criminal with no further harm to innocent victims. I definitely do *not* wish to have the energy of a criminal bound to me, but feel that I have a magickal responsibility to serve my community by ensuring that innocent bystanders are no longer victimized, and the criminal is brought to justice. I feel strongly about crimes perpetuated against people, animals, and the earth, and work for justice in each of those cases.

In the case of abuse, if you are being abused, I do not think it is ever wise to do a binding! First and foremost, follow sound mundane action and get away from the abuser immediately. File police reports, find a safe haven, and seek professional therapy to help you cope and stop the pattern of abuse. Sorry, magick will not stop a bullet, blade, or fist. Once you are safely away, then go ahead and banish the abuser from your life magickally.

How to Create a Binding Spell

When it comes to the subject of bindings, it is important to look deeply at the situation and not act in haste.

Ask yourself a few questions:

- Is this someone I want to have a bond with?
- Would I be better off without this person or thing in my life? If so, then a banishing may be the best course of action.
- Am I willing to see the situation through to the end?

Binding spells utilize different colored cords corresponding to the intention of the spell. Yarn, ribbon, string, and embroidery floss can all be used. So your next step is to choose a cord in a color appropriate to your intention.

When doing a binding spell, envision yourself tying up the problem and keeping it close to your heart. Next, visualize yourself knotting the problem up within the cord, stopping the situation.

The best time to do a binding spell is during the waning moon, up until the dark moon. The waxing period would be a fantastic time to do a binding of a positive nature, such as a handfasting, or a binding as a form of commitment—commitment to a new diet, or determination to finish something started. Working magick of this nature during a new moon is very powerful as well.

Sample Binding Spell

Sample binding to bring a project to completion:

- Get a piece of yarn, ribbon, or cord in a color that represents your goal (for example: yellow for creative projects, green for money, and so on).

- Tie the knots, while saying the corresponding lines:

  First knot: By the knot of one, my project has begun.

  Second knot: By the knot of two, distractions are few.

  Third knot: By the knot of three, my work is glee.

  Fourth knot: By the knot of four, I let it soar.

  Fifth knot: By the knot of five, for excellence I strive.

  Sixth knot: By the knot of six, my goal is fixed.

  Seventh knot: By the knot of seven, it is sent to the heavens.

  Eighth knot: By the knot of eight, it is my fate.

  Ninth knot: By the knot of nine, completion is mine!

- Again state your purpose, and affirm it with, "So mote it be!"

- You can keep the cord either on your altar, in a charm bag, or worn around the wrist or ankle as a reminder of your goal.

- When the project is completed, untie the knots and either bury or burn the cord, while giving thanks to deity for helping you.

Ethics of Banishing and Binding

Every single type of magical act carries the ethical question: "Am I manipulating the free will of another?" With banishing or binding spells that involve other people, we find this a most difficult choice.

We have the right to a happy life, without the antics of negative people to spoil our contentment. However, there is always a downside to either a banishing or binding spell.

When we do either type of spell, we need to keep in mind that both, indeed, manipulate another's free will. With that said, ask yourself if you are willing to accept the responsibility and whatever karmic payback you might experience as a result of this magickal act. Is it worth it? Can you settle the matter without taking such drastic magickal action? Again, look at the situation from all angles, taking your time to see if a binding is what the situation calls for, or if there is some other type of magick that might work more to your advantage.

Binding and banishing spells can be very helpful tools in many diverse areas of your life. Knowing the best way to put them into use will save you from unexpected results and possible unsavory karmic repercussion. When we learn to look at magick from every angle, we begin to see the potential within every situation. Used properly, both binding and banishing spells are helpful tools that can be used to enhance our lives.

Breaking and Reversing Spells

There are two forms of spell reversals. The first type would be to break or ground a spell that you as the magickal practitioner have cast. The second type is reversing or sending back a spell someone else has cast on you.

Breaking a Spell You Cast

We all make mistakes. To err is human, right? Magick is something not to be taken lightly (although it can be fun!), but every so often we react to a situation before sitting down and thinking things through. With the guidance from the various authors found within this book, you can hone your spell skills and learn the importance of planning, so that you will never need this section at all. But what do we do when we really mess up and have cast a spell we want to take back?

Take a Close Look

Sit down and take a very close look at the original spell that was cast.

- At the time you cast the spell, why did you feel that that was the correct avenue to take?
- Were you acting on a strong emotion, without thinking things through?
- Was the spell cast before you were provided with all of the information about the situation?
- Do you feel that you messed up in some way and cast the spell incorrectly?
- Was the original spell not thought through in detail?

It is important to get to the root of why you feel the spell needs to be broken. Write down your findings to help you to figure out the circumstances.

This is a situation where your Book of Shadows will really come in handy. If you took notes when you originally cast the spell, you will have the resource at your fingertips. Your notes may also help to spark any other feelings you might have had when you set out to cast the spell, and may bring added insight to the situation. As you read through your notes, your Book of Shadows may also show the moon and astrological phases that were in effect at the time of the working. This will give you a further look into what you might want to change.

Cover Every Angle

Now that you have the reasons why you cast the spell originally, you need to take some time and ponder each possible manifestation of the spell. While contemplating the possible outcome, make sure to take notes. Look closely to see if the spell really needs to be broken.

Perhaps your present desires are not really that far off from the original intention. On the surface, the situation may seem to have changed drastically, but after dissecting it you may find that at the core the final goal remains the same.

Look at your notes and weigh the pros and cons. If both your intention and the situation remain the same, then you do not need to do a spell to break the original. But if you find that the intention and situation are dramatically different, then you will have to create a spell to break the original.

Deity has a way of getting us to do things that may not make sense, but in the long run are for our benefit. There very well could be an unseen reason why you cast the spell you now believe needs reversing, and it may lie in your best interest to sit tight and wait it out.

Now that you have analyzed the original spell to see if it was indeed miscast, and looked at every possible manifestation of the spell, you are ready to see if you need to do a breaking and grounding spell.

Breaking a Miscast Spell

This method will work if the spell was done incorrectly or if you cast a spell without having all the information at hand. It will not work if the spell was done correctly, but has manifested in a way that is unsatisfactory. Magick *always* works. You may not like the results, but spells work the way they should work. This technique will also work for breaking a spell that was cast on you.

The first thing to do is to ground the energy you created with the first spell. This can be done very simply, with visualization or a few simple props.

You may need some optional items, such as a spray or mister bottle filled with clean, fresh spring water.

Sit quietly and ground. Take a few cleansing breaths to relax your body. If you wish, cast a circle and call the quarters to help you focus and direct the energy.

Once you feel comfortable and relaxed, begin to envision the energy you created with the first spell as a gentle rain cloud gathering over your head. It might help to envision the energy as wind gathering into the cloud.

When you have this picture clearly in your head, envision the rain cloud beginning to drizzle down a gentle cleansing rain upon the earth. You might say something like this:

Here and now I place a call.
Ground this energy for the good of all.
Return to the earth, cleansing and nourishing,
leaving only life enriched and flourishing.
With harm to none, so mote it be!

The most important thing to remember while doing a spell to break up energy is to envision the energy gathered up and then dissipating into something nourishing. I prefer to send energy to the earth, as we all know how badly she needs it; but feel free to send the energy where you feel it may be best utilized—perhaps consider a gentle cleansing rain to enrich and heal the wild animals of the world. Make sure you send the energy to a natural setting; otherwise you might manifest flooding and broken plumbing!

Once you have finished this spell, you may go on to create a new spell to manifest the proper energy needed. Personally, I give myself three days to make any magickal decisions, and I would institute a waiting period rather than beginning another spell right away.

Magickal Loopholes

Many witches build into their spells something that would be considered a "magickal loophole." This can be as simple as a line to ensure that the energy does not turn negative and bring harm, or more elaborate such as timing the spell to conclude at a specific point.

The following popularly used loophole line is attributed to the late Sybil Leek: "May this spell not reverse, nor bring upon me any curse." This gives the practitioner a kind of magickal insurance against possible mishaps he or she may not have foreseen.

"With harm to none, and for the good of all" is another common loop-hole that comes to us via the Wiccan Rede. Again, this is to prevent any unforeseen negative manifestations of a spell.

Another option is to set the spell to conclude at a specific time. This is employed as a technique for two specific reasons. The first, most obviously, is that you have a time limit and need the spell to manifest within a certain time frame. The second reason would be that the situation is so volatile that it can change drastically from the time you cast the spell to the time it will manifest. Timing a spell is done very easily—simply state the time you wish the spell to conclude. Additionally, adding a line or two regarding where the energy should go should the spell not manifest completely will give further magickal insurance against errant results.

It is important to remember that using these magickal loopholes without forethought may still muddle and confuse your results. They should be used when you have thought carefully about your spell, and not with abandon. The gods know when we are sincerely seeking positive change and can be quite forgiving. But they will also send us challenges or, as the saying goes, a "cosmic clue by four" to thump us on the head and force us to take heed and pay closer attention.

Things to Remember

- Think long and hard before casting any spells to be sure you have investigated all the angles.

- Trust your instincts. If deep down you feel you need to do or not do magick for a situation, *listen*!

- Divination helps a lot of people decide if they should or shouldn't do magick. Try to familiarize yourself with at least one form of divination that can be used as a tool to help you make the best magickal choices.

- Don't forget to leave yourself a magickal loophole!

Detecting Magick

I am a fairly practical witch, and instead of suspecting that magick is involved in all occurrences, I tend to look for ordinary reasons for things happening as they do. In my experience, 99 percent of the time there wasn't a nasty curse placed; it is simply life serving us another lesson we need to look at and learn from. However, there are cases where some unbalanced person is going about casting wicked spells on people, and if you live in an area with a lot of "witch wars" going on, you could possibly get caught in the crossfire!

Divination can help you to discern whether or not a spell has been cast on you. If you seek a reading from someone else, please go to an ethical reader to be sure you do not get sucked into a scam where the reader sees a curse that was not otherwise there!

Do not discount your instinct. If you have a strong gut feeling that something was done, then it could very well be the case. Make sure to view the feeling as dispassionately as possible, so that you can discover where your feelings may be coming from.

You may also have physical evidence of a curse or negative spell having been cast on you. If so, destroy the item immediately. Burn, bury, or throw it in moving water, off your premises, as soon as possible!

Reversing a Spell Cast on You

There are various techniques for reversing energy that has been sent to you. These can be broken down into two categories: grounding and returning.

Grounding Spells

Grounding energy can be done as described under the Breaking a Miscast Spell section (page 228). Many people do not feel comfortable returning negative energy that was sent their way. If you feel this way, you may use the technique described in the aforementioned section for collecting and grounding the energy. Protection spells cast for yourself, loved ones, and home or business may also be employed to boost your intention. There are books written specifically about protection spells, so I will not repeat any protection spells here. Refer to Resources on page 257 to see a list of many books you might find helpful.

Additionally, you may wish to create a shield to keep from being on the receiving end of any negative spells. Our astral and physical bodies have natural defense mechanisms, and consciously creating a shield is simply a booster. This can be done with visualization. Envision a shield surrounding your whole body. The shield can be made from any protective material you wish, such as armor. Work at keeping the shield up around you, starting at first with short periods and later building to longer periods. Eventually, you will be able to pull the shield up quickly without much forethought.

The only problem you may encounter with shields is that you may create a shield so strong that positive energy can't get through. Go back to your visualizations and see any positive energy as a type of refreshing and energizing mist that can permeate anything. Working on this a little should clear up the problem and allow the positive to flow through your life.

Returning-to-Sender Spells

Personally, I have no problem returning negative energy that was sent to me. But then again, I have no problem returning an unwanted gift! It is extremely important to remember not to add to the negativity when you are returning to the sender, even though you may be angry or distressed. Send back only what was sent to you, otherwise you will perpetuate a cycle of negativity and will have to deal with receiving back what you sent out.

A shield made of mirrors facing outward can be employed as a technique to return a spell back to the sender. Envision your shield constructed of mirrors facing outward, so that anyone looking at you is instead seeing himself or herself. This method is simple and very effective; you will find that the negativity stops pretty quickly once the sender realizes what is happening.

Rubberized shields can be used to great effect as well. Simply envision your shield rubberized, and everything bounces back to the sender.

To best illustrate how to create a return-to-sender spell, I will use a very simple childhood rhyme that nearly every child knows. "I'm rubber, you're glue. Whatever you say bounces off me and sticks to you!" Change the words slightly, and you have a great return-to-sender spell: "I'm rubber, you're glue. Whatever negativity you send bounces off me and sticks back to you. So mote it be!" I know this seems a bit sophomoric, but since just about everyone knows that saying, it becomes even more effective with the power boost of a collective consciousness! (Besides, kids do the best magick without intellectualizing!)

Methodically thinking magick through is a skill that will serve you well. It becomes easier with time, as you condition yourself to ponder every possible angle and manifestation. When you have honed this skill, you will be able to create effective magick quickly and simply without having to resort to grounding the energy. And you will not have to send negativity back, as you will be prepared to keep it from permeating in the first place. Think first, cast later!

The Choir Sings

THE SPELLWEAVER COLLECTIVE

We began this book with a concern about how magic and spells are portrayed and marketed, and with an invitation to experience spellcraft as an all-encompassing spiritual path. Throughout this book there are unique perspectives and paths, preferred tools, pantheons, and timings, but there is also an openness and willingness to embrace others' ways of working. We wanted to offer you the chance to explore our worlds and beliefs, to share what we have learned, to offer you the benefit of our experiences. We hope that what you have found in these pages inspires you to explore your own ways of working.

There is already a broad range of "how-to's" on the market, varying from quick fixes to the elitist writings that deter the beginner. We felt it was necessary to redress the balance a little by exploring exactly what spells are and why we work them: what we believe about how they work, the ways we construct and perform them, and the ethical considerations. All these things are bound up in our personal beliefs about the world we see around us, what we believe about ourselves, the teachings we have received, our history and philosophies.

There are many books, Internet sites, and other inspirations that we have found useful whilst walking our respective paths, and for those we refer you to our Resources section.

We may honour different gods and goddesses, use different magical systems, techniques, and language, but essentially we are all following a path set by nature. All of us have been drawn to the rhythm of life—the planetary movements, the phases of the moon, the daily and seasonal tides. This is an extraordinary gift that all of us have worked hard to attain and appreciate being able to sense. It is a gift that everyone has inside, and is not reserved for the select few. We recognise that we are *part of* nature. Like the phases of the moon, each of us expresses a unique energy, yet we cannot be separate nor separated from each other nor the rest of life.

For all of us, there is a sense that magic is with us every day. Magic is a prayer, a wish, a yearning for change, a ritual putting on of our lucky socks. Magic is in everything we do and think, and sometimes we are unconsciously working it. Magic is carefully planned rituals and impromptu castings. Magic can be immediate and direct, or gentle and worked over a period of time. Magic is deep, instinctive, Otherworldly, and ordinary. It is natural rather than supernatural.

> *Magick is a deeply personal thing; it is something that most people do unconsciously all of their lives, instinctively, and without any need to be taught or told when to do it.*
>
> —MARTIN WHITE

Magic isn't something locked into the past. Nor should we seek to imitate the past. We can seek to eke out the teachings of our ancestors and see what works for us in the here and now. Some of us are drawn to the ancient ways and beliefs because we can see the intrinsic value and values within them. Sometimes this can lead to the belief that we are somehow out of touch with the modern-day world. In society today it is all too easy to feel divorced from the natural forces at work, to be shielded from the ravages of nature, to forget, ignore, or simply not have time for the natural rhythms. In turn, this sense of separation has caused great harm to the planet, and also to our own evolution. The ways of science and magic and idealism and reality do not have to be at odds. Like the Crone who has seen and witnessed aeons of experience, so each of us can learn from experience. Society is not something outside of us—*we* are society. We are here and now, and our history (herstory) has brought us here.

The Path

Throughout these pages there are many paths within the path. Inspiration comes from Gardenarian and Alexandrian witchcraft, Traditional British witchcraft, Wicca, druidry, northern traditions, shamanism, Western Mystery Tradition, wildcraft, Fae, and Hermeticism. Beyond these there are many other paths. Among us, we are drawn to certain magical systems that have aided us on our journeys—runes, the tarot, astrology, numerology, herbs, healing, and dreams. We have been taught by both physical teachers and those who work in the unseen worlds, and are in gratitude to both. We have recorded our experiences, made mistakes, reached plateaus in learning, and climbed further again. Magic has not made our lives "perfect." Instead, magic has offered us a way to live life with appreciation.

Magic is a fully comprehensive system of living and life. There is a consensus among us that we all sense a presence, an intelligent force that resides both within and without. Some of us refer to this as Deity/Creator. Some name this deity using gods and goddesses from particular pantheons—Celtic, Norse, British. Some of us choose not to name this intelligence but appreciate it symbolically, maybe choosing names that represent specific attributes that we connect with—or need to connect with. Creation can be unknowable yet tangible. There is an overwhelming sense of reverence and awe in all cases.

With these thoughts of Deity/Intelligence in mind, all of us describe or implicitly refer to the Web of Life, the Greater or Cosmic Pattern, and it is this that we work with in our spellweaving. It is precisely this attachment and connection between all things that offers the ability to cast spells. Spells are often seen in isolation from all other aspects of the Craft, yet in many ways spells are an extension of living a magical life.

This part of the divine within everyone and everything is connected by a series of fibres and forms a web of being, a net of power that links and gives life to the cosmos.

—ANNA FRANKLIN

The Craft

What Are Spells?

We are in agreement that spells are the ability to manifest our will. We believe that by focusing intent, raising energy, and directing that intent, our vision will become visible. Many of us refer to the macrocosm and microcosm, the "as above, so below" principle that illustrates that what happens on one level happens on another level. What we create on the inside is what we create outside. We are all aware of the invisible worlds, the unseen astral realms and other dimensions as well as this earthly physical plane. For some of us this physical realm is not "fixed." It vibrates at a slower rate than other realms, but it is still malleable.

A consensus is found in our belief that magic is neither good nor bad, black nor white. It is simply a force or energy that is neutral, in the same way that the weather does not have intention—it just is. The positives and negatives are an implication of the intent of the practitioner or the possible consequences of action. For some, "black" magic may be a description used when someone meaningfully does a spell to cause harm to another. For others, not only does this apply, but they also believe that even if the intent were "good," a spell that changes some aspect of another's life without his or her request is still considered harm. In either case, it is something that must be decided by each individual.

What Are the Natural Laws?

There are certain laws in the universe—karmic laws, laws of destiny and alignment—that cannot be broken. There are patterns in the great cosmic web that must remain as they are.

—LEAH WHITEHORSE

In our experience we have learned that there are certain natural laws that must be taken into account when practising spellcraft. The following is a summary of those laws.

- There is an innate balance within the universe.
- Magic takes the path of least resistance.
- You cannot break the laws of the physical universe.
- Magic is not an exact science—people use different methods for the same results.
- Magic comes at a price—there are always consequences, and you don't get something for nothing.
- For every action there is a reaction.

What Are the Ethical Laws?

Because magic touches the sacred, it should only be put to sacred use.

—ANNA FRANKLIN

The Law of Return

The ethical laws we have discussed in our individual chapters for the most part centre around the nature of harm. In the natural laws, "For every action there is a reaction" is the natural law connected to the ethical law commonly termed the Law of Threefold Return. This is an ethic held strongly by the Wiccan community.

Some of us differ on the interpretation of this law. In the wider community there are some who do not recognise the natural law of return at all, and therefore have few ethical dilemmas when considering the intention of their magic. However, I think it is safe to say in our combined experience that many magical practitioners do have ethical considerations, and we would advise that path.

When we harm one on the web of life we harm all by connection.
The energy of harm is sent into the world. It is that simple.

—POPPY PALIN

It seems we are in unity that "For every action there is a reaction," but whether this return is tripled or not is debated. For some, the threefold refers to physical, spiritual, and karmic; for others, simply three times the energy (positive or negative) is returned. For others still, this tripling of energy seems to go against the natural principle of balance in the universe—that what energy is put out comes back in equal measure. It has also been suggested that as magic is linked with the divine it attempts to work in service to the world, regardless of what the practitioner seeks to achieve. It is perhaps only in belief and experience that you can decide which are the right interpretations for you.

Magic Is a Last Resort

Despite encouragement from the various products on the market, magic is not a quick fix. It is not to be used in lieu of effort. Our voices sing in a chorus here that one cannot consider magic until all other avenues are entirely closed. Even then, it is wise to spend time in further consideration to make sure that what you believe about your situation is actually the truth.

Certainly there are times when magic can and must be performed on the spot—such as when in immediate danger, for example. However, even then it is wise to run first!

Why Do We Do Spells?

There are as many reasons why people decide to perform spells as there are people in the world, but here are the most common reasons:

- To bring ourselves in line with universal patterns
- To remove blockages and obstacles
- To find things hidden or lost
- To manifest change internally and externally
- To bring forth in us capabilities shrouded by fears

- To emphasise abilities we already have
- To encourage personal development emotionally, physically, intellectually, or spiritually
- To protect ourselves, others, and places
- To return unwanted energies from others
- To cast out illness or negativity
- To commune with Otherworldly entities
- To unite mind, body, and spirit
- To transform some aspect of ourselves or our lives

How Do We Perform Spells?

The theory behind envisioning your goal as completely manifested comes from quantum physics. The very basic context of this theory is that all time is happening now, and if we tune ourselves in we can "plug into" various planes of existence. Therefore, on a different plane, your goal has already manifested itself.

—MORGANA SIDHERAVEN

For some of us spells have become a part of everyday life, a knowing and attunement to the cosmic pattern. For all of us, however, there are perhaps still times when we wish to cast a specific spell, and despite differing ways of practicing, our spellweaving processes are remarkably similar. Here we have summarized the main aspects of each part of that process.

The Reason

Think first, cast later!

—MORGANA SIDHERAVEN

Be sure of your intention. Think about why you want to do a spell. Have you tried all avenues open to you? Look deeply into yourself. Is there internal conflict about what you desire? Is what you want to do appropriate and ethical? Is the focus of the spell a want or a need? What would you offer the universe in exchange for your desire?

Meditate or sleep on the problem. Listen to your dreams. Divine using runes, tarot, or another magical system. Consult people recommended to you, such as a reader or magical shop owner, if you feel too emotionally involved to be detached from the problem. Do a pathworking or visualization to consult with your own guides, familiars, power animals, or ancestors. Consider the type of magic you will do, and carefully consider if you are thinking of binding, banishing, or reversing. Also think long and hard before casting a spell for someone else.

> *Sometimes we aren't meant to ask for certain things, as life has other*
> *things in store for us on our path, and it is good to know this, too.*
>
> —POPPY PALIN

The Goal

Once you are clear that you wish to do the spell, you need to set a clear goal that can preferably be reduced into a simple phrase, poem, or chant. Try not to make the spell too restrictive. Think of what precautions you can take to remove unnecessary risks and harmful consequences, such as employing the use of "magical loopholes" or the "harm none" adage. Consider whether you want to add a time limit to the spell: "I need this to manifest by October 7," for example.

The Ways

Once you clearly know the purpose of your spell, consider how you are going to do it. Are you going to use visualization alone, or sympathetic or contagious magic? Look at the correspondences that have an affinity with your goal. Ask permission from the spirit of the objects you wish to use, such as crystals and herbs. Remember that in sympathetic magic, like attracts like. How can you symbolize your spell becoming manifest? Work with those things that you feel comfortable with rather than simply using what is suggested in a book. Really *feel* that what you are using is right for you, and understand why you are using it. Consider colour, symbols, oils, herbs, incense, numbers, tarot cards, runes, and so on.

The Tools and Consecration

What tools, if any, do you wish to use? Some typical magical implements include candles, athame, cauldrons, and cords. Any items you wish to use need to be cleansed and consecrated before casting a spell. Once blessed, keep them apart from other objects.

The Timing

As we have seen discussed in these pages, timing can be a very important factor. Even with spells cast immediately without planning, the tides of the universe may dictate whether that spell works.

Consider the rhythms you attune to—daily, lunar, seasonal, natural rhythms such as weather phenomena, or animal or bird movements. Planetary and other cosmic events may also be considered.

The Purification

Where will the work be done—outside or inside? Preferably it will be somewhere you can be safe and secluded. Make the space sacred in an appropriate way. Some people sweep widdershins just before the ritual to clean away negative vibrations. Rooms or areas can be smudged using sound, incense, or movement. Salt and healing energy such as Reiki may also be appropriate.

For yourself, purification may be through abstinence from toxins such as caffeine, fasting, or bathing using ritual oils.

The Protection

All of us work within a circle—even if it is a quick and simple circle of protection cast over ourselves in the street. The circle represents eternity, equality, wholeness, and perfection. The circle is a sacred space between the worlds—a place to contain the energy you raise and repel any negative entities or energies.

A circle can be cast with a wand, finger, or purely with the mind, from east to east in a deosil (sunwise) motion. It may be a white light, a blue-gold flame, a silver cord. You may call on elementals to watch over you, guardians, and deities. This is always done with great respect and recognition that none of these beings is at our beck and call.

The Energy

> Whether we are wide-eyed in wonder or moved to the core, we
> must feel whatever we do.
>
> —POPPY PALIN

The energy of the spell comes through you from the universe. You are a conduit, a channel. It is very unwise to use your own energy in a spell. That way leads to depression and sickness. Power comes from the universe, the elementals, guardians, and deities.

Energy can be raised through the drum, chant, rattle, circle dance. Energy can be transferred to the object/focus of your spell by shouting or pointing or touching. Energy can be released into the universe by burning a piece of paper with a spell written on it.

The Afterward

- Ground any excess energy by putting your hands onto the floor.
- Remember to thank all entities for attendance.
- Snuff out (don't blow) candles, and either draw back the circle or leave it to dissipate. Eating or drinking a little can help you reconnect with the physical world. Dispose of items used in the appropriate way.
- We are in agreement here that it is wise to keep silent about your spell until it has come to pass. Make notes of your experiences, but endeavor to release the spell from your mind.

The Manifestation

If you haven't set a time limit within your spell, expect to wait at least one lunar cycle, sometimes three. Sometimes a whole season's passing is necessary. Remember that the concept of time is very different in the Otherworlds. Be patient. Spells can be repeated, but you need to consider why they may not have worked in the first place.

Once a spell does manifest, any objects you still have linked to the spell need to be disempowered.

Raising an Octave: Transformation

> . . . by utilising an expanding vocabulary of symbols in our magic, we begin to initiate deep changes within ourselves that have far-reaching effects on our psyches, leading to growth and change, whether or not that was our original intent.
>
> —ELEN HAWKE

Without exception, we have discovered that walking a magical path has changed us. The practice of spellweaving not only changes things in the outer world, but also the inner world. As you begin to walk the path it is natural to question such things as:

- Is there a creator?
- Where does this energy come from?
- How do spells work?
- What is my place in the world?
- What is my service?
- What are my gifts?
- What do I believe about myself?

The process of casting a spell in itself changes you. You change via a deeper understanding of the forces of life, a formalization of your beliefs about how the universe works, and, ultimately, you choose who you are. The process is never complete. There is always more to learn and experience.

The primary business of the magician is the transformation of the magician himself.

—ANNA FRANKLIN

Solo Voices

It is not to walk the path; it is to become the path.

—ANNA FRANKLIN

. . . magickal practise is an extremely viable way for people to make direct contact with deity, and discover for themselves what that word really means to them.

—MARTIN WHITE

Magick will not stop a bullet, blade, or fist.

—MORGANA SIDHERAVEN

Magic impels; it does not compel.

—MARTIN DUFFY

Perhaps it could be said that the journey of a witch is toward self-healing, self-understanding, and self-acceptance—being wise within and without.

—LEAH WHITEHORSE

Wildwitches consider the Craft to be part of them—not only some-thing that they do but something that they are.

—POPPY PALIN

Be a conscientious magician with an awareness of the earth we live on, as well as respecting the rights of other people. Consider not only what you can take from the world, but what you can give to it.

—ELEN HAWKE

Magic comes in many forms and guises—each time wearing the face of those who seek to add an extra harmony to the eternal chorus of the universe. Your magic wears your face: the face you show to the outside world and the face that only you (and the gods) see. If you have seen a picture that shows a human face made symmetrical through reflection, you would have seen that there are subtle differences in the left and right side. No face is symmetrical, no face completely balanced. In both magic and life we strive for balance.

Walking the magical path is like walking into a hall of mirrors. You will be taught to see yourself from all different angles. You will see the things you loathe about yourself and the things you love, and you will learn to see those aspects that you were previously blind to.

Your magic is like a gene weaving its way throughout the body of time and space. It bears an imprint of you and carries a potential. Like a baby that carries the genes of its mother and father, your magic is an unknown quantity until it is made manifest on this place; until it matures. The innocent babe can grow up to become a Nobel Peace Prize winner or a warmonger, depending upon the kind of nurturing the baby receives from his or her parents, peers, and the wider world, as well as the baby's own internal genetic pattern. Nature and nurture create anew.

Your spell's intent is the vision of what might be and how you would like it to be, rather like the new parents' as they gaze into the newborn's eyes. We learn discipline and structure, read to increase our knowledge, and practice what feels right for us. Yet amidst this is the incredible human desire to be free, to guide without restricting, to allow the personality to develop unhindered, to revel in inspired thought, action, and discovery. Sometimes life and magic are about taking a risk, the risk to simply be who you are.

We are seven faces in the endless diversity of humankind, and our intention has been to share some of the things we have learned along the way. Our Magical Ways as described in these pages say as much about us as people as they do about spellcrafting. They say something of our uniqueness, yet also express a commonality. Our words are stones cast into the ocean of knowledge; our thoughts ripple toward you. They may make waves, and you can choose to dive over or under them, or simply let them wash over you.

Like the seven colours of the rainbow we bow to our teachers—those who have walked ahead of us and those who will follow. Refracted light is a part of the whole. We are all both light and prism.

Maybe you have already found a voice you resonate with, but be open to new voices. As ever, be tuned in to that internal voice that whispers deep inside of you, for it is the one that all others need to harmonise with.

End Word

It is clear that the paths to successful magic are many and varied. Each has its own song to sing, each has its own wisdom to impart to the open-hearted seeker of the truth. It may have struck you that although the tune and feel of each path may be different, often the lyrics or what is being said have a consistent theme.

By now you should have realised that real magic involves hard work and persistence to achieve results, and that there are no quick fixes; that real magic involves an exchange of energy, and that nothing is for nothing; that real magic has consequences that need careful consideration before casting spells; and that the act of becoming involved with real magic often changes the budding magician on a deep and spiritual level.

We hope that you, the reader, have enjoyed the journey through these pages, and that you have found something within them that resonates with you and inspires you to create your own magic. Whether it be the silky, flowing prose of natural magic, the beautiful symmetry of Hermeticism, the wild call of the north, or the simplicity and structure of the Wiccan path, we hope that you have been inspired to believe in your own judgment—to believe in yourself enough to put aside the prewritten off- the-peg spell and instead let your own creativity shine through, forging effective spells, tuning in to *your* specific needs.

Most of all, though, we hope that this book has made you really *think* about magic and spells for yourself, and to question received wisdom, especially where it jars with your own intuition. We at the Spellweaver Collective wish you well for the future, whatever path you tread, because for the magical current to remain healthy and vibrant, it needs nourishing with new thoughts and ideas. In this sense you are all the future . . .

Blessings.

Author Biographies

Leah Whitehorse

Leah is a writer, musician, singer, dreamwalker, healer, and witch. She is inspired by nature—the woods, the sea, and she listens to the whisper of the stars wheeling above. Her path is eclectic, influenced by shamanic practice, druidry, and Wicca.

Her writing credits include contributions to *Praise to the Moon*, by Elen Hawke, *Sacred Hoop Magazine,* the newsletter of TABI (Tarot Association of the British Isles), as well as her own website.

Away from the keyboard she has run workshops and given talks in the northwest of England on a variety of topics: practising witchcraft, astrology, tarot, healing, shamanism, and dreams. She has run several self-help groups in Manchester; in these groups, people with mental health needs are able to express and discuss their own spiritual experiences and beliefs in a safe place. She has also appeared on Radio 5 Live's show *Afterhours*.

She tends to follow her own path. Dreams are what brought her to this journey, and these remain her personal passion. She lives in Manchester, UK, but her soul is still running in the fields—true to her Romani heritage.

Elen Hawke

Elen is a British witch living in Oxford, England. She has studied many religious paths, among them Hinduism, Buddhism, Taoism, Gnosticism, and Druidry (in which she was initiated to Ovate grade). She is a Craft elder, a Wiccan initiate, a professional astrologer and tarot reader, and a professional illustrator and photographer, producing work with a strong pagan theme.

Elen is the author of four books by Llewellyn: *In the Circle: Crafting the Witches' Path*, *The Sacred Round: A Witch's Guide to Magical Practice*, *Praise to the Moon: Magic & Myth of the Lunar Cycle*, and *An Alphabet of Spells*. She is a regular contributor of both articles and illustrations (including cover art) for the *Children of Artemis Witchcraft & Wicca Magazine* and a contributing columnist for the award-winning online magazine *Echoed Voices*.

Martin White

Martin is a professional tarot and rune reader, and is also a Reiki master. He runs courses in meditation and relaxation throughout Britain for adult education, as well as for a local charity that supports handicapped people. He lives in a wonderful part of England: at the edge of the peak district in Derbyshire.

Martin formally studied the Western Mystery Tradition with Marian Green, and owes her a huge debt of gratitude for sharing her wisdom and guidance over the past few years. Although he avidly reads anything and everything occult, he has a particular interest in the Norse/Saxon pantheon of gods as well as the runes, and this heavily influences his approach to magic. This is not to say that he is exclusively of the Northern Tradition, nor is he a purist in any sense. For Martin, a spell is judged not by its prose or aesthetic quality, but by its results alone, and to get those results he will happily mix and match from a variety of sources.

He is a member of the Pagan Federation, and runs a small training group for people interested in ritual.

He also favours the use of amulets and talismans, and finds them an excellent focus for spellcasting. His "angle," therefore, is the creation of amulets and talismans empowered by runic script and the old gods of the north, which may then be used as a magical lens to focus the mind. One thing he has come to realise is that the practice of truly effective magic and self-transformation go hand in hand.

Martin Duffy

Martin lives on the south coast of Sussex, in the south of England, with his partner, Dan, and his Jack Russell, Lucy. Although he is essentially a solitary practitioner at heart, he runs a small coven that practices its craft at sacred sites in the Sussex countryside.

Professionally, he is a holistic therapist (qualified in beauty therapy, aromatherapy, reflexology, Indian head massage, kinesiology, and electrolysis), and in this field he has an extensive knowledge of both technique and esoteric philosophy (subtle bodies, chakras, meridians, elemental theory, the four humours, polarity, and so on). He is a member of the Federation of Holistic Therapists, which represents the International Federation of Health & Beauty Therapists, the subsidiary body of which Martin is a member. Outside of this his time is nearly entirely devoted to witchcraft and the teaching of it (with the occasional bit of violin playing!).

Martin is quite fortunate to have been exposed to much local folklore and the odd bit of paganism in his formative years, and this has flavoured his path. He works with local deities, utilises country folk magic, and has a keen interest in his local landscape and its places of power. His craft also has undertones of West Country witchcraft, shamanism, and Celtic spirituality. He likes to experiment with his own ideas, most notably the incorporation of hermetics and occult philosophy into an earthy path.

Anna Franklin

Anna Franklin lives in a village in the English Midlands. She is the High Priestess of the Hearth of Arianrhod and a Third Degree witch. She has been a priestess of the British Pagan Tradition since the age of eighteen, initially training with first a Gardnerian/Alexandrian coven, learning the craft of herbalism and healing, and then the Hearth of Brighid, a traditional coven of the Coranieid, under Sara and Phil Robinson. Anna founded The Hearth of Arianrhod, a coven of the Coranieid, in 1986. The Hearth runs training and teaching circles, discussion groups, and postal networks for distant members. It also publishes a pagan magazine, founded in 1988, called *Silver Wheel*.

Anna trained initially as a photographer and artist, gaining an honours degree in fine art in 1980. She worked as a photographer, illustrator, and community artist, exhibiting and teaching both subjects. In the mid-1980s she found that the spiritual side of her life began to push itself more and more to the forefront of her activities, and she was soon a familiar sight at many psychic fairs with the Silver Wheel Craft Supplies stall, selling occult goods, homemade incenses and magical oils, and reading the tarot. She retrained as a therapist in reflexology and aromatherapy, the better to help the people she came into contact with, and with Sue Phillips and Amazon Riley she opened the Holistic Healing Centre.

Anna now spends much of her time contributing articles to other pagan magazines, and writing pagan books.

Poppy Palin

Poppy is a qualified and experienced artist, writer, tattooist, and teacher who illustrates her own work. Her *Waking the Wild Spirit Tarot*, a combination of magical fiction and inspirational artwork, is published by Llewellyn. She is an illustrator for magazines such as *The Triple Spiral, Wood and Water,* and *Enhancing Your Mind, Body, Spirit.* Her artwork graced the first front cover of *Pentacle*, a new pagan magazine.

Poppy illustrated Rae Beth's book *The Hedge Witch's Way*. She has written and illustrated four nonfiction books on her life and work as a natural psychic, all published by Capall Bann. Her most recent books include *The Greening*, the first of her series of enchanting fiction, *Craft of the Wild Witch*, and *Wild Witchcraft*. For fun, she writes modern horror fiction.

Poppy currently lives in Glastonbury, UK, but hopes to escape with both her cat and her sanity in the near future.

Morgana SidheRaven

Morgana owns Morgana's Chamber, a Pagan/Wiccan shop in New York City, along with her husband. She's been studying witchcraft-related subjects since the late 1970s and practicing as a witch since the early 1980s. In 1997 she became part of the Black Forest Clan, headed by Silver RavenWolf. She works both solitary and with a coven. Her path has been blessed with many wonderful Craft teachers and Elders, both in New York City and the surrounding area, and in the UK, who have given their knowledge and guidance freely and humbly. For this, she is forever in their debt, and hopes she has made them proud.

Shortly after opening the shop, Morgana created and wrote a unique ongoing series of basic and intermediate level classes called Witch Workshops, designed specifically for Solitary Eclectic use. Morgana has taught hundreds of people with these Witch Workshops and has also taught classes in Connecticut and New Jersey. She is a certified Usui Reiki Master Teacher. Her recipes and spells are published in *Silver's Spells for Protection*, *Silver's Spells for Prosperity*, *Silver's Spells for Love*, and *Halloween*, all by Silver RavenWolf. She has been featured in articles that appeared in the *New York Times*, *New York Post*, *New York Daily News*, *Village Voice*, *New York Resident*, UK and Australian editions of *New Woman* magazine, *Italian Vogue*, and the German magazine *Brigitte*.

She is currently working on a book of incense, oil, and herbal charm recipes. The most magical part of her life is her family.

Resources

General Witchcraft and Paganism Organisations

British Druid Order

www.druidry.co.uk

P.O. Box 1217

Devises, Wiltshire

SN10, 4XA

Great Britain

SparrowHawk@britishdruidorder.co.uk

An organisation that honours native British spirituality. Produces a quarterly journal called *Tooth and Claw*. Coordinates a network of Groves and Seed-groups and organises events.

Children of Artemis

www.witchcraft.org

On- and offline organisation for witches. Promotes a positive understanding of the Craft, an ethical approach to practice, and offers a safe place to network. Large online community and lots of resources available. Produces the magazine *Witchcraft and Wicca*.

Liferites
www.liferites.org

An organisation to serve people who wish to celebrate the important times in life and also death. Liferites is not an exclusively pagan organisation but caters to people who follow nature-based spiritualities. Training to become a celebrant is also available.

Order of Bards, Ovates and Druids (OBOD)
http://druidry.org

Members of the Order follow a path of training in three stages: Bard, Ovate, and Druid. The Order also holds events and camps for members.

The Pagan Federation
www.paganfed.demon.co.uk

Promotional and educational organisation for pagans. Produces *Pagan Dawn* magazine.

WiccaUK
www.WiccaUK.com
BM WiccaUK
London
WC1N 3XX
England

WiccaUK is a networking organisation for Wiccans, witches, and pagans in the UK whose aim is to provide a safe and secure networking platform (both in real life and online) and to promote acceptance of pagan beliefs in the UK.

Books

Adler, Margot. *Drawing Down the Moon.* Boston: Beacon Press, 1986.
An exploration of neo-paganism in the United States today.

Agrippa, Henry Cornelius. *Three Books of Occult Philosophy.* St. Paul, MN: Llewellyn Publications, 1994.
A fantastic resource for discovering much of the occult philosophy that underlies modern magic thought.

Ashcroft-Nowicki, Doloris. *The Ritual Magic Workbook: A Practical Course in Self-Initiation.* Wellingborough, Northamptonshire: Aquarian Press, 1986.
A full year of training in ceremonial magical practice.

Bardon, Franz. *Initiation Into Hermetics.* Salt Lake City: Merkur Publishing, 2001.
This book contains a brief outline of some of the basics of hermetic thought and contains a vast programme of exercises to help develop abilities useful for occult activities.

Beth, Rae. *Hedgewitch: A Guide to Solitary Witchcraft.* London: Robert Hale, 1995.
Written in the form of letters to two apprentices, this book explores the path of the solitary.

———. *The Hedge Witch's Way.* Illustrated by Poppy Palin. London: Robert Hale, 2002.

Budepest, Zsuzsanna E. *The Grandmother of Time.* New York: HarperSan-Francisco, 1989.
A month-by-month guide to the Goddess; celebrations, rituals, spells, and personal reflections from the author.

———. *Grandmother Moon.* New York: HarperSanFrancisco, 1991.
An exploration of the thirteen full and new moons that occur each year to help women tap in to their own connection with the lunar goddess. Contains spells, rituals, and personal reflections from the author.

Crowley, Aleister. *Magick.* Book 4. York Beach, ME: Red Wheel/Weiser, 1998.
Contains loads of material for practical use in magic, and gives the reader plenty to think about (not really for beginners!).

Farrar, Janet, and Stewart Farrar. *The Life and Times of a Modern Witch.* London: Headline, 1987.
Answers the questions most people ask about living the life of a Witch.

Fitch, Eric L. *In Search of Herne the Hunter.* Chieveley, UK: Capall Bann, 1994.
Covers the lore and legends of the British god of witches.

Flowers, Stephen. *Fire & Ice*. St. Paul, MN: Llewellyn Publications, 1994.
Covers German occultism from the early twentieth century, in particular the activities and rituals of the influential Fraternis Saturni.

Fortune, Dion. *The Sea Priestess*. Wellingborough, Northamptonshire, UK: Aquarian Press, 1989.
A classic occult novel by one of the most influential occultists of her time. The novel takes the reader on a journey of esoteric discovery.

————. *The Mystical Qabalah*. Wellingborough, Northamptonshire, UK: Aquarian Press, 1987.
Possibly the best book on the Qabalah ever written, by the famous British occultist.

Franklin, Anna. *Fairy Lore*. Illustrated by Paul Mason. Chieveley, UK: Capall Bann, 2000.

————. *The Fairy Ring*. Illustrated by Paul Mason. St Paul, MN: Llewellyn Publications, 2002.

————. *Familiars: The Animal Powers of Britain*. Chieveley, UK: Capall Bann, 1996.

————. *Herb Craft*. Chieveley, UK: Capall Bann, 1995.

————. *The Illustrated Encyclopedia of Fairies*. Illustrated by Paul Mason and Helen Field. London: Vega (Chrysalis), 2002.

————. *The Little Book of Fairies*. Illustrated by Paul Mason. London: Vega (Chrysalis), 2002.

————. *Magical Incenses and Oils*. Chieveley, UK: Capall Bann, 2000.

————. *Midsummer Magic*. St Paul, MN: Llewellyn Publications, 2001.

————. *Personal Power*. Chieveley, UK: Capall Bann, 1998.

————. *Wise Woman/Cunning Man*. Earl Shilton, Leicestershire, UK: Lear Books, 2004.

Franklin, Anna, and Pamela Harvey. *The Wellspring*. Chieveley, UK: Capall Bann, 2000.

Franklin, Anna, and Paul Mason. *Lammas*. St Paul, MN: Llewellyn Publications, 2000.

Franklin, Anna, and Sue Phillips. *Pagan Feasts*. Chieveley, UK: Capall Bann, 1997.

——. *Real Wicca for Teens*. Chieveley, UK: Capall Bann, 2002.

Graves, Robert. *The White Goddess*. London: Faber and Faber, 1986.
A classic text exploring the myth of the Goddess in literature and poetry.

Green, Marian. *A Witch Alone*. London: Thorsons, 1995.
A book to help sole practitioners connect with the natural cycles and rediscover their magical abilities.

——. *A Modern Magician's Handbook*. Loughborough, UK: Thoth, 2001.
Excellent beginner's book covering most aspects of magic.

Harner, Michael. *The Way of the Shaman*. New York: HarperSanFrancisco, 1990.
A classic text following the journey of anthropologist Michael Harner.

Hawke, Elen. *An Alphabet of Spells*. St Paul, MN: Llewellyn Publications, 2003.

——. *In the Circle*. St. Paul, MN: Llewellyn Publications, 2001.
The author eloquently uses her own personal examples as she takes the reader on a journey through the ritual year of the witch with clear instruction.

——. *Praise to the Moon*. St. Paul, MN: Llewellyn Publications, 2002.
Thoroughly covers the lunar phases, cycles, and lore, the moon in astrology, and illustrates how the reader can tune in to his or her own lunar rhythms.

——. *The Sacred Round*. St. Paul, MN: Llewellyn Publications, 2002.

Hutton, Ronald. *The Triumph of the Moon: A History of Modern Pagan Witchcraft*. Oxford: Oxford Paperbacks, 2001.
A scholarly, amusing, and vastly informative historical account of nineteenth-century to modern-day witchcraft and paganism.

Lévi, Eliphas. *Transcendental Magic*. York Beach, ME: Red Wheel/Weiser, 1982.
This contains much material of practical use that can be assimilated into one's practice.

Macbeth, Jessica. *Moon over Water*. Dublin: Gateway, 1990.
Details many meditation techniques; most people should find at least one that suits them.

McTaggart, Lynn. *The Field*. London: Element, 2001.
Covers a number of esoteric phenomena from a scientific perspective. Of particular interest is the statistical research that shows a definite link between consciousness manipulating reality.

Nataf, Andre. *The Wordsworth Dictionary of the Occult*. Hertfordshire, UK: Wordsworth Editions, 1994.
A guide to the various famous figures of the occult world, plus schools of occult thought and a glossary of terminology.

Palin, Poppy. *Craft of the Wild Witch*. St. Paul, MN: Llewellyn Publications, 2004.

———. *The Greening*. Book 1 of the Wild Spirit Trilogy. Glastonbury, UK: Wild Spirit, 2005.

———. *Season of Sorcery*. Milverton, UK: Capall Bann, 1998.

———. *Soul Resurgence: A Guide to Reincarnation*. Milverton, UK: Capall Bann, 2000.

———. *Walking with Spirit: A Guide for the Natural Psychic*. Milverton, UK: Capall Bann, 2000.

———. *Wildwitch*. Milverton, UK: Capall Bann, 1999.

Regardie, Israel. *Tree of Life*. St. Paul, MN: Llewellyn Publications, 2000.
A great introduction to magic and some of the theory that underlies it.

Romani, Rosa. *Green Spirituality*. Illustrated by Poppy Palin. Sutton Mallet, Somerset, UK: Green Magic Publishing, 2004.

Shallcrass, Philip. *Druidry*. London: Piatkus, 2000.
A clear introduction to druidry by the joint chief of the British Druid Order.

Stepanich, Kisma K. *Faery Wicca*. Book 2. St. Paul, MN: Llewellyn Publications, 1995.
Focusing on the shamanic practices in connection with the faery tradition, plus instruction in the "cunning arts" (divination, spellcraft, and herbs).

Walker, Barbara G. *A Woman's Dictionary of Symbols and Sacred Objects.* New York: HarperSanFrancisco, 1988.
A huge reference book exploring the myths around objects connected with women and the feminine, including symbolism, herbs, animals, birds, plants, trees, and more.

Websites

Anna Franklin
www.annafranklin.net

Information on books, plus news of appearances, talks, and workshops, and general information on Wicca, the sabbats, magic, rituals, and fairies.

Anna Franklin's Online Hearth
http://communities.msn.com/HearthofArianrhod

Hearth of Arianrhod is an Internet community where you can discuss the author's work, magic, and witchcraft in general, plus access articles and resources.

Archives of Western Esoterica
www.esotericarchives.com

Online historical writings by famous figures such as Agrippa, Trithemius, John Dee, and others.

Avalonia
www.avalonia.co.uk

Run by Sorita, who is well-known for her contributions to various magazines and other work regarding witchcraft. Avalonia offers free 101 courses and provides accurate information about paganism and witchcraft. Many resources on the site.

Belief Net
www.beliefnet.com

Has a large earth-based spirituality section.

Boudicca's Bard

www.boudicca.de

Articles on chaos magic.

Encyclopaedia Mythica

www.pantheon.org

Information on myths, legends, and folklore around the world.

The Hermetic Library

www.hermetic.com

Library of hermetic texts (including many on magic).

The Internet Sacred Text Archive

www.sacred-texts.com

A vast site containing writings on religions and spiritual paths across the world, including paganism and witchcraft.

Jaq D. Hawkins

www.jaqdhawkins.com

Jaq D. Hawkins's own website. Useful articles on working magically with elementals and sigils. Also lists her books, which are very good.

The Modern Antiquarian

www.themodernantiquarian.com

Based on the monumental book by Julian Cope, this huge site offers information and visitor reviews of ancient and sacred sites across the UK and Ireland.

Occult Forums

www.occultforums.com

A great place to ask questions and find out what others are up to!

The Online Books Page

http://digital.library.upenn.edu/books

Public domain books available to read on the Internet. Includes a large amount of occult and paranormal books under the Psychology section.

Spelwerx

www.spelwerx.com

Contains loads of information on traditional witchcraft and magic, designed for practitioners of all levels—novice to adept.

Symbols.com

www.symbols.com

An encyclopaedia of symbols and their meanings.

UK Pagan

www.ukpagan.com

Internet community discussion forum.

UK Pagan Links

www.ukpaganlinks.co.uk

A directory of websites connected with Wicca, druidry, shamanism, and witchcraft.

The Witches' Voice

www.witchvox.com

Possibly the largest witchcraft website on the Internet. Based in the United States, but catering to pagans and witches around the world.

Magazines

Echoed Voices E-zine

www.echoedvoices.org

An online magazine aimed at all aspects of contemporary spiritual traditions.

Pagan Dawn

The Pagan Federation's own magazine (see Organisations).

Pentacle

www.pentaclemagazine.org
Marion Pearce
Pentacle
78 Hamlet Road
Southend on Sea
Essex
SS1 1HH
Great Britain

Britain's leading independent glossy pagan magazine, emphasising the positive aspects of paganism.

Quest

BCM—SCL Quest
London
WC1N 3XX
England

Produced by Marian Green of the Invisible College, which also runs excellent correspondence courses.

SacredHoop

www.sacredhoop.org

The leading magazine for shamanism, animism, and earth wisdom.

Silver Wheel

www.silverwheel.co.uk
P.O. Box 12
Earl Shilton
Leicestershire
LE9 7ZZ
Great Britain

Published by Anna Franklin four times a year. Craft, druidry, shamanism and folklore, rituals, pathworkings, recipes, and much more.

White Dragon
www.whitedragon.org.uk

A quarterly magazine, but the website contains many articles, a gazetteer of sacred sites, and more.

Witchcraft and Wicca
Produced by Children of Artemis (see Organisations).

Astrology

Books

Arroyo, Stephen. *Astrology, Karma and Transformation: The Inner Dimensions of the Birth Chart*. Sebastopol, CA: CRCS Publications, 1978.
Explores the karmic and transformative effects of the outer planets' positions in the natal and progressed charts, plus transits. The author focuses on spiritual and psychological growth through understanding the karmic teachings of the planets. Possibly best suited to intermediate level.

Beckman, Howard. *Mantras, Yantras & Fabulous Gems*. N.p.: Balaji Publishing, 1996.
A wonderful book, giving remedial measures to be used to counteract negative karma and help one work positively toward resolution of difficulties. It is particularly useful for its information regarding the gems to be worn for the planets in Vedic astrology.

Braha, James T. *Ancient Hindu Astrology for the Modern Western Astrologer*. Miami, FL: Hermetician Press, 1986.

Casey, Caroline W. *Making the Gods Work for You: The Astrological Language of the Psyche*. London: Piatkus, 1998.
The author has created her own form of psychological astrology: Visionary Activist Astrology. It encourages the reader to connect with the planetary energies within and without.

Defouw, Hart, and Robert Svoboda. *Light on Life: An Introduction to the Astrology of India*. New Delhi: Penguin Books, 1996.
An inspiring introduction to Indian astrology.

Frawley, David. *Astrology of the Seers*. Twin Lakes, WI: Lotus Press, 2000.
A deeply spiritual approach to Vedic astrology, with a slight flavour of Theosophy. The book explores all aspects of Indian astrology, including the use of Ayurvedic remedies such as herbs, chants, and gemstones.

Greene, Liz. *Saturn: A New Look at an Old Devil*. London: Arkana Penguin Books, 1990.
The author is a psychological astrologer and, drawing on Jungian analysis, takes the reader through the myths connected with Saturn and the wisdom that comes from understanding this planetary influence.

Huber, Bruno, and Louise Huber. *Moon Node Astrology*. York Beach, ME: Samuel Weiser, 1995.
From the Huber School of Astrology, this book looks at the karmic influence and psychological patterns of the moon's nodes.

Louis, Anthony. *Horary Astrology: The History and Practice of Astro-Divination*. St. Paul, MN: Llewellyn Publications, 1991.
Considered the "Bible" of this branch of astrology. Horary astrology is the art of using astrology to answer questions.

Mayo, Jeff. *Astrology: Teach Yourself Books*. Sevenoaks, Kent, UK: Hodder and Stoughton, 1977.
This is a good general introduction to astrology by the founder of the Mayo School of Astrology.

Patterson, Helena. *The Handbook of Celtic Astrology*. St. Paul, MN: Llewellyn Publications, 1995.
Celtic astrology is based on the thirteen lunar month cycle. In this book the author combines the lunar zodiac with the druid's ogham (tree calendar) and offers a rich interpretation of each of the signs and its associations—including the fixed stars.

Sutton, Komilla. *The Lunar Nodes, Crisis & Redemption*. Bournemouth, UK: The Wessex Astrologer, 2001.
Excellent book, focusing on the role of the lunar nodes in Vedic astrology, but equally relevant for Western astrologers. The material goes deeply into the psychological, emotional, and spiritual impact these little-studied astrological points have on the birth chart, both natally and by transit.

Websites

American Council of Vedic Astrology

www.vedicastrology.org

A nonprofit organisation devoted to bringing knowledge of Jyotish (Vedic or Indian astrology) to the West. The site has information about software, books, and courses.

Astrodienst

www.astro.com

Resources, information, and online charts.

British Association for Vedic Astrology

www.bava.org

Nonprofit organisation that aims to promote knowledge of Vedic astrology in Britain.

The Centre for Psychological Astrology

www.cpalondon.com

Founded by Liz Greene and Howard Sasportas, the centre offers a professional training programme combining astrology with the humanist school of thought and transpersonal psychology.

Dirah Academy International

www.dirah.org

Excellent correspondence course in Vedic (Indian) astrology, either via e-mail or ordinary mail. This gives you points toward American Council of Vedic Astrology accreditation. The site also furnishes articles, recommendations for books and software, and a list of useful links.

Faculty of Astrological Studies

www.astrology.org.uk

Founded in 1948, this organisation is considered one of the leading teaching bodies in astrology.

Halloran Software

www.halloran.com

Professional-level Western astrology software at a budget price. This superb programme contains all the options you could wish for, including multiple house options, Arabic parts, an accurate ephemeris, and the ACS Atlas. Sadly, it is PC only, so Mac users can use it only via Virtual PC.

The Mountain Astrologer

www.mountainastrologer.com

Articles and resources from one of the best-known astrology magazines.

Parashara's Light

www.parashara.com

Site for the excellent Vedic calculation software Parashara's Light. Mac and PC compatible.

Soul Healing

www.soulhealing.com

Hank Friedman's site where he reviews many astrological software programs, both Western and Vedic. He gives hints and advice on buying software, and offers tutorials, courses, a reading list, and much more.

Sri Jyoti Star

www.vedicsoftware.com

Home of Sri Jyoti Star, Vedic astrology software used by many well-known Vedic astrologers and authors. The site also has information regarding courses in Vedic astrology, Tantra, meditation, retreats, and so on.

Dreams

Books

Bro, Harmon H. *Edgar Cayce: On Dreams.* Edited by Hugh Lynn Cayce. Wellingborough, Northamptonshire, UK: Aquarian Press, 1989.
A fascinating examination of the case histories of Edgar Cayce—the sleeping prophet.

Harary, Keith, and Pamela Weintraub. *Lucid Dreams in 30 Days*. Wellingborough, Northamptonshire, UK: Aquarian Press, 1990.
A step-by-step process to trigger lucid dreaming.

LaBerge, Stephen, and Howard Rheingold. *Exploring the World of Lucid Dreaming*. New York: Ballantine Books, 1997.
Creative exercises and techniques are offered to readers so they can learn to control their dreams (achieve lucidity) and make use of this state of consciousness. LaBerge is one of the worldwide leading authorities in this area of dream research.

Melbourne, David F., and Keith Herne. *The Dream Oracle*. New Holland, London: 1998.
Experts in dream research, the authors have devised a code for deciphering the messages of dreams. This book teaches readers how to use the code and resolve life issues through understanding dreams.

Signell, Karen A. *Wisdom of the Heart: Working with Women's Dreams*. New York: Bantam Books, 1990.
A fascinating study on the symbolism contained in women's dreams.

Ullman, Monague, and Nan Zimmerman. *Working with Dreams*. London: Hutchinson, 1979.
A good general work on learning to interpret your own dreams. Explores symbolism, recall techniques, recording of dreams, and working in dream groups.

Vance, Bruce A. *Dreamscape: Voyage in an Alternate Reality*. Wheaton, IL: Theosophical Publishing House, 1989.
Equips you with the tools you need to explore the landscape of your dreams.

Websites

The Association for the Study of Dreams
www.asdreams.org

The Association for the Study of Dreams is an international, multidisciplinary, nonprofit organization dedicated to the pure and applied investigation of dreams and dreaming.

Dream Gate

www.dreamgate.com

Global virtual community on sleep and dreams.

The Dream Tree

www.dreamtree.com

An online resource centre for those interested in all aspects of dreams and dreaming.

The Lucidity Institute

www.lucidity.com

Founded by lucid dream researcher Stephen LaBerge.

Patricia Garfield

www.patriciagarfield.com

One of the world's leading experts on dreams and dreaming.

Runes

Books

Aswynn, Freya. *Leaves of Yggdrasil.* St Paul, MN: Llewellyn Publications, 1990.
Scholarly yet full of personal experience and spirituality, the book investigates the meaning of the runes and offers constructive advice on working with this fascinating system.

Websites

Irminsul Ættir

www.irminsul.org/ru/ru.html

Part of the Irminsul Ættir Ásatrú website offering a huge list of resources for those interested in learning more about the runes.

Freya Aswynn

www.aswynn.co.uk

The author's homepage. Includes information about Freya, rune resources, and details of her correspondence course.

Tarot

Books

Matthews, Caitlin, and John Caitlin. *Hallowquest: Tarot Magic and Arthurian Mysteries*. Wellingborough, Northamptonshire, UK: Aquarian Press, 1990.
The companion book to the Arthurian Tarot *by the same authors, this text gives an in-depth look at the Arthurian Mysteries and Celtic Lore in connection with tarot magic.*

Pollack, Rachel. *Seventy-Eight Degrees of Wisdom: A Book of Tarot*. London: Thorsons, 1998.
A classic text exploring the meaning of the tarot cards. Using the Rider-Waite deck as a focus, the author examines the psychological, mythical, and spiritual associations of the cards.

———. *Tarot: The Open Labyrinth*. Wellingborough, Northamptonshire, UK: Aquarian Press, 1986.
A collection of commentaries and interpretations on tarot readings the author has given to querants, which deepens the readers understanding of the cards.

Wang, Robert. *Qabalistic Tarot*. York Beach, ME: Samuel Weiser, 1983.

Decks

Franklin, Anna. *The Celtic Animal Oracle*. Illustrated by Paul Mason. London: Vega (Chrysalis), 2003.

———. *The Oracle of The Goddess*. Illustrated by Paul Mason. London: Vega (Chrysalis), 2003.

———. *The Sacred Circle Tarot*. Illustrated by Paul Mason. St. Paul, MN: Llewellyn Publications, 1998.

Palin, Poppy. *Waking the Wild Spirit Tarot*. St. Paul, MN: Llewellyn Publications, 2002.

Websites

Aeclectic Tarot

www.aeclectic.net/tarot

Dedicated to the diversity and beauty of tarot. See images of tarot cards, read reviews of tarot decks and books, learn about tarot, receive a tarot reading, or join the tarot community.

The Tarot Association of the British Isles

www.tabi.org.uk

Online tarot organisation with classes, forum, links, and so on, and even a free reading done by a real person, not software.

Shopping

The Goddess and the Greenman

www.goddessandgreenman.co.uk

Wonderful shop in Glastonbury, England. Visit their website and see what they have to offer. They have one of the best collections of statues and images we have seen, along with books, jewellery, and more.

The Henge Shop

Avebury

Marlborough

Wiltshire

SN8 1RF

England

Gift shop in the heart of Avebury village, which is surrounded by the largest stone circle in Britain. Stocks esoteric books, Avebury and surrounding area souvenirs, crystals, jewellery, cards, and more.

Hocus Pocus

www.hocuspocus.co.uk

38 Gardner Street

Brighton

BN1 1UN

England

A large variety of metaphysical goods including books, tarot decks, crystals, posters, and spellkits. Readings available.

The Inner Bookshop

www.innerbookshop.com

They do worldwide mail order on occult books, incense, and some equipment. But the shop itself is well worth a visit, and afterward you can go next door to the Magic Café for a meal or coffee. A map and full details on how to contact the shop or go there in person are given on the website.

Morgana's Chamber

www.morganaschamber.com

MorganasChamber@aol.com

242 West 10th Street

New York, NY 10014

telephone: 212-243-3415

Morgana's Chamber is a full service Pagan/Wiccan/Witchcraft supply shop. They offer classes and workshops, networking evenings, open rituals, and psychic readings, and host author events. Special services with Morgana include spell consultations, customized oil and incense service, hand-carved spell candle service, and handmade talismans created for every intention. Local New York City authors can frequently be found at Morgana's Chamber offering classes and readings. They have New York City's largest selection of tarot cards! If you are interested in receiving updates of classes and events, please visit their website and be sure to sign up for the e-mail announcement list. Mail order available; see website for details.

Mysteries
Monmouth Street
Covent Garden
London
WC2H 9DA
England

Long-established mind, body, spirit shop with a large stock of books, paraphernalia, tools, and gifts.

New Aeon Books
www.newaeonbooks.com
95 Oldham Street
Manchester
M4 1LW
England

Established occult bookshop in the heart of Manchester.

New Moon Occult Shop
www.newmoon.uk.com

One of our favourite online occult shops! Huge range of products available.

Occultique
www.occultique.co.uk

Antiquarian esoteric books and occult paraphernalia.

SoulJourney
www.souljourney.com
sandi@souljourney.com
9 Main Street
Butler, NJ 07405
telephone: 973/838-6564
fax: 973/838-1471

New Jersey's longest continuously running metaphysical shop, SoulJourney has Pagan/Wiccan/Witchcraft merchandise, classes, author events, readings, and spell consultations. Offers a large variety of goods such as tarot and divination, tools, herbs, candles, and more. Mail order available; see website for details.

The Speaking Tree
www.speakingtree.co.uk
5 High Street
Glastonbury
Somerset
BA6 9DP
England

Stocks a huge range of esoteric books at bargain prices.

Places to Visit

The Harbour
Boscastle
Cornwall
PL35 0AE
England

A large collection of witchcraft regalia and artefacts. The website has a searchable database of their exhibits and is well worth a visit!

Glastonbury Goddess Temple
www.goddesstemple.co.uk
2–4 High Street
Glastonbury
Somerset
BA6 9DU
England

A space to honour the Goddess in her many aspects. Rites and ceremonies, healing, and prayer.

Museum of Pagan Heritage
11–12 St John's Square
Glastonbury
Somerset
BA6 9LJ
England

Exhibition dedicated to pagan cultural and spiritual heritage.